Kit

MW00881197

MISSIONARY
and the
WITCH

Mythology comes to life
in rural Transylvania

KIT AND DREW COONS

MISSIONARY
AND THE WITCH

Mythology comes to life
in rural Transylvania

Missionary and the Witch

© 2023 Kit and Drew Coons

ISBN: 9798392823321

Library of Congress Control Number: 2023910022

Illustrations by Julie Sullivan (MerakiLifeDesigns.com)

First Edition

 Printed in the United States

24 23 22 21

20   1 2 3 4 5

"It isn't what we don't know that gives us trouble, it's what we know that ain't so."

Will Rogers

Acknowledgments

This novel would not be possible without professional editing and proofreading by Jayna Richardson. The artwork and cover by Julie Sullivan. We also thank our reviewers Leslie Mercer, Judy Burrows, Jane Campbell, Jess Moore, and Marlys Johnson who read the manuscript and made valuable suggestions.

Special thanks to Laurentiu and Clara Barbulescu and Gina Teodorescu who have been our close Romanian friends for twenty-six years. They have taken us to every part of Romania to enjoy the richness of their people and culture.

Primary Characters

Ioana Nagy – A midwife, medical practitioner, and farmer in Horvata, Romania. Her cat is named Vlad.

Christina – Ioana's mother. Seventy-five years old.

Gideon Dixon – American church-sponsored Christian missionary to Romania.

Aaron Dixon – Gideon's father and senior pastor of the Bible Belt megachurch, which has sponsored Gideon as a missionary.

Madeline Dixon – Aaron's wife and Gideon's mother.

Sofia – A secret admirer of Ioana. Sixteen years old and an orphan living on her own.

Baal – The most powerful evil spirit.

Spiritual Warriors

Florin – Widower who operates a shoe-repair shop in the village.

Claudia – Seventyish-year-old widow.

Andrei – A large, strong man who does road repair for the government. His big dog is named Dragon.

Luca – Seventeen-year-old boy who works on his parents' farm.

Daniela – A middle-aged shopkeeper's wife.

Bears

Pastor Raphael – Bi-vocational pastor of a small Protestant church in Horvata.

Eugen – A tough blacksmith and winemaker.

Father Marcă – Novice Orthodox priest. Twenty-three years old.

Maria – Sixteen-year-old schoolgirl who lives at home.

Nadia – The best of Gideon's English students. Eighteen years old.

Werewolves

"He Who Kills" – Leader of a pack or gang of werewolves.

Darius – Young Romanian nicknamed "Bloodthirsty."

Vampires

Father Flavius – Senior Orthodox priest in Horvata.

Primar (mayor) Serban – Former communist party member and ruler of the local collective farm.

Prefect (county administrator) Lazar – A former communist official remaining from the Ceauşescu regime.

Ceauşescu – Executed communist dictator of Romania.

Places

Horvata – Fictional village of about five hundred residents in the Carpathian Mountains of Transylvania.

Transylvania – A region of Romania noted for its mysterious beauty and medieval structures. The Austrian-Hungarian empire ruled Transylvania until 1918. Many Hungarian speakers remain today.

Braşov – A medieval fortress town and crossroads in Transylvania ringed by the Carpathian Mountains. Braşov is known for its medieval Saxon (Germanic) walls and bastions and the medieval Black Church.

Bucharest – The capital and largest city of Romania, located south of Transylvania. Before the twentieth century wars and communism, it was known as "Little Paris of the East."

Bran – Location of picturesque "Dracula's Castle" built in the late 1300s to defend Transylvania from invaders from the south. Now Romania's most popular tourist attraction.

Comănești – A town north of Brașov that has an annual festival in which residents dress up in bearskins to recall ancient traditions of warding off evil spirits.

Setting and Foreword

Transylvania conjures up thoughts of a mysterious and exotic locale. We first visited there to speak at a conference in the 1990s. We found Romania, of which Transylvania is part, frozen in time back to the 1930s. Rural areas reflected even earlier times. Today Romania and her people have progressed tremendously since the 1989 Romanian Revolution, especially since joining NATO in 2004 and the European Union in 2007. The cities have become as modern as Western Europe. Still, in rural areas horse-drawn wagons are common on the roads.

In 1989, Romanians overthrew the communist government set up by the Soviet Union after World War II. The communist regime under dictator Nicolae Ceaușescu had maintained brutal control of the people with secret police, informers, and torture. Captured during the 1989 fighting, Ceaușescu was executed by firing squad.

Our story begins four years later in 1993. Romania then had instituted the basic elements of democracy. The country struggled mightily to transition to a free-market economy after forty-two years of economic decay under communism. Inflation devalued the Romanian currency to more than two hundred leu to the American dollar.

The new elected government maintained federal control over twenty-three million Romanians, most of whom lived in smaller towns and rural villages. Forty-one județe (counties) and the municipality of Bucharest are administered by federally appointed prefects from regional centers.

A commune (comună in Romanian) is the lowest level of administrative subdivision in Romania. The commune consists of one or more villages that do not themselves have an administrative function. A primar (mayor) is elected to represent the commune's needs before the prefect.

Many Romanians have maintained belief in spirits, particularly in rural areas since ancient times. Customs in 1993 reflected traditions originally intended to ward off evil spirits. Although the seriousness of those customs varies widely, certainly Romania—like many countries—has a heritage of believing in the supernatural.

Prologue

"Thank you for coming from so far, Florin," an anxious Romanian mother said to her older brother. "I do not have anybody else to help me. Maybe you can talk some sense into Audi. Until recently, he was always a loving son and a good student, especially since we lost his father."

"How is Audi different now?"

"One of his teachers asked to speak to me. She says that he has been disruptive in class and argumentative with her and other teachers." Florin's sister hesitated then spoke with difficulty. "The teacher said that some of the girls complained that Audi made suggestive comments and sometimes brushed up against them inappropriately." She hung her head in shame before adding, "He never did such things before."

"He is seventeen years old now. Teenagers frequently test boundaries."

Florin's sister shook her head. "No, this is more than that. I think maybe he's keeping bad company while I work. Even when I am home, some men I don't know come to summon him. I tell him to stay home and do his homework, but he goes with them anyway. I lie awake listening until he comes home, sometimes very late even on school nights. His clothes smell of tobacco and alcohol."

"Where is Audi now?"

"In his room."

Florin went into the shoddy government-built apartment's second bedroom. There he found Audi awake, lying on his narrow bed while looking at a lewd magazine. "Your mother would be disappointed to find you with that," Florin began. "I understand you are having troubles adjusting to—"

A deep, throaty laugh from his nephew cut Florin off. The young man before him seemed nothing like the nephew he had known. This Audi sneered at him with a dark and angry expression.

Florin felt inexplicable horror and fear. He wanted to run away but love for his sister forced him to resume. "—adjusting to your father's death."

Audi laid down the magazine and swung his feet to the floor. "What do you know about death?" a deep, resonating voice demanded.

"My wife died in the revolution in Timisoara—"

"No, I mean someone's death by your own actions." Audi rose to his feet. His father had been a big man. Audi stood a foot taller than his uncle. "Death is glorious—the end of a meaningless life."

"That's not true, Audi. Jesus came to—"

14

Audi's face showed rage. "Mention not your pathetic God to me," he shouted. Audi advanced toward his uncle with clenched fists and violent intent. "Who are you, a thief who stole tools from his employer, to lecture me?" Foul language and curses flowed out of his mouth.

"Don't blaspheme, Audi, or—" A blow from Audi's fist above Florin's ear cut his words off. "Help me, Jesus!" Florin pleaded reflexively.

The teen paused and appeared uncertain. Suddenly Florin knew that the creature he faced wasn't his sister's child. "Leave this boy alone, spirit," he demanded in desperation. "In the name of Jesus, let Audi go."

Moments of confusion followed. The boy screamed and his body crumpled to the floor, where it convulsed. Florin felt dizzy from the blow but repeated, "In the name of Jesus, let Audi go." Florin thought he saw a dark shadow leave Audi then shrink away into nothingness.

Florin staggered over to the bed and sat down. He closed his eyes as ringing in his head subsided. After a minute, a high-pitched boy's voice made him look up.

"Uncle Florin, why are you here?" Audi rose to his feet. "I had the most terrible dream. At least, I think it was a dream."

Chapter One

No amount of money could adequately compensate a midwife for a summons late at night, followed by all-day care, and then another sleepless night at a rural farmhouse without electricity or running water. And no amount of money was exactly the amount Ioana had received for her efforts. With Romania's currency scarce and nearly worthless, she preferred the jar of home-grown honey she received instead of money anyway. *Seeing a healthy baby with her proud parents rewarded me enough,* she consoled herself.

After walking six miles home to her mother's farmstead outside of Horvata, Ioana began a full day of chores—milking twenty-three nanny goats, feeding eighteen chickens, and minding a quarter-acre hand-tilled garden. After eating the garden refuse, her two nearly-grown pigs ambled to the woods to root for themselves. Ioana then started churning the cream, which she had separated from the goats' milk, to make butter. What butter she couldn't trade or use would be rubbed into curing goat cheeses which, along with the chickens' eggs, served as her year-round bartering currency. The pigs would have skimmed milk and the buttermilk remaining after churning for their supper. During the fall butchering season, a fresh ham could be traded for a recently killed calf stomach. Rennet from that stomach would allow her to make next year's cheese over the following winter.

As she churned, Ioana's seventy-five-year-old mother, Christina, kept her company while happily knitting socks. *Christina is the perfect name for Mama,* Ioana thought. A grandmother Ioana never met had named her daughter Christina, the female form of Christian, and bequeathed a strong faith and loyalty to the Orthodox Church. Christina lived her faith through knitting socks for the needy.

"Ioana, I'm nearly out of yarn again. Can I buy some more?" asked Christina.

"We don't have any money, Mama," Ioana explained. Remembering that Christina regularly walked past the wool merchant in the village when visiting widowed friends, she suggested, "Why don't you offer to trade some cheeses for yarn?"

"I will," Christina agreed.

"We'll have honey on our porridge tonight," Ioana promised.

As Christina repeated village gossip, Ioana couldn't avoid dwelling on her circumstances. *I could have been a fully-fledged doctor living in a city by now. As a doctor, I would probably have a loving husband, maybe a child. People wouldn't be suspicious of me then. Now I will never finish medical school.* She remembered the few serious suitors who had come to the farm. *A drunkard, an opportunistic land seeker, a man who would have beaten me, all of whom I rejected. My bold demeanor and the stories about me frightened other would-be admirers away. My strange-looking eyes made me even more suspect. Now I am past prime bridal age with an obligation to help even those who resent or fear me.* For the thousandth time, Ioana reminded herself, *Having no husband is better than having a bad husband.*

Suddenly Ioana knew that something would change and soon. Unlike her normal premonitions, she couldn't discern what.

* * *

Through an open window of a decrepit bus, Gideon Dixon stared in eager anticipation of brooding castles on craggy peaks surrounded by foreboding forests. After years of preparation, he had finally arrived as a Christian missionary in Transylvania, an ominous land of legends. Gideon's bus shared the road with low hay-laden wagons drawn by horses. Unlike wagons with wooden-spoked wheels shown in American films, Romanian wagons used inflated car tires mounted on old auto axles. The bus only occasionally encountered motor-driven cars, usually clunky Russian-built Ladas or Romanian Dacias. Despite Gideon's expectations, the narrow winding road passed through rolling hills and sunny green countryside. Robust people working the midsummer fields with horses and homemade implements cheerfully returned his waves. The landscape reminded Gideon of Amish country in Pennsylvania, albeit surrounded by alpine forest-covered mountains. Rural Romania seemed more like a Disney-like land of happy fairytales than of dark medieval mysteries.

Trees with whitewashed trunks lining the road announced the approach of small towns. Picturesque steeples of centuries-old churches marked communities in the foothills of the Carpathian Mountains. Reddish tiles covered nearly all the roofs. In larger towns, concrete stucco houses painted in multiple pastel colors sat shoulder-to-shoulder along the main road. In many places, the concrete plaster had broken away to reveal bricks underneath. Stout oaken gates guarded entrances to walled residential enclosures and provided privacy. Through one gate left open Gideon glimpsed multiple doors to rooms opening off of a courtyard shaded by a grapevine arbor. Occasionally houses displayed Romania's tripart blue-yellow-red flag.

The bus driver finally announced their arrival at Gideon's destination, the village of Horvata, a community of about five hundred residents. Descending the bus steps with his two large suitcases, Gideon thanked God that he'd followed his father's advice and attended language school to learn fluent Romanian. Linguistics had been the one thing at which Gideon had ever excelled. Romanian being based on Latin—the people even considered themselves the inheritors of ancient Rome or Constantinople—had made their language easy for him to learn. Gideon could communicate fluently with Romanians, albeit with a twangy American accent.

Townhouses and shops boxed in Horvata's cobblestone-paved square, which was dominated on the east side by an ancient stone church. A white marble memorial commemorated fifty-nine men from the village killed during the 1940-45 war. Away from the square, haphazard fences enclosed vegetable gardens surrounding freestanding cottages. Gideon spotted one garden that had been turned into a mini vineyard through which a stone walkway led to a cottage door. Window boxes filled with flowering geraniums and petunias made the village charming. Jumbled storks' nests topped some utility poles. *I'm living in a different world now*, Gideon marveled.

That night Gideon slept in a bare-bones room of the village's tavern. At breakfast, he inquired about renting a house. Before he could finish eating—dense brown bread with jam and butter, wedges of cheese, a slice of cured ham, and strong coffee—several house owners had approached him to offer a residence in exchange for American currency. He suspected most planned to rent their own home and find lodging elsewhere. Hyper-inflation of Romanian's currency, the leu, in 1993 made anybody with access to American dollars wealthy.

A group of potential landlords and curious onlookers followed as Gideon examined several housing candidates. He looked twice at a concrete-floored brick cottage with a whitewashed exterior. "This would be fifty-five dollars a month in American currency," the owner offered after Gideon returned to the outside.

When Gideon agreed, glances the Romanians gave each other indicated they thought him a sucker for paying so much.

A low fence with a swinging gate separated the small property from neighboring residences. Several aged and neglected plum trees with wormy-looking fruit struggled to survive within the fence. One large room, two sleeping compartments with cot-like beds, a small kitchen with a tank-fed propane burner for cooking, and a simple bathroom with an old tub completed the cozy interior. One rough table with five hand-made wooden chairs and a sagging couch comprised the furniture. A built-in wood-fired brick stove between the kitchen and main room would heat the cottage and bake food in winter. The stove's narrow brick chimney protruded through the tile roof.

Surveying the house after the departure of his landlord, Gideon felt pleased to be standing in his own first home. He remembered his previous job as a shelf stocker for a large grocery store. *I'm finally at my place of calling. I can—I will—make my father proud here.*

* * *

Gideon spent the afternoon exploring Horvata and chatting with anybody willing to talk. Plenty would converse, including a few pretty and flirtatious young women. Most had narrow faces, dark brown eyes, straight Roman noses, and long black hair. Gideon imagined them in the streets of ancient Rome. *They probably see me as a potential ticket to America and a wealthy lifestyle,* he told himself. *To most, I'm a curiosity, an American speaking fluent Romanian.* The villagers appreciated him buying household supplies, though. With Romania's economy struggling to transition from communism to a free market, prices seemed absurdly low—a large loaf of locally baked bread for fifteen cents, a kilogram of beef for a half dollar; two dollars bought a used set of porcelain dishes and utensils.

Shops closed as the workday ended and villagers headed home for supper. Gideon returned to his rented cottage and made scrambled eggs on the propane burner using an iron skillet he had purchased for fifty cents. After eating, he shook out wrinkled clothes taken from his suitcases and hung the shirts on nails in the bedroom. Under a lightbulb hanging by its wire, he made the cot-like bed with linens bought in the village and shoved his two suitcases underneath. *I'll need a chest of drawers to store clothes,* he told himself. *And a desk to make the other bedroom into an office. An easy chair with a floor lamp would be nice.*

His accommodations put in order, Gideon's thoughts turned to his father, an influential pastor in America's Bible Belt, and his father's expectations. He had once overheard his father confiding in his mother, "Gideon loves God and probably knows the Bible better than me. But he becomes ambivalent applying Scripture beyond the basics. People just don't want a wishy-washy Bible preacher."

His mother had tried to spin her son positively by answering, "Gideon *is* very analytical and open-minded."

He sat down at the table on one of the chairs to apply his analytical skills. *I learned to speak Romanian, but don't know much about the country,* he reminded himself. He opened a guidebook about Romania he had purchased near the Bucharest train station. He discovered that Romania was about the size of Georgia and South Carolina combined with a similar number of people. But unlike Georgia, where most people lived in or around the metropolis of Atlanta, most Romanians lived more thinly dispersed in small towns and villages.

The book's section on culture claimed that many Romanians retained ancient beliefs about spirits and witches, especially in rural areas. Country people customarily used garlic, bearskins, roof decorations, burning tires, and even sheep heads hung in trees to ward off evil spirits. On this issue, Gideon felt assurance and thought, *No knowledgeable twentieth-century Christian would fall for claims of magic. The supernatural ended after Christ and his immediate disciples. About this I can be certain. Who could be better than me to expose baseless superstitions as a form of idolatry?*

A surge of confidence made him restless and eager to begin. He ventured into the night and found the village streets dark with only a few dim lights showing through curtained windows. Above his head the clear sky revealed the Milky Way cloud of stars that dimly illuminated the streets even without the moon. Only barking of distant dogs and the gentle buzz of summertime insects disturbed the quiet. A momentary burst of boisterous voices rose from the tavern where he had spent the previous night, then the noise died away. Despite the peaceful surroundings, an uncanny feeling of unease affected Gideon. He returned to his cottage, entered, and locked the door.

That night Gideon suffered a disturbing dream. His dream-self wandered the streets of Horvata during the day. Nobody would talk to him until he accidentally bumped into a little girl and knocked her over. She started to cry. The girl's mother, a large woman with an angry face, began to berate him. "See what you've done, worthless foreigner!" An angry crowd gathered in Gideon's dream. People heaped on criticism. "You are careless." "You shouldn't be here." "Why don't you go someplace else?" Behind the crowd, Gideon saw the image of his father shaking his head in disapproval.

The dream image of his father became darker and darker until it became a featureless man-like shape outlined by greenish lights emanating from behind. *I must be having a nightmare*, he thought. *Wake up! Wake up!*

Chapter Two

Gideon awoke in the dark room chilled and feeling a sense of horror. He lay awake and motionless on the cot-like bed until morning light streaming through the windows fully illuminated the room. *You're too old to fear monsters under the bed,* he told himself and forced his legs to swing to the floor. After standing, he put ground coffee beans into a pot, added water, and turned the propane flame on underneath. With bread and boiled coffee, he spent the early morning praying and reviewing Old Testament scriptures related to forbidden supernatural activity. He hoped this would return the assurance he had felt the previous evening. But the dream had taken away his confidence.

He ventured out and found a bi-weekly open-air market in progress around Horvata's square. Even decades of communism hadn't suppressed that ancient custom. At rough wooden tables, vendors sold and bartered items, especially locally produced foodstuffs. The availability of used items reminded Gideon of a yard sale back home. But chatting with

Romanians seemed more difficult than the previous day. Buying and selling occupied people, and his strange face no longer evoked curiosity. "I'm hosting a Bible study at my home this Sunday," he told vendors and shoppers as he passed them. "I'd love to see you there." Most people replied politely or feigned interest. Many claimed that they would be attending church on Sunday.

He sat down on a public bench by an older lady bent with age who appeared befuddled and frail. When Gideon mentioned God, she replied, "Do you love God too? So nice to see in a young man. I knit socks for the less fortunate." Then she lamented about being out of yarn and that the wool merchant would not trade for cheese. "His wife also makes cheese," she explained. "Would you like to buy some cheese? It has a nice sharp flavor. I could buy knitting wool with the money."

Why not? he thought. "Yes, I could use some cheese."

"Wonderful! You'll need to walk with me to collect it."

As Gideon followed, the lady introduced herself as Christina and chatted about people he didn't know. After a third of a mile, she left the road where whitewashed rocks revealed the entrance to a farmyard. Gideon saw an old single-story house and several dilapidated out-buildings. "We'll need to find my daughter," Christina said and angled toward a rustic barn. Inside, sitting on a three-legged stool, a woman in tattered work clothes milked a nanny goat. A dozen other goats waited their turn. A large gray cat watched nearby, expecting a saucer of milk.

"Ioana, this young man would like to buy some cheese."

Christina's daughter stood up. Gideon saw a striking woman that he guessed to be about his own age—mid-twenties—and nearly his height. Although thin, her body appeared wiry and strong. She had sharp symmetrical features and chocolate-brown hair pulled back from a long face into an untidy bun. Unlike most Romanians, exceptionally light blue eyes with black pupils set in a light complexion gave her an unworldly look. He stood mesmerized, trying to decide if she was hideous or the most beautiful female he'd ever seen.

"How much cheese would you like?" the woman asked with a husky voice.

Still startled by her appearance, Gideon extended five dollars. "How much will this buy?" He couldn't avoid wondering, *Is she married?* His continued evaluation of her shifted toward impossibly beautiful.

The woman's eyes widened, and she blinked while accepting the American money. "Come with me." She led Gideon to a cool root cellar where dozens of cabbage-sized cheeses cured. She selected five and loaded them into his arms. "Can you carry these?"

Ioana suppressed a smile as the stranger struggled to hold onto five round cheeses. He could, only with difficulty since they totaled over twenty pounds. She noticed him to be lean and handsome with fine features and warm brown eyes. *He's*

about my age, she thought. Curiosity caused her to prolong the transaction. "Your money and accent are American. Why are you here?" she asked while watching him trying not to drop the cheeses.

"My name is Gideon. I'm here to tell people about God."

"We have plenty of churches in Romania. What makes you think you can teach us about God?"

Gideon fumbled for an answer. "I can warn people about superstitions and dabbling with the supernatural."

"Our churches already do this."

"They do? And they teach people that from the Bible?"

Ioana didn't want to discourage a man she perceived as sincere. And she hadn't talked to a sincere man her age for a long time. "Mostly the church just warns about the occult. The Orthodox expect people to do what the priests say, with or without the Bible. And most Romanians are Orthodox."

Gideon tried not to stare but couldn't help glancing at Ioana repeatedly. "That's too bad." He then quickly clarified, "I didn't mean too bad about being Orthodox. I meant about not using the Bible."

Ioana could tell that Gideon felt uneasy, almost apologetic, around her. *Not a typical American. Not a typical missionary, either. Rather shy,* she thought. After noticing his glances, she realized, *He is attracted to me.* She enjoyed the feeling of being admired and extended their conversation. "How did you find Horvata?"

The American smiled as he confessed, "I closed my eyes and put my finger on a Romanian map." Apparently wishing to prolong the conversation himself, he then asked, "Your mother called you 'Yo-anna.' Does that name have a meaning?"

"Yes, my name is Ioana. It means graced by God. Mama and Poppa had no children until Mama was nearly fifty. Then Mama became pregnant with me. Following the example of John the Baptist's elderly parents, Mama named me Ioana, the Romanian feminine form of John."

"Have you always lived here?" While balancing the cheeses, Gideon used his elbow to indicate the farm.

"No, I had attended medical school in Bucharest until Poppa died three years ago. This is Mama's home. She deserves to stay here during her older years. I left school and came back to care for her."

Gideon nodded appreciation and said, "I'm starting a Sunday Bible study at my house tomorrow. Would you be interested?"

"Inviting strangers into your home is unusual in Romania. And most people attend church on Sunday," Ioana answered. "I'm too busy tomorrow anyway. But my mother is deeply religious. I'll ask her." *Something harmless for Mama to do,* she thought. *Maybe he'll buy more cheese later.* "Do you need help carrying the cheese home?"

"I can manage. Thank you anyway."

31

Walking home with cheeses cradled in his arms, Gideon enjoyed the afterglow of having talked with an attractive member of the opposite sex. Then he considered Ioana's comments about church attendance and reconsidered his calling. *People here are going about their business and are no longer holding out their hands for Bibles as I had expected. And Romanians already have churches. All the stories I heard of Romania following the fall of communism made me believe that everyone would be eager to learn spiritual truths from me, but that doesn't seem to be the case. My father expects me to be teaching the Bible and gathering a following. Were my sacrifices—Bible college, seminary, a girl who dumped me for a medical intern, six months of language school—justified? Did I come to Romania for the prestige of being a foreign missionary? Will I ever find people who want and need me?*

Doubts and worries followed him to bed. His gloomy thoughts led him to recall prior failures until the guilt and shame of past mistakes felt almost unbearable. Then he heard distant howling like a wolf. Listening closely, he detected slow footsteps in the kitchen. *Has somebody broken in?* Glimmers of greenish light reflected from the main room. Although the night remained calm, he heard a wooing sound like wind encircling the house. *Ghosts aren't real,* Gideon assured himself. Even so, he felt horror building within his chest. Breathing became difficult as he lay frozen in fear in his bed. Then a black shape formed at the doorway to his sleeping cubicle. Greenish glimmers outlined the man-like figure from his nightmare. Terror paralyzed Gideon. He could feel the being's cold presence. Hollow words as if two voices spoke in unison came to Gideon's ears, or maybe into his head: "You are a failure and always will be." An inhuman guttural laugh followed. "Your father is embarrassed by you. God has abandoned you. You will always be alone."

A pounding noise from his front door drew Gideon's attention. But he could not move. A male voice shouted through the door, "In the name of Jesus Christ, begone, evil one." The shape and glimmers rapidly shrunk in size for a second or two until they disappeared entirely. Silence followed. A gentle breeze stirred the window curtains. Gideon wondered, *Have I woken up? Was that just a terrible dream?* After an extended period, he summoned the nerve to leave his bed and open the front door. He found nobody outside.

The American means well and seems like a decent man. Mama will be safe with him, Ioana thought as she walked her mother into the village the following morning. Residents helped her locate the American's cottage. She knocked until Gideon opened the door, looking disoriented, like he hadn't slept much. His eyes widened when he saw Ioana.

"Yes?" he asked.

"Did you invite Mama to a Bible meeting?"

"Oh, right," Gideon answered. "Please come in."

Ioana observed Gideon's home with curiosity. In typical male fashion, the interior was sparsely furnished and unadorned. She glanced through a doorway to see his unmade bed and clothes hanging on pegs. Unwashed dishes filled the kitchen sink. The five cheeses Gideon had purchased rested on the table.

"You had a visitor late last night," Ioana commented.

Gideon's face showed tension as he turned to face her and spoke deliberately. "Why would you think that?"

"I just do."

He shrugged before asserting, "Well, I'll be fine."

"If you say so."

Gideon hastily arranged chairs and lit propane under a pot with water to boil before adding ground coffee. He waved toward the chairs. "Please sit down. I'll pour coffee."

Ioana shook her head. "I need to go into the forest. A man has been injured cutting wood. Could you see that Mama gets home after your Bible meeting?"

Gideon appeared disappointed but answered, "Sure. Are you a doctor?"

"More of a medical practitioner. I did not finish medical school."

"Oh, right. I remember now."

Ioana elaborated, "I set bones and stitch wounds. Deliver babies. Offer a few herbal remedies." As she departed, she whispered to Gideon, "Mama loves stories." As she walked away, Ioana laughed to herself and thought, *The American would probably call me a witch doctor.*

Chapter Three

No others Gideon had invited arrived for the Bible study. While Christina waited and patiently knitted, Gideon realized that his planned lesson debunking magic would be inappropriate. Rather than teach, he served Christina coffee and cookies. Then remembering Ioana's advice, he started retelling Moses' story: the baby hidden in the bulrushes, the Pharaoh's daughter, Moses' flight, the confrontation with Pharaoh, the golden calf. His gestures grew bolder as Christina responded with increasing attentiveness. Gideon started using exaggerated voices to depict the characters. Christina laid down her knitting, leaned forward, and giggled at the story's twists and turns. Seeing her enjoy the Bible gladdened Gideon's heart.

Escorting Christina to her home, Gideon discreetly asked about her daughter. Christina told about Ioana rebuffing men of dubious character, working diligently, and helping all who needed her.

"She is smart and knows things others do not," Christina said proudly. According to Christina, Ioana had inexplicably uncovered embezzlement by authorities, brutality of violent husbands, and sexual abuse of children. Christina lowered her voice to a whisper. "People accuse Ioana of being a witch. But whoever heard of a witch who takes such diligent care of her mother?"

* * *

The following week, Gideon resumed trying to network in the community. He kept one cheese to eat and distributed the others to some impoverished widows and orphans. When he saw people struggling with a difficult job, he offered to help and enjoyed the physical effort. He sensed the Romanians warming up to him, but most appeared happy with their Orthodox church or one small church in town that appeared Protestant from the exterior. However, not everyone welcomed his presence in the community. A grubby man threatened him, saying, "You have no business being here, American. Leave Romanians alone, or something will spill your blood in the night."

"I'm only here to help—" Gideon started until the man abruptly turned away.

After that encounter, Gideon felt unsettled and, despite reassuring himself of God's protection, made a point to lock his door securely after dark. Although he didn't experience the same waking dream with the man-like figure again, each night he lay awake battling fear and anxiety. Thoughts came to make him doubt himself and his mission. He anticipated the shame of going home a failure.

Daytime dispelled most negative thoughts. Gideon started ranging out from the village, walking unpaved roads and paths in the lovely countryside. Gray and white farm geese honked to announce his passing. He hiked in groves of beech trees, through fields of wildflowers, and along clear babbling creeks. Above him a few white clouds clung to steep hillsides covered with dark forests of fir trees. People greeted him with curiosity. Several warned him to beware of wolves and bears. Others, without specifying a cause, cautioned him to stay out of the mountains at night.

Once Gideon walked alongside a wagon caravan of Romani people known as Gypsies in America. Stout ponies pulled their camper-like homes. The tinkle of harnesses and creak of the wooden wagons had a soothing effect on him. Circled around a common campfire that evening, the Romani served Gideon thick, bitter coffee and told ancient tales of wandering in which spirits meddled in their lives. Although he didn't contradict his hosts, their legends strengthened Gideon's resolve to expose the notion of spirits as superstition.

*　*　*

Ioana carried a live chicken, given as payment for midwifing a baby, as she walked home from a remote farm after a late-night summons. She saw a familiar figure, the American missionary, on the path ahead of her. After quickening her steps to catch up, she called, "Hello, American Bible storyteller."

Gideon turned and, recognizing Ioana, waited for her to catch up. "Nice chicken."

"An old rooster. We will eat him." Ioana smiled at Gideon for the first time. "Mama enjoyed the Bible story you told her. But she loves the grandeur and ritual of the Orthodox church and would never leave it. Are you getting any Romanian interest in your religion?"

"Hardly any," he confessed. "I'm not a very convincing leader."

"Do not be hard on yourself. It is hard to live up to your father. I *know* you can do great good. Only that will happen very differently from your father's example."

"How do you know anything about me and my father?"

Ioana clenched her teeth as they walked together. *You slipped that time,* she realized. *Be careful, or he will guess your secret.* Rather than answer, she laughed and changed the conversation.

"Mama has been telling her friends about your Bible story. Others are talking about your generosity with the cheese and willingness to help them."

"Your mother is sweet and thoughtful." Gideon paused, unsure what to say next. "Christina says people call you a witch." He laughed to show he thought that ridiculous.

If you only knew, Ioana thought but smiled as if bemused. "Well, that would depend on how you define a witch. I do not live in a gingerbread house and eat children. I cannot fly on a broom, although that *would* be convenient to visit patients. And I never place curses. However, some men I publicly rebuked for doing wrong described me as a witch afterwards. Although I am not a licensed physician, people call me for medical help. In that sense, you might say, I am a witch . . . doctor."

After Gideon laughed, Ioana prompted, "How did you decide to become a missionary?"

"My father is a great man, a Christian leader in America. Dad draws huge crowds to his megachurch and big TV audiences by delivering unwavering and authoritative sermons with his powerful voice. Dad named me, his only son after two daughters, Gideon. He hoped I would become a great warrior for God. But I took after the other side of that biblical hero— that is, 'show me some proof.' I didn't excel at Bible college or seminary. Maybe because I frequently cited alternative scriptures or historical records to question my teachers' theology. I just felt discomfort with closed-minded certitude about complex spiritual matters. My lack of assurance denied me the confidence required to be a successful preacher. After graduating from seminary, and still hoping to make my father proud through a Christian vocation, I instead found myself working as a shelf-stocker at a grocery store."

Ioana sensed his angst but kept that to herself. "You still have not told me how you came to Romania."

"The disintegration of communism in Eastern Europe provided an opportunity. Christian organizations rushed in. Videos showed hundreds of hands outstretched for Bibles. I felt confident that anybody could be successful in such a spiritually starved environment. Even me. My father agreed. 'Those people need the basics of Christian faith,' he said. Dad urged his congregation to provide funds for me to become an independent missionary."

Ioana sighed. "After the poverty of the communist era, people would accept anything free. We already had churches and Bibles here. Romania is already Christian."

"I know that now. Maybe I should just go home," Gideon returned.

Ioana could feel Gideon's despair and thought, *This is a good man. He could even make a good husband.* She gently placed her free hand on his shoulder as they walked. When he didn't react negatively, she urged. "No, do not go home, Gideon. God has something important for you to do in Horvata. Believe me, I know."

"Thank you, Ioana. I hope you're right."

Ioana removed her hand. To keep the conversation going, she told Gideon about how she had treated a young boy with a chronic sore throat earlier that morning using the last of her antibiotics. "The little rascal was excited about the ice cream his father had made to ease his throat pain. Only he did not want to share with his sister." She glanced over at Gideon and felt gladdened that her story made him smile.

When their paths parted, Ioana waved the doomed rooster and made him squawk. "Would you like to stay for lunch when you escort Mama home after your Bible meeting on Sunday?"

Gideon's face showed surprise, but he answered, "Yes, I would. Thank you."

* * *

After returning home, Gideon realized, *Ioana didn't exactly deny being a witch.* But despite that, he couldn't resist being drawn to her energy and capability. *She's quite a woman. Though mysterious for me.*

Three additional widows joined Christina for the Bible meeting on Sunday. None of them had brought Bibles. So, after serving coffee and cookies, Gideon told and acted out the Bible story of Jacob. The widows knit with yarn Christina had purchased using some of the cheese money. They expressed obvious enjoyment of his antics.

As Christina's thoroughly entertained friends departed, one in her late sixties whispered to Gideon, "I know night spirits are trying to deceive you. I am awake each night praying for your protection."

How does she know about my anxiety? Gideon wondered. After the departure of the newcomers, he found a raw egg, four slices of bread, and a large onion remaining on his table.

"Weren't my friends nice?" said Christina as she laid a pair of thick wool socks she had knitted with the other gifts.

Christina and Gideon walked together to her cottage while she bubbled with enthusiasm about the Bible story. "I never knew the Bible could be so interesting."

At the farm, a different-looking Romanian woman met them in front of the cottage. She wore a traditional loose white blouse made of linen with red, black, and blue embroidery and a ruby-red ankle-length Romanian skirt. A linked bronze belt holding trinkets like a charm bracelet hung low on her hips. Her long, brown hair dangled down her back under a red and black scarf that framed her face. An eye-catching blue choker fit closely against her thin neck above a traditional necklace of old brass coins. Her eyebrows had been plucked and tapered outwards to a point. Dark red lipstick made her even more striking. Gideon detected a touch of perfume and stood mesmerized. A bit of gray eyeshadow highlighted dramatic blue eyes. Then he realized, *This gorgeous woman is Ioana.*

Ioana appeared embarrassed but pleased by his stare. "You like my costume?" she asked. "This is how I dressed as a girl for special holidays."

"You look very nice," he managed. "Lovely."

"I am a silly woman for dressing like a young maid. Let me bring in the bread."

Gideon watched Ioana use a wooden peel to remove two large crusty loaves of bread from an outdoor oven with an arched brick opening. He had seen pizza makers cook like that and charge extra for "wood fired."

Ioana gestured toward the house's front door. "Please come inside."

Although Christina and Ioana's house looked similar to Gideon's cottage on the outside, colorful plates and artwork decorated the brightly painted interior walls. Fat candles burned in chest-high wrought-iron candlesticks from a century earlier. Braided wool rugs made from old fabrics covered a floor of dressed stones set into concrete. Comfortable embroidered pillows made a couch look inviting. Pictures showed a younger Christina with her husband and Ioana as a child. Smells of chicken and paprika permeated the house.

"Lunch is ready." Ioana pointed toward a seat at the head of the table. "Our custom is for the man to sit there. This was my father's place. Mama and I will sit on the table's sides." To Christina, Ioana said, "Sit down, Mama. I will serve you both."

"Romanians always start with soup," Ioana explained as she placed a pottery bowl before Gideon. "I boiled the rooster first to collect broth for soup and to make his meat tender. Help yourself to bread." She placed one of the still-warm loaves with a knife on a cutting board alongside a mound of soft goat butter.

Ioana worked in the kitchen over a propane burner while Gideon and Christina enjoyed chicken soup made with onions and potatoes. The soup's sour flavor from a dash of apple vinegar pleasantly surprised him. When they finished the soup, Ioana served a bowl-like plate with chicken and small dumplings cooked in tomato sauce blended with paprika and homemade sour cream. Gideon waited until Ioana fixed a serving for herself, took off her apron, and sat down opposite Christina.

"I hope you like this. This is a Hungarian recipe I learned from Mama."

"Transylvania used to be part of Hungary, you know," Christina explained. "My father's family was Hungarian. My mother made paprika dishes for him. Would you thank God for us, young man?"

After a short prayer, Gideon tasted the sauce and found it zesty and delicious.

Ioana and Gideon remained silent as they ate. Ioana noticed his curious one-handed American manner of eating. Christina talked endlessly about her parents and other relatives, the tough times they had endured, and the changes Romania had experienced in her lifetime. Gideon kept glancing at Ioana and looking away when their eyes met. *This man is not like those I rejected,* Ioana thought and visualized him sitting in that chair every night. She imagined Gideon and herself living and working together to make a good life for their children. She wondered what sleeping next to him and having him touch her would be like.

Chapter Four

After eating, Christina nodded off to sleep in her favorite rocking chair. Ioana motioned for Gideon to join her outside. They sat together on chairs in the shade of an enormous beech tree listening to the gentle wind in the branches and the hens clucking as they poked around the farmyard.

Gideon broke the silence. "So, you're part Hungarian?"

"Yes, my father's side had some Magyar roots. And I'm a quarter Saxon from Mama's mother."

"You're part Saxon?"

"Germanic people settled in this area in the early Middle Ages. They built the city of Braşov and the famous castle in Bran. The Russians transported many of them to Siberia after the war. My grandmother married a Romanian who had fought against the Germans and so was left here."

"I thought Romanians descended from the ancient Romans."

"Most Romanians are a mixture of Roman and Dacian, the people the Roman legions conquered. I have an even wider genetic mixture. Somehow my genes combined to give me these strange eyes."

Gideon unobtrusively examined Ioana's face as she talked. "I think your eyes are beautiful."

Ioana's heart soared at the compliment. "Do many American women have eyes like mine?"

"No," Gideon admitted. "But many would wish for such eyes."

Ioana felt uncomfortable at the unaccustomed praise and searched her mind for an escape. "How is your work going?" she asked.

"Slowly," he confessed. "Except for one man who threatened me, I think most people like and accept me now. But they aren't very open to new spiritual ideas."

Ioana felt his frustration and hesitated before speaking carefully. "Religion here is very traditional. People are afraid to take chances with things they do not understand."

"But I can help them understand. Dispel their superstitions."

"Maybe some of their beliefs are justified."

Gideon looked skeptical. "Like what?"

"Most believe in spirits."

He shook his head. "Ghosts aren't real."

"No, the spirits are not the souls of dead people remaining on this earth. But spirits can disguise themselves as ghosts to frighten people."

"What spirits?"

Ioana thought carefully before speaking. *This man must know about you, if ever you might have any possibility of a future together.*

"Good spirits seek to protect and enlighten people. But angels are not the only living spirits. Evil spirits hate all that is good. They deceive and use people to harm others. They especially try to prevent being recognized for what they are by religious leaders. Dark spirits have visited you in the night. God gives a few select people special abilities to oppose them. He is protecting you using human helpers."

"Why does God use helpers to protect me rather than just protect me Himself?"

"I do not understand all of God's ways. I do know that God is not our genie. He wants people to make their own choices, good or evil. Protecting you is good. Evil spirits use humans to do harm by deceiving them. The deceived frequently dabble in sorcery. Spirits make some believe themselves vampires or werewolves. The man who threatened you may have been so tricked. You should be careful of him."

"Do you believe in vampires and werewolves?" Gideon asked.

Ioana shrugged. "I think deceived people might act like vampires or werewolves."

"You mentioned special abilities. Do you have special abilities, Ioana?"

"Not all the time. I cannot choose what I want to know. But sometimes I do know things not evident to others. Terrible things people do in secret. Events before they

47

happen. I know evil spirits have been tormenting you at night."

Gideon spoke earnestly, "Ioana, Christians should avoid becoming entangled in occultism. People who do so become idolaters. The Bible warns us clearly."

Ioana nodded. "Romanian churches also teach this. They are right in doing so. Most people should avoid the supernatural world. But the church does not always recognize that God grants a few people special abilities to oppose evil spirits. Maybe because church leaders rarely have the abilities themselves. We have lost warriors to the forces of darkness. We need a pastor to teach and encourage us."

"There are others besides yourself?"

"Yes. Brother Florin, who came to your house one night to drive away an evil presence. Mama's widow friend, Claudia, who senses evil spirits and prays for you is another. Those who use magic-like abilities for God, we call supernatural warriors."

Gideon shook his head. "This is not what I've been taught, what I believe."

Ioana nodded again before answering. "I understand that."

"Thank you for the wonderful lunch," he said and made an excuse before leaving. "People have free time to talk on Sunday afternoons. I should be trying to meet other villagers."

At that moment, Ioana's hope died. She felt certain she had chased Gideon away with her talk of spirits. Her fate was clear: she would remain alone unless she gave in to marry an inappropriate man. Other than wanting to live to care for Mama, she would have wished to die.

* * *

That night, Gideon suffered another horrifying experience. The ordeal started with a dream. In the dream, he saw and heard his father. "You're failing as a missionary, Gideon, just like you fail at everything," his dream-father accused. "All you've accomplished is a knitting circle of old women. Now you are colluding with a witch. She'll lead you astray with lies and spells. You must condemn her or be pulled into a netherworld apart from God. Your mother and I will be ashamed of you. The church will withdraw your funding. All you'll be fit for is stocking shelves. No woman will ever marry you."

Dad would never speak in such a manner, Gideon thought within the dream. *You must be having a nightmare,* his horror-filled mind concluded. He struggled to wake himself and forced his eyes to open. He saw the cottage interior, dark and peaceful. Far away a summer storm sent flashes from lightning through the windows. Distant thunder rumbled. Gideon took deep breaths as his thumping heart started to slow. Then he heard footsteps inside the cottage as he had before. Glimmers of greenish light started outlining a man-like shadow. The presence grew larger, loomed over Gideon, and radiated coldness. Fearing the apparition, he squeezed his eyelids together, but heard a sound like slow and heavy breathing nearby. The hollow, guttural laughs from his previous experience returned.

"This is not a dream," a deep voice claimed. "I represent the true god. Your attempts to be a missionary are pathetic. Serve me and I will give you a devoted following. Otherwise, the witch, Ioana, will send a spirit to enter your body and control your thoughts and actions."

As Gideon anticipated his heart stopping due to terror, a man's voice came from outside the cottage again. "In the name of Jesus Christ, begone, evil one."

The ominous voice and coldness ceased. Gideon cowered in fear for a moment wondering, *Am I awake or asleep?* An urge within him demanded, *You must determine what is real.* With resolution foreign to him, Gideon opened his eyes, forced himself out of bed, darted to the front door, and jerked it open. His sudden reaction startled a smaller, terrified-looking man outside. Gideon had seen the man in the village at work in a shoe-repair shop.

"You must be Florin," Gideon said. "How did you know to come?"

"Claudia sent me. You should sleep now. I will watch outside and protect you."

Gideon slept without interruption through the remainder of the night. In pleasant dreams, he hiked through the Romanian countryside with Ioana. She guided him in collecting wild mushrooms. After sleeping until well after the sun came up, he went outside to thank Florin, but found him gone. *Was Florin here or part of my dream?* he wondered.

Gideon hurried to the farm to see Ioana. But Christina told him that Ioana had responded to a summons in the night to help a woman in difficult labor. As he started to leave, Gideon heard plaintive *baaa*s from nanny goats waiting to be milked in udder-extended discomfort. The pigs and chickens made noises, hoping to be fed. He didn't know anything about farming, but Christina did. "Can you teach me how to milk a goat?" he asked.

Christina sat down on a three-legged stool. She demonstrating two-handed goat milking by holding teats, pulling gently, and squeezing with her index fingers followed in succession by the other fingers. After a couple of squirts, she struggled to her feet. "I cannot sit so low for long," she explained. "Now you try."

Gideon approached the nanny, which stared suspiciously at him. Her strange rectangular pupils unnerved Gideon. But he reached out and grabbed two surprisingly warm teats. With Christina's coaching, he managed after several tries. The gray cat came as before. Gideon wondered if he might be Ioana's familiar and gave him still-warm milk.

A young woman, still a teenager, screamed as she attempted to give birth to her first child. Hours of labor as Ioana tried to turn the breech baby had completely exhausted the mother-to-be. The umbilical cord had become twisted. The baby's weakening movements made Ioana fear it wasn't getting enough oxygen. She prayed for help and reminded herself, *God helps those who act.* She quickly gave the young mother a strong dose of pain medication. In her head, she reviewed the hospital procedure she had observed a surgeon perform during medical school. Without confidence, she used a sterilized knife to cut the mother's abdomen then uterus to perform her first cesarean delivery. The baby came out of the womb blueish as the young mother gasped in pain. The baby remained still for some seconds while Ioana scissored and tied the umbilical cord. Then quick slaps made the baby bawl.

"You have a son," Ioana told the sobbing mother.

Ioana wiped and wrapped the baby in a clean cloth. Then she called in the nervous father. "This is your son. Hold him close to keep him warm." She waited for and then checked the discharged placenta. Finding it whole, Ioana thanked God. After cleaning the mother, she used some dissolvable thread carried on calls to stitch the incisions. Next, Ioana took the baby from his father and laid him next to the mother, who stopped sobbing to admire her child. Continuing to bawl, the baby gained a healthy pink color. He quieted while Ioana cleaned up the mess.

She waved to the baby's maternal grandmother, who had anxiously watched the delivery through the partially open bedroom door. Handing her the infant, Ioana instructed, "Keep him warm. Let the mother rest a while, then start the child nursing. Coach your daughter about nursing and caring for your grandson."

Before starting home, Ioana spoke to both new parents. "I am out of antibiotics to prevent infection from the cutting. You must go to the hospital in Braşov and let the doctors treat mother and child. I am leaving you a few more painkillers to help until you reach the hospital."

Already exhausted, Ioana began the two-hour walk home. Sadness at her circumstances nearly overcame her. *I'll have a mountain of chores to complete when I get home. The goats are long overdue for milking. And Gideon thinks of me as an idolatrous witch.* But she then felt a rare inner peace saying, *Well done, Daughter. Both mother and baby would have died without your help.*

Ioana staggered a little from fatigue as she hurried the last mile home to start the chores before dark. There in the twilight, she found that Gideon, guided by Christina, had completed all her chores, tended the garden, and even churned the milk. The goats acted unsettled after being milked by an awkward stranger but were relieved, nevertheless. Ioana collapsed to a sitting position on the ground in wonder and exhaustion.

Gideon saw her and hurried over. "Are you alright, Ioana?"

"I'm just completely tired out. Thank you for helping us." Ioana shifted her gaze to Gideon's eyes and reiterated, "Thank you for helping *me*." As Gideon assisted her to her feet, she added, "How are *you* doing?"

"I enjoyed working on your farm today."

"I meant about the spirits we discussed yesterday."

"I think I saw something last night. The man Florin came again . . . I don't understand what happened."

Ioana sensed Gideon's confusion with what he believed to be true versus what he had experienced.

He continued, "I just can't accept that you can somehow supernaturally know things others don't. I would need evidence before I could believe."

"The Bible tells a story about your namesake in the Bible. The biblical Gideon demanded evidence. God gave him the wet fleece and then the dry fleece. Now God will offer you proof through me. Tomorrow, you take the bus down the mountain to Braşov. Use a phone there to call your mother. Today a tumor will be found near your father's heart. He will go into emergency surgery tomorrow after your call. The following day you will phone again to learn that the surgery was a success, and the tumor was benign."

Chapter Five

Gideon sagged in relief after hearing his mother's exclamation of joy. As Ioana had predicted, his first phone call preceded his father's dangerous surgery. The second phone call revealed a successful operation and a benign tumor. His father would fully recover. Astonishment quickly replaced his relief. This proved Ioana had supernatural foreknowledge.

Upon returning to Horvata, Gideon found the village in turmoil. The mother who had undergone the caesarian had developed abdominal pains after her husband delayed taking her to the hospital. Before accompanying his wife in a car to Braşov, the young husband in his fear and grief had lashed out to anyone who would listen.

"The midwife who cut her is not a doctor. That woman is a witch."

A hysterical mob had grabbed Ioana as she bartered cheese and eggs for flour and oil at the village market. An immediate public trial of sorts began. Held between two strong men, Ioana looked terrified. Men she had exposed for doing wrong accused her of witchcraft, saying, "Devils speak to her." Suitors she had rejected called her unnatural. Nobody asserted that the evils she had exposed had been accurate. Nobody mentioned the babies Ioana had successfully delivered or patients who had recovered from injuries she treated.

Agitators in the crowd clamored for ancient tests of witchcraft. Among the loudest, Gideon noticed a cheese-making competitor demand, "Bind her and throw her into water. If she floats, she is a witch."

"Undress her and look for the devil's mark," yelled another male. "Stick her with pins until the mark appears."

Gideon recognized the grubby man who had threatened him. "Burn the witch before she can put curses on us all," the man insisted. A murmur of voices agreed.

Terror filled Ioana as angry faces surrounded her. A frightened mob demanding trial by bonfire created feelings of ultimate fear and helplessness in her.

She saw Gideon pushing through the crowd. He shouted, "Listen to me!" After getting attention, he spoke with determination and defiance. "No one will harm this woman unless you kill me first. The U.S. Embassy would want to know the circumstances of my death. Your newly elected government wants to partner with America. Romanian authorities will find you and charge you with my murder."

Others in the mob insisted, "We can confiscate the witch's property. Then banish the witch and the old woman, Christina."

Gideon spoke firmly again. "Without Ioana, who would deliver your babies? Who else would come at any moment to treat the injured? Who else is willing to risk your rejection for exposing thievery, seduction, and child abuse? Think of the socks knit by Christina." A few unconsciously glanced down at their feet.

"Witches are evil. God will punish us for allowing a witch to live among us," loud voices clamored.

"Let God Himself destroy Ioana if she's an evil witch. But this woman does not practice sorcery like witches condemned in the Bible. I believe her abilities are a gift from God. In the Holy Bible, godly men and a woman named Deborah knew things before they happened. Others had the ability to recognize evil spirits and discern falsehood. The Holy Bible says that you shall know prophets by their fruits. What but good has Ioana done among you? Even in this case, she saved the baby. What mother do you know who would not want her own life risked to save her child?"

After a silence, a man called out, "The American is trustworthy. He speaks our language and takes cheese to orphans."

"He helped repair my roof," another man added.

"After I twisted my ankle, Gideon spent two days hoeing my garden."

"Ioana delivered my baby even when we had nothing to pay her," a woman reported.

"If the American is right that God has gifted Ioana, we must not oppose Him," suggested the butcher.

"Release Ioana," a woman asserted. A chorus of voices consented.

Ioana saw the crowd melt away, leaving her alone with Gideon in the market square. She looked long at him. Then she nodded her gratitude and smiled.

"I guess this would be the wrong time to tell everybody that I know the mother will quickly recover with treatment at the hospital."

Gideon returned her smile and shook his head. "I wouldn't say anything prophetic to those who accused you right now."

She laughed aloud. "I better get home. Mama will wonder where I am."

"Please remind her of Bible study Sunday."

"I will, Gideon."

Walking back to his house, Gideon received an impression like none he had ever experienced. *Well done, Son. You spoke for one who could not speak for herself.*

That night Gideon slept peacefully the entire night for the first time in Romania. On Sunday, all the knitting widows attended his Bible study, as well as Ioana, who accompanied

Christina. Florin entered Gideon's home along with two men and one woman of various ages whom Gideon didn't know. He presumed the others to be spiritually gifted. Without sufficient chairs, the newcomers sat together on the floor, leaning against a wall. Ioana took a seat by her mother.

After serving coffee and cookies, Gideon started by quoting Ephesians 6:12, "For we are not contending against flesh and blood, but against the principalities, against the powers, against the world rulers of this present darkness, against the spiritual hosts of wickedness in the heavenly places." He followed with dramatic stories of Moses, Elijah, and Jesus, who knew things that would happen. He explained the biblical gift of discernment by which gifted men and women could supernaturally determine the difference between truth and deception. The group listened attentively. Several, including Ioana, shed tears of relief for the affirmation they received.

As the attendees departed, Gideon found a cardboard box containing a dressed duck, a bag of wild mushrooms, a jar of honey, and a basket of cherries left for him. Ioana stood waiting until all the others had departed.

"You acted quite forcefully yesterday. I cannot imagine your father being more courageous," she said.

Gideon felt a surge of joy recalling his own boldness and words. He had finally found his voice. But he answered simply, "The situation warranted directness."

"You are open-minded. Be our pastor," demanded Ioana in her forthright way.

Gideon remembered his mother's words praising his open-mindedness. "Whose pastor do you mean?"

"Florin and the others are spiritual warriors who oppose evil spirits on the edge of darkness. To remain strong, they need somebody to love, teach, and care for them. Those gifted who have lost heart and faith, you may be able to restore. None of us asked for the burdens we carry."

"And you, Ioana?"

"Yes, I am also one who needs a pastor."

The enormity of the calling—Pastor of Supernatural Spiritual Warriors—overwhelmed Gideon. He told Ioana, "I'm not trained for that."

"Nobody is trained for this. We need you."

"Must the pastor have magic-like supernatural abilities of his own?"

"The abilities to tell Bible stories and defend others in their calling are also important gifts."

For three minutes of silence, Gideon considered her pastoral challenge with trepidation. Ioana stood frozen in suspense. Gradually he realized, *Mystery, not certainty, makes faith rich.* An impression came from outside him. *Accept the flock that wants and needs you.*

Then Gideon heard his own voice whisper, "I'll do my best to love, teach, and care for you all."

Ioana slumped a little in relief and moved closer, then shyly rested her head on his shoulder. Gideon felt overwhelming confidence that he had found God's place for him.

* * *

Ioana felt Gideon put his arms around her and gently squeeze. No man but her father had ever hugged her. And her Poppa's last hug had been the last time she left home to attend medical school years earlier. Gideon's arms felt lovely. She could feel his heart beating. The stirrings of genuine love started creeping into her as she thought, *I could stretch the feelings of this moment over eternity and always be content. Thank you, God,* she silently prayed. Then Ioana felt relief. A major issue had been settled. The spiritual warriors would have a pastor.

Suddenly another thought intruded. *You are still an unmarried woman in a house alone with a man. He is even embracing you. As if the village gossips need more about you to discuss.* Ioana lifted her head and stepped back. Then she took Gideon's hand and led him outside as was proper for a single Christian woman in rural Romania.

Outside, Ioana reverted to a more reserved demeanor. She dropped Gideon's hand and looked up to see the sun at midday. "I sent Mama home. She will be expecting lunch. Will you join us?"

Gideon nodded. "Okay. Let me lock the door first."

While Gideon locked the cottage door, Ioana realized, *I have nothing prepared to feed him.*

They started walking together in silence, neither knowing what to say. Ioana's mind raced, searching for a lunch menu.

Mama would be satisfied with porridge or boiled potatoes from the garden. Gideon deserves something better. I can take the eggs we had saved for trading and make an omelet.

Gideon's voice disrupted her domestic thoughts. "Can we talk about the pastorate you've challenged me to?"

"Yes, of course."

"Please explain to me more about the gifts you and the others have. I really don't fully understand."

"None of us understand either. I had always wanted to help people and intended to become a doctor. At about age twenty, I developed awareness of dreadful things that people did. I believed the information came from God because the things needed to be stopped. When I exposed people, I made enemies. Rumors about me being a witch started then. Maybe I am a witch."

Gideon shook his head. "You sound more like a prophetess to me. Have you ever tried to do magic?"

"You mean like spells? No, never. But I have prayed to God for things to happen, and they did."

"What about knowing the future, like when you predicted my father's operation?"

"That has only happened a very few times and recently."

"What about the others you call 'supernatural warriors'?"

"Everybody's gift is different. Claudia, Mama's widow friend, knows those who are being spoken to by good and bad spirits. She identified the warriors to each other. Florin confronts evil spirits disguising themselves as ghosts or mentally tormenting someone in the night. But he needs help from the rest of us to know when the spirits will attack. Of the others, Luca can occasionally heal. Daniela senses people's true intentions versus what they say. Andrei can identify people influenced by spirits to do evil, especially those who consider themselves vampires or werewolves."

Gideon shrugged. "The supernatural gifts you describe—knowledge, discernment, healing—aren't unbiblical. They *are* mentioned in the New Testament, especially in chapter twelve of First Corinthians. But the next chapter suggests that gifts will cease. In America, most—but not all—Christians consider the most dramatic gifts like yours and Florin's to have ceased or at least greatly declined a generation or so after Jesus' death."

Ioana laughed and put her hand under Gideon's arm as they walked. "Maybe we are keeping the gifts alive here in Romania."

"Perhaps Romania needs the gifts more than America does."

"Could be," Ioana agreed. "Or maybe America needs them more than they realize."

Chapter Six

At the farm cottage, Gideon listened to Christina's chatter while waiting for lunch. After bustling around in the kitchen, Ioana approached the dining table carrying plates of omelets made with goat cheese and tomatoes from her garden. After serving him and Christina, Ioana collected a plate of omelet for herself, sat down, and waited expectantly. Gideon took the hint and bowed his head.

"Thank you, Lord, for this food and for the hands that made it."

Gideon noticed his portion to be larger than the women's. He took a mouthful that included a blend of egg, cheese, tart tomato, and a hint of paprika for added zest.

"This is delicious, Ioana."

Ioana nodded demurely.

The gray cat came purring and rubbing against their legs as they ate in silence. Gideon spoke in jest to break the quiet. "Is the cat your familiar?"

Ioana laughed. "I wish. But Vlad only makes himself

familiar with warm places to sleep and food." She scooped a spoonful of egg and cheese from her plate and placed it on the stone floor for the cat. "Vlad knows how to take care of himself."

"Where did you get the name Vlad?"

"The historical person Vlad was a fifteenth-century warlord in Wallachia, or south Romania. He sacked villages in our Transylvania and cruelly killed prisoners by impaling them on posts. He is called 'Vlad the Impaler' and was so bloodthirsty that he became the inspiration for the vampire stories. Vlad's father was named Dracul, meaning 'dragon.' Dracula means 'little dragon,' which people called Vlad as his father's son."

Ioana reached down to rub the purring feline behind his ears. "Our cat is mostly lazy and only kills when he has no other food. I named him Vlad because he sometimes plays with his prey. But Western Europe and America distorted all the vampire legends. Traditional vampires are not necessarily after blood, but they do drain a victim's life force. Like con men cheating older people of their money or those who sexually abuse
children."

Christina nodded and added, "The worst like Vlad are aided by evil spirits."

Ioana nodded in agreement.

Gideon thought about vampires and evil spirits as he walked back to his cottage after lunch. He prayed about how he could possibly be a pastor to those who were trying to fight something he didn't understand. *What would my father think?* he wondered.

* * *

The next morning Gideon went into the shoe repair shop where he had seen Florin working. Past a curtain at the back of the shop, he saw a small room being used as living quarters. The smaller man emerged in response to a bell over the shop door.

"Can I help you?" When he recognized Gideon, Florin's face broke into a smile. "Welcome, Mr. Storyteller. I enjoyed your Bible meeting yesterday. Did Ioana convince you to become our pastor?"

Gideon extended his hand. "Yes, she did. I hope to serve you . . . spiritual warriors."

"God bless you," said Florin and gripped Gideon's hand. "Ioana is a good woman, isn't she? And pretty?"

"She is a good woman," Gideon agreed without acknowledging the subtle hint. To himself he thought, *Pretty isn't adequate to describe Ioana.* "Florin, I don't intend to interrupt your work. Would there be a time we could meet? You could tell me about your service for God and about Romania. Would you come to my cottage for coffee?"

"Yes. Tonight, I will come."

That evening Gideon served extra-strong coffee along with pastries to Florin. He sat down at the table across from his guest. "Thank you for coming to my rescue when a spirit threatened me."

"Ioana and Claudia had warned me. Then when I got close, I could sense the evil one."

"How did you receive the ability to repel spirits?"

"My widowed sister in Bucharest asked me to talk to her son. He had been staying out late with strange people and changed from a good son into a bad person. When I confronted him, horrible, blasphemous words came from his mouth. Then my nephew made a terrible face and spoke to me about tools I had taken from the factory where I worked. How could this boy know about the tools other than by a spirit? When he hit me, I asked Jesus for help. Then I remembered a story about Jesus facing demons, and I used his name. The boy cried out and a dark shape left him. My nephew has since resumed being a good son to his mother.

"Later, Claudia visited me and talked about others afflicted by spirits. Sometimes the possessed react with violence and throwing things. It is best if you repel the evil spirit before it inhabits the person and causes them to hurt themselves. Other times, spirits disguise themselves as ghosts to frighten people. I am afraid but also know I must help the people."

"Why are you afraid, Florin?" Gideon asked with respect.

Florin gestured to himself. "You can see I am small. Someday a powerful spirit may make a person injure or kill me."

Gideon sat amazed. Had he not seen the apparition and experienced Florin's help, he could not have believed the story. Having nothing to add, Gideon asked, "How did you learn shoe repair?"

"Under the communists, I made shoes in a factory near Timisoara. But there was never enough leather available. The machines broke down. No spare parts for repairs. Our pay came infrequently. After the revolution four years ago, some former communists used their connections and bribery to gain positions in the new government. The former secret police frequently do their dirty work.

"The former communists in the new government sold the shoe factory where I worked for a pittance to a former comrade. He had Western money collected by bribes banked in Switzerland. Communists converted into capitalists and became millionaires overnight by buying government assets with money stolen before the revolution. That is when I took the tools the spirit knew about and moved back to quiet Horvata, my childhood village. Since new shoes are so expensive, I have enough business repairing old ones to live and to sometimes help my sister and nephew, Audi. A few people pay with leu, but most give me farm produce. Potatoes are our money in Horvata," Florin joked.

Gideon laughed in sympathy. Florin—all the Romanians—lived in a world previously unimaginable to him. "How did the communists take over Romania?"

"During the worldwide Depression of the 1930s, an anti-Semitic and fascist party called the Iron Guard gained influence over the government, just like in Germany. They naturally leaned toward Hitler. We have oil fields on the other side of the mountains near Ploiesti. Germany had to have our oil for their wars and moved five hundred thousand German soldiers into Romania without opposition. After that, our government openly sided with the Nazis. Our King Mihai was only nineteen years old then. I think evil spirits incited both the Iron Guard and Hitler to great evils.

"A million Romanians fought with Germany against the Soviet Union. But the war went badly at Stalingrad. About a hundred and sixty thousand Romanian soldiers died there. Using supplies provided by America, the Russians then pushed the Germans and our Romanian armies back and killed hundreds of thousands more. With the Russians approaching our borders, King Mihai, who was then twenty-four, organized a government coup ousting the Nazi sympathizers. Then he surrendered to the Russians. Afterwards, Romania's remaining armies fought against Germany and lost a hundred and fifty thousand more men. After the war, Russia set up a Stalinist government with Ceauşescu as dictator. That communist government executed or deported to Siberia hundreds of thousands of ethnic Germans living in Romania. Communists forced Mihai to abdicate the throne and move to Switzerland in 1947.

"Ceauşescu made Romania a police state. The secret police monitored everyone. They encouraged children to report their parents for any statement critical of the government. Secret police came by night to arrest anyone suspected of anti-government feelings and torture them. In 1989, Romanians revolted, especially in Timişoara and

Bucharest. A cannon shell killed my wife during the conflict. After ten days of fighting, our revolutionary fighters captured and executed Ceaușescu by firing squad."

"What will Romania do now?" asked Gideon.

"We want to join NATO for protection against the Russians. That is also necessary to attract foreign investment, which we need to become modern."

The two men sat quietly for a minute after the grim lesson in Romanian history. "Will you tell me about America's history?" Florin requested.

* * *

Ioana scrubbed dirty clothes with soapy water in a trough made from a hollowed tree trunk. Her blissful thoughts, mostly about Gideon, made the routine drudgery of farmwork less dismal. *Gideon is a good man. Many American girls, younger and more sophisticated than me, must want him as a husband. I wish he wasn't so handsome. Then he might court me.*

A stocky teenage girl with her hair under a scarf and wearing sandals interrupted Ioana's daydreams of a future with Gideon. "Are you the nurse and midwife, Ioana Nagy?"

I wish I could be Ioana Dixon, Ioana thought, but answered, "Yes."

"You are needed. An accident on the highway leading into the village."

Is a narrow and winding two-lane road considered a highway? Ioana asked herself. But she answered, "Give me a minute to collect my supplies. Then I will follow you."

A brisk two-mile run-walk brought Ioana to the scene. A speeding car, new and imported, had rear-ended a horse-drawn hay wagon on a curve. The crash had thrown four farm workers, who had been riding eight feet off the ground on top of the hay, onto the asphalt. The horse, an older mare, stood shaken in a field nearby. Ioana could see lesions on the animal's legs where she had fallen. But the horse stood steadily.

None of the human injuries appeared to be life threatening but would require treatment. A woman and a young man had ghastly lacerations of their skin. One man had a clean lower arm break. The fourth and most serious, a young woman, had suffered a compound fracture of her thigh. Her husband, who had been working in fields nearby, had run to the scene at the sound of the crash. He now knelt beside her. The car's owner and driver, a short and overweight man of about fifty years old, stood smoking a cigar and examining scratches on his new Mercedes.

Ioana prioritized the woman with the compound fracture, who groaned hysterically due to the pain. "You will need to go to the hospital for proper care. Let us immobilize your leg and get you into the car. Take this pain killer."

"Wait a minute," complained the car's owner. "The hospital in Braşov is ninety kilometers away. I'm already late for a meeting. Just clear these people off the road so I can go."

"This woman could be permanently crippled unless she has surgery and traction. Surely your meeting is not that important."

"That's for me to decide. Now I order you to get these people off the road."

Ioana did not flinch. "You are driving that woman to the hospital. If you refuse to take her, I will commandeer your car due to an emergency and leave you walking to your meeting."

"You think *you* can take my car?" the driver sneered.

"No, but these men can." Ioana pointed to four additional men who had come out of an adjacent farm field to watch. Each man nodded affirmation to Ioana.

Chapter Seven

Thirty minutes later, the car headed to the hospital. The woman, with her leg strapped securely to a board, rode still crying in the spacious back seat along with her husband. In the passenger seat sat the strongest and youngest of the field workers.

"If he isn't cooperative," Ioana had pointed at the fuming driver, "smash his face and take the car. He can collect his car when we finish with it."

For two more hours, Ioana cleaned, treated with antiseptic, and stitched wounds. She set and carefully cast the clean arm fracture. "Come see me in ten days for the stitches, three weeks to have the cast removed," she told her patients.

The farmer who had been driving the wagon approached her apologetically. "Missus, if you don't mind." He pointed to the mare now grazing but with lesions still visible.

"Of course. I will need help holding her," Ioana said to the crowd that had collected.

In another hour, Ioana walked home with about two

dollars' worth of leu contributed by those she had treated and the promise of a load of hay from the horse's owner. She thought about the situation she had experienced. *Who is that callous car driver? Somebody called him Primar Serban. Daniela, who senses motives, told me that our primar participates in bad things. Something about money. Daniela could not understand what.* The word "Caritas" came to Ioana. *I will ask Gideon.* Then her thoughts returned to wistful thoughts about her future.

* * *

Darius reveled in the comradery of men like himself. After a hard week working as a hired laborer, he needed a diversion, hopefully an adventure, on Saturday night. "Hired" would be a generous description of his employment. Food and a place to sleep in a shed were his only compensation. As a former orphan, he hoped for no more.

Now he could enjoy the company of men in similar situations. He had joined nine of them in the light of a bonfire built in a remote glen of the mountains. Darius saw horsing around, impromptu wrestling matches, and hilarious scenes acted out. He laughed at ribald and sexist jokes. Jars of homemade liquor passed from hand to hand. Anybody who coughed after swallowing the alcohol straight became the object of ridicule. When Darius coughed, he enjoyed being the center of attention that lasted until someone else failed the swallow test.

One man, older than the rest and grim-faced, watched with a more reserved demeanor. Darius noticed the others gave him deference. The man approached Darius. "Having fun, brother?"

Darius straightened up and tried to look more mature than his nineteen years. "Yes, sir."

The grim-faced man nodded acknowledgment of Darius's respect. "Well, we have a sort of team here. I'm the leader. I have heard that you're a take-what-you-want type of man."

"Yes, sir!" Darius spoke with enthusiasm.

"Would you be interested in joining our pack of brothers? We are called The Werewolves. Warning though, if you pass the initiation and join us, you are always in. No backing out."

"Yes, sir. I mean, no, sir! I would not back out."

The man patted Darius on the back and laughed. "Then we will determine if you have what it takes to be a werewolf later tonight. If you do, you will get a special name."

The group's boisterousness slowed as the men became more intoxicated. The bonfire died to a red glow. But a full moon made the glen bright. The werewolves' leader hushed the men and then called out, "We are ready to meet you, spiritual protector of the pack."

The men quieted. Darius saw the werewolf leader staring at a darker shape in the shadow cast by a fir tree in the bright moonlight. Several men instinctively shied back from the black shape. Gradually, greenish gleams of light coming from behind the shape outlined a man-like figure.

The figure spoke in a hollow voice like two voices in unison. "I sense a newcomer. Step forward, Darius."

Darius felt his knees weaken with fear. A chill passed through his body. He resisted the urge to flee and forced himself to take five steps toward the apparition.

The hollow voice spoke directly to Darius. "I saw you break your employer's wheelbarrow by overloading it. Then you blamed another. You have dark desires for the fourteen-year-old milk girl. You stole the widow's bread."

Darius gasped in surprise. He wondered, *How could anyone know so much about me?*

"You want to be a werewolf? You must pass an initiation in front of the pack brothers," continued the spirit.

The grim-faced man opened a previously unnoticed bag lying on the ground and removed a live chicken by its feet. "To join us, you must bite the head off this prey." He handed the chicken to Darius.

When grabbed by the feet, the rooster squawked and flapped. Darius became aware of snickers from the men. He clutched the bird to his chest, pinning its wings. He looked up in surprise and confusion. The men roared in laughter.

Darius had no idea how to bite off a chicken's head. He first thought about putting the entire head into his mouth. Fear that the bird would peck his tongue stopped him from trying. He decided to try for a neck bite and used his hands to stretch the bird's head away from its body. He took a deep breath, placed the neck in his jaws, and bit down. The chicken struggled but pressure from Darius's teeth stopped its squawking. Darius couldn't bite through the skin and bones, though. He grinded his teeth, bit down harder, and felt bones crushing. Hot blood flowed into his mouth, almost choking him. As the chicken's body spasmed, he released his bite grip, leaving the chicken's neck unsevered, and spit the blood out.

The werewolves circled within feet of him, shouting encouragement. In desperation, Darius clamped the neck with his teeth and used his hands to tear the bird's body away. He dropped the head and carcass. Men pounded Darius's back in approval and roared with laughter as he leaned over to throw up.

The werewolf leader pushed through the men congratulating Darius and handed him a jar of liquor. "Welcome to the pack. You can call me He Who Kills."

Darius swigged a mouthful of the liquor, glad for anything to take away the foul taste of chicken blood. Swallowing, he felt his throat burning but clenched his teeth to not cough. The men roared again and renewed the back slapping. For the first time in his life, Darius felt like he belonged.

When the tumult quieted, the men looked back at the dark man-like shape that He Who Kills had called their spiritual protector.

"Well done," the figure said to Darius. "I name you Bloodthirsty." The men shouted approval, then became silent.

Next the spirit warned the werewolves. "We have a foreign cult challenging our Romanian traditions and values," the spirit said using low-pitched, deliberate words. "The cult comes from America, who supplied arms to the Russians who ravaged our country and killed our finest men. If you intimidate and silence the witch-woman named Ioana, the cult leader will return to America. We will be pure again." The dark figure gradually grew smaller and disappeared.

* * *

The morning after talking with Florin, Gideon told himself, *You need a break to think everything through.* The late-summer Transylvanian countryside drew him. A path led him through farm fields with cut hay drying in the August sun. He remembered his pleasant dreams about hiking with Ioana.

A distant call interrupted his thoughts. "Hello, Bible teacher!"

Gideon looked to a nearby field and saw a sweat-covered teenager holding a handmade hay rake. The tall young man looked nearly as thin as the rake handle. He dropped the rake and ran to join Gideon on the path.

"Do you remember me?" he asked. "I came to your house to hear Bible stories. My name is Luca."

"I'm glad you came, Luca. Did you like the stories?"

"Yes, I had heard about Joseph before. But not as exciting as you told it."

"Where did you hear before?" asked Gideon.

"In Pastor Raphael's church. My family is Protestant, like you."

Gideon nodded acknowledgement. "How did you know to come to my house?"

"Claudia invited me. She thinks I'm part of a special group. She calls us 'spiritual warriors.'"

"Are you part of that group?"

Luca shrugged. "Maybe. I can't sense spirits or anything. I just want to help people."

"How do you help?"

"This is my father's farm. Once I found an ewe with a broken leg. She bleated so piteously that I prayed from my heart for her. Then she jumped up and ran away on a healed leg. I've since prayed for people that Claudia told me had been hurt by spirits. But I tell no one. If people knew, they would think I'm strange."

No matter what country, teenagers never want to be labeled as strange, thought Gideon. "You are not strange, Luca. But you may have a special gift from God."

"Do you think so?"

"Yes, I do. Is every person you pray for healed?"

Luca shook his head. "No, not all. But I sometimes get a confident feeling deep inside me. Then I pray hard, and they are healed every time."

After spending an hour talking to Luca and discussing Bible passages that dealt with healing, Gideon ventured back into Horvata.

Gideon sat at the table in his cottage with an open Bible during the late afternoon. He wrote notes about the story of David's sins against Bathsheba and Uriah and the troubles that ensued. In his mind, he rehearsed voices and gestures he would use to bring the story to life.

A knock on the door broke his concentration. Opening the door, he found a large, well-built man in his early thirties dressed in work clothes that smelled faintly of tar. The man's face angling downwards gave him an apologetic demeanor. A huge, friendly-eyed dog without signs of any recognizable breed accompanied the big man.

"Hello, Mr. Dixon. I like the stories you tell. The ones from the Holy Bible."

Gideon recognized the man as one who had attended Bible study with Florin. "Please come in and sit down. Let me make some coffee." The dog followed his master inside. When the man turned to force his companion out, Gideon added, "I don't mind your dog coming in."

"You mean inside your home, Mr. Dixon?"

"Sure. He looks well behaved. And you can call me Gideon." Gideon put water on to boil while the man sat down uneasily at the table. The dog quietly lay down at his feet. "And your name is . . . ?"

"My name is Andrei," the man returned. "We start work early in the hot summer. I am finished for the day now."

"And what work do you do, Andrei?"

"Road repair."

Gideon added ground coffee into the heated water and

opened a package of cookies. He extended one hand with a cookie to the dog, who gently accepted it and chewed quietly. "What's your dog's name?"

Andrei looked fondly at his canine friend. "I named him Dragon because I like dragons. He has been my friend since my wife died."

More mythology, thought Gideon. *But considering what I've seen since coming to Romania, who knows?* "Have you ever seen a real dragon, Andrei?"

"No, but I would like to."

"The Bible mentions dragons in the book of Revelation. I'd like to see one too." Andrei perked up at Gideon's biblical reference. "How did your wife die?" Gideon continued.

"Childbirth." Andrei looked down and paused before he could continue. "We had no doctor here until Ioana came home."

"I'm very sorry, Andrei." Gideon poured coffee for both, pushed the plate of cookies forward, and sat opposite Andrei. "Are you a friend of Florin's?"

"We look out for each other. Him and the others who battle spirits."

"And how do you battle spirits, Andrei?"

"Me? I just know who the spirits direct and how. I tell Florin, who forces them away. Or Claudia, who prays for protection for those afflicted."

"You mean you have the gift of discernment?"

"I don't know. I just want to help people. Florin, Ioana, and Claudia do the real battling."

"And what do you discern about spirits?"

"I can tell how the spirits are directing people, especially vampires and werewolves, sometimes witches. I know that a werewolf threatened to 'spill your blood in the night.'"

Andrei's knowledge of his encounter in the village surprised Gideon. "Who else do you know is being directed by spirits?"

"The local primar named Serban and Prefect Lazar. They are like vampires. Taking people's life force. The Orthodox church's older priest, Father Flavius, is one too. And a man who calls himself 'He Who Kills.' He leads a group who call themselves werewolves."

"How about you, Andrei? Do the spirits bother you?"

Andrei hung his head. "Only in my head, like they do all of us. They make me afraid."

"What do you do to deal with your fear?"

"I have come to you for help."

Andre's words staggered Gideon. He remembered that he had agreed to pastor those with supernatural gifts. *What would Dad do?* he wondered. He could not imagine his father in this situation. Still, he needed to offer comfort to Andrei.

Chapter Eight

Gideon's open Bible remained on the table. "You and I will read some scriptures together," he said. Then we can memorize a couple."

"I am not very good at learning things in books."

"I'll memorize the verses with you. Then we can repeat them to each other. When spirits bother either of us, we should quote the scriptures."

"Thank you, Pastor."

Gideon busied himself looking up scriptures. He dared not try to use his throat at that moment for fear of choking up. He had never before been called "Pastor."

Finding his voice, Gideon read, "'Resist the devil and he will flee from you. Draw near to God and he will draw near to you.' That's James chapter four verse seven. Now I'll say the first few words to you, and you'll repeat them to me. We'll add a few words at a time until we can say the whole verse. Now repeat, 'Resist the devil . . .'"

An hour later, Andrei took Dragon and departed with his

head held high, mumbling scriptures to himself.

* * *

Low on coffee from serving guests, Gideon needed to replenish his supply. At a village food shop smaller than his cottage, he found himself the only customer. Shelves higher than his head formed narrow aisles. The merchandise mostly consisted of bulk foods and local produce.

"We have more access to Western foods since the revolution," the matronly woman who waited to check out customers explained. "But they are too expensive for most people in Horvata."

Gideon recognized her from the previous Sunday. "You came to the Bible study at my cottage."

"I didn't know if you would remember me," she answered. "I am Daniela. This is my husband's and my store."

Gideon placed a large, prepackaged bag of coffee beans on the counter. "Could you grind these for me?"

"Of course." Daniela opened the bag and poured the beans into the grinder's hopper. She put the bag under the chute to be refilled as the blade chopped the beans. Odors of ground coffee filled the air.

"Ioana told me that you're one of the warriors. That you can sense people's motivations. Is that accurate?"

"It seems so. And I know they all want to do good. The warriors, I mean. I do sense that motivation in them."

"How about me? What do you sense about me?"

"You also want to do good. But even more, you want to prove yourself to your father."

Gideon felt naked and vulnerable having a woman he didn't know verbalize that which he had hardly acknowledged himself. He remained silent for a long moment while Daniela waited for his agreement or denial.

He smiled and nodded. "That's enough to convince me your gift is genuine."

"Your honesty with yourself convinces me you will be a good pastor for us. I can also sense evil people's motives."

"Do you mean those who are influenced by evil spirits?"

"Yes. You see, spirits can also sense people's inner motivations. They use those motivations to manipulate them."

Gideon remembered Andrei's identification of the primar as being a vampire. "What does Primar Serban want?"

"Money. And the things or people money can buy."

"How about Prefect Lazar?"

"He wants to control people. He bribed his way into the government to gain power."

Gideon thought about the Orthodox priest that Andrei had named. "What does the priest Father Flavius want?"

"The glory of God for himself. And sex with young girls."

"Do you know a man calling himself He Who Kills?"

"I know he exists and considers himself a werewolf. He wants to be a leader of men who respect no law or decency." Daniela looked away. "I know these things but am afraid to tell anyone. I want to help people, but don't know how."

A burly man came out from an office at the rear of the

shop. "My husband. He is a good man but is not very religious," Daniela whispered. She hastily sealed the coffee bag. "That will be four American dollars," she said aloud.

"Thank you," said Gideon as he handed her the money.

"I'll see you on Sunday," Daniela whispered as Gideon departed.

Once Gideon had met each of the spiritual warriors, he made a list of them and the abilities they claimed. He found the gifts didn't fit what he had been taught about biblical gifts exactly. *But then scriptures don't define the gifts exactly either,* he thought. *Or maybe the spiritual gifts listed in various places are meant as examples. Believers could have hybrid gifts based on their personalities and circumstances. Obviously though, the warriors have supernatural abilities from God.* He studied the list he had made.

<u>Warriors with supernatural gifts</u>
Ioana – prophecy
Claudia – faith and prayer, ability to sense spiritual attacks on others
Andrei – distinguishing spirits
Luca – healing
Daniela – wisdom to discern motives
Florin – faith to expel evil spirits

What do they have in common? Gideon asked himself. He remembered their words, "I just want to help people." *Maybe God has given greater gifts to those who have a passion to help others. Or maybe God gave that passion as part of their gift.*

* * *

Creeping single file in darkness late on a Saturday-night mission with his werewolf brothers excited Darius. Together they would defend Romanian culture against a foreign cult. He knew werewolves should not allow the morality of commoners to restrain them in defense of Romania's way of life. They would take what they wanted. They would spill blood that night. Maybe even human blood. A jug of liquor passed up and down the line.

The pack followed He Who Kills through the woods and onto Ioana's farm. "This is where the foreign cultist witch lives," said their leader. "Our spiritual protector is expecting us to punish and intimidate her. Spread out and see what you can find."

Darius explored the dark farmyard. He heard the creak of an opening door. The voice of one of his brothers called softly, "Anybody hungry? I found cheese in the root cellar."

Darius hurried to find his brothers each holding a spherical cheese. He Who Kills broke his open and bit into it. The other werewolves followed his example. Darius had never enjoyed the luxury of all the cheese he could eat. After filling their stomachs, the werewolves crushed the remaining cheese with their feet. Entering the barn, the intruders found livestock. Frightened in the darkness, the two-hundred-fifty-pound pigs broke through their attackers and headed for the woods. Trapped in their enclosures, the goats and chickens couldn't escape so easily. One of the wolfpack handed Darius a live chicken.

"Here Bloodthirsty, want something to drink with your cheese?"

Darius pushed the terrified bird away and tried to speak convincingly. "I want something bigger."

The werewolves chased the chickens and goats into the barnyard. There they cornered a half-grown kid.

A loud ruckus in the barnyard woke Ioana. She heard her pigs squealing and running. Then came sounds of chickens squawking and goats bleating. The frantic cries of a goat kid in distress broke her heart. Ioana started to hurry outside in her bedclothes. To her surprise, Christina blocked the door.

"Don't go outside, Ioana," Christina ordered in an authoritative voice that Ioana hadn't heard since childhood.

Ioana shouted through an open window, "Who is out there? Stop what you are doing! Leave our farm!"

A chorus of human throats mimicking wolf calls and growls answered her. "Come outside and stop us, witch-woman," one voice answered.

Rather than leave the cottage, Ioana started screaming "Help!" out the window for her neighbors to hear.

Thrown rocks broke three of the cottage's windows. Someone rattled the locked door, trying to get inside. Ioana heard a male voice say, "Find an axe or something to break down the door."

Ioana looked for a weapon and picked up a fire poker. Then the lights of neighboring houses started coming on in response to her screams. Dogs in the area barked. Male voices yelled from nearby houses. Ioana heard feet running as the attackers withdrew.

She looked around for Vlad and found the cat cowering under her bed. "A lot of good you are," she told him. He replied with a cautious *Rrrow.*

Christina abandoned her spot blocking Ioana from the door and sat down in her rocking chair, distraught and weeping.

"They are gone now, Mama. You stay inside while I check for damage."

Ioana turned on a rarely used outside light and then, seeing no one, opened the door. She stepped into the barnyard still carrying the fire poker and a flashlight. There she found one of her young goats killed and partially eaten raw. Bloody human fingerprints and footprints fouling the ground and surfaces showed in the flashlight's beam. Elsewhere items had been turned over, tools broken, cheeses ruined, and all her animals had disappeared.

* * *

The frightened goats and pigs drifted back in the early morning light. Ioana milked the nanny goats and gave the pigs the despoiled cheeses. Her chickens remained spooked. Several sat in low branches of nearby trees but wouldn't come down. Ioana scattered cracked corn on the ground to coax them back.

Christina remained frightened and needed comfort. So they dressed and walked together to attend Gideon's Bible study. All nine who'd attended the previous week were there, plus two more villagers who had heard about Gideon's entertaining stories. Seeing Gideon's facial expressions and gestures mimicking possible reactions of the disciples to stories told by Jesus did seem to reassure Christina and made everybody laugh.

After the stories and a discussion about how to apply Jesus' teaching, the warriors lingered in Gideon's cottage. Ioana sent Christina home with one of Christina's widowed friends. Then Ioana described with dismay their late-night fright and the destruction left behind by the intruders. Everyone looked alarmed.

"This is the first time any of us has been attacked," said Florin.

"Don't you have a guard dog?" asked Daniela.

Ioana shook her head. "We can hardly feed ourselves. Big dogs eat a lot."

Andrei looked down at Dragon curled at his feet. "One man may be afraid of a dog. A group of marauding men could have quickly killed any dog you had."

"I'll start sleeping in your barn," Gideon offered.

"No," Ioana answered. "You need your rest here." She gestured toward the warriors and herself. "And we all need to know you are available at your cottage in case of an emergency."

"Wasn't *this* an emergency?" Gideon countered.

"Yes. But future emergencies are likely to occur elsewhere," Ioana explained.

The others nodded in agreement with Ioana. Gideon spoke to them firmly. "Alright then. Anytime one of you is threatened or senses a potential attack, you must try to summon me. I will come and bring with me any of you who could provide aid." The group nodded assent.

"I'll stay awake praying all night and sleep during the day. Maybe God will show me where a nighttime attack will occur. Then I can tell Pastor Gideon," Claudia offered.

"Thank you, Claudia," said Gideon. Then he asked everyone, "Who do you think did this?"

"The howls and dead goat sound like a pack of werewolves," answered Andrei.

"But there wasn't a full moon last night."

The warriors, except for Ioana, politely laughed, thinking Gideon had tried a joke. Ioana stopped their laughter with a stern look. Then she spoke to Gideon. "I tried to explain before. Werewolves are not like those depicted in your

Western books and cinema. They do not change shape and grow wolf teeth under a full moon. They are humans influenced by spirits to conduct bloody rituals in the forest. The troublemakers kill animals and eat the flesh raw. God almost always restrains Satan and his evil spirits from harming humans directly. But because God gives free will to humans, the spirits can incite humans to commit violence against other humans. Those who voluntarily become werewolves under the direction of evil spirits can be extremely dangerous."

Andrei said, "A man who accused Ioana in the square of being a witch is a werewolf who calls himself He Who Kills. He had nearly convinced the mob to burn her alive. Then Pastor Gideon defended and saved her. I was there but afraid to do anything."

Gideon stepped forward, put his hand on Andrei's shoulder, and looked the big man in the eyes. "We are all afraid, brother. I am the most afraid because spirit activities are new to me." He looked at each of the warriors in turn. "We are all safest if we depend on and defend each other."

Andrei reached with his arms and embraced Gideon. All the others joined the group hug. After a long minute, they stepped back and exchanged glances of commitment.

* * *

Gideon saw Florin remaining after the others departed. "Ioana needs more protection, Pastor."

The title of pastor gave Gideon's heart a little thrill and yet humbled him. "I offered to sleep in her barn."

"A single woman having a single man staying at her home, even if he sleeps in the barn, is not proper. People would talk. Their talk would affect your ministry and make those of us who follow you presumed of condoning immorality."

Gideon lifted his hands in a show of frustration. "What can I do?"

"You could marry Ioana," replied Florin directly. "You will not find a finer woman. You and Ioana need each other."

Gideon could hardly believe his ears. "Isn't this rather fast?"

"I know American ways of romantic courtship are different from ours. Ioana has let you see all she is. You know enough about her to decide."

Gideon remained silent for a long minute. "Ioana *is* wonderful. Too good for me." Internally, Gideon struggled. *What would Mom and Dad think? They could see Ioana as a witch. And why would Ioana marry me? Would I set myself up for a humiliating refusal? Create an awkward situation among our group?* After another quiet minute he asked, "Do you think Ioana would accept?"

"I do. Talk to her, Pastor."

Chapter Nine

The following morning Ioana leaned her cheek against a nanny goat's side while milking. She couldn't stop thinking about the goat kid the werewolves had killed. Tears ran down her cheeks. Gideon showing up so early surprised her.

"Why are you crying, Ioana?" he asked.

Ioana felt embarrassed and wiped her face on her sleeve. "I'm sad about the young goat killed by the werewolves. I had helped the nanny deliver her kid. I named her Daisy. She would have had a good goat life here and given us much milk."

"I'm sorry," Gideon returned. "Would you like me to bury Daisy for you?"

"Mama and I can't afford to waste meat. I butchered the carcass last night. The meat is in the root cellar. The pigs ate the rest."

"Uh . . . okay, then."

"Why are you here, Gideon? You look tired."

"I lay awake all night," he confessed.

Ioana finished milking one nanny, patted the goat's bottom to move on, and started milking another. "Were spirits bothering you?"

"No. I was thinking about you, Ioana."

"Thinking about me?"

"I wouldn't want to see anything happen to you. You need protection. I could take care of you."

Ioana stopped milking and partially turned on the milking stool to face Gideon. "What are you saying?"

"Have you ever thought about getting married to someone?"

Of course I have, Ioana thought. *What unmarried Romanian woman has not? Is this a clumsy proposal? If it is, do not make it hard on Gideon.*

Ioana stood up. "Yes, I would very much like a husband to be my friend and partner. Someone kind, generous, and strong . . . like you. I would be a good wife to that husband."

Gideon's heart soared at Ioana's words, "like you." His voice wavered a bit as he asked, "Do you love me, Ioana?"

She smiled and shook her head. "You Americans allow feelings to make your decisions. In Romania, we are more practical. I respect you, Gideon. You are a good man. I would give you my whole heart after I knew you wanted me for a lifetime."

"I'm not experienced at love myself, but I know that you're the best woman in the world for me. Would you marry *me,* Ioana?"

Ioana felt elation, but more powerfully, relief, that she had—or would have—a fine husband. "Yes, I will marry you," she answered without hesitation. As Gideon approached and wrapped her in his arms for a prolonged hug, Ioana felt unreserved acceptance. At that moment, Ioana knew she could do, would do, anything to be a good wife for Gideon.

After they parted from the embrace, Ioana smiled at her intended and said, "We have a lot to talk about."

"Yes . . . we . . . do," he returned. "I've never been engaged before," Gideon managed to say. "What should we talk about first?"

"You are not officially engaged yet. Our custom is for you to ask my father for permission to marry me. Then, should he agree, he tells me that I am betrothed and welcomes you to the family. In my father's absence, you will need to ask Mama. She will be delighted, of course. If you are ready, you could do that while I am fixing lunch. Then we could talk about our wedding and marriage." Ioana held her breath waiting for Gideon to affirm his commitment.

"I'm ready. I'll ask her before lunch," Gideon answered.

Ioana felt a second surge of relief followed by a surge of feelings toward him. *This must be the beginning of genuine love,* she thought.

"Then help me finish the chores," she told Gideon. "Then I will make a special lunch to celebrate the day of our betrothment. How about some fresh goat?"

*   *   *

Gideon sat on the couch waiting for lunch with Christina. Sounds of rattling cookware came from the tiny kitchen where Ioana prepared goat stew. He could smell meat browning in a skillet. Christina rocked in her chair and chatted about her friends and bits of village gossip.

"Mrs. Nagy, I have something to ask you," he interrupted. "You have a lovely daughter."

"She would make some young man a wonderful wife," Christina agreed.

"What about me? Could I have the honor of marrying Ioana?"

Christina looked at Gideon and smiled. "Certainly. I do not need to ask her. I can see in her eyes that she would agree. She probably already has accepted." Christina turned toward the kitchen. "Ioana, come in here."

Ioana appeared, wearing an apron and holding a wooden spoon, which she had been using to stir the stew. "Ioana, I have given you to Gideon as his wife."

Gideon saw Ioana exhale deeply, a reverse gasp. She glanced at Gideon and winked before respectfully nodding. "Yes, Mama." Ioana smiled shyly at Gideon and hurried back to the kitchen.

"Welcome to the family, Gideon," said Christina and resumed her chatter as if nothing monumental had happened.

Minutes later Ioana returned. "Please sit at the table, Mama and Gideon. Lunch is ready." Gideon took the place at the head of the table as he had at their previous lunches. Ioana had made a Hungarian stew with potatoes, onions, carrots, black pepper, flour for thickener, and of course a bit of paprika. A dash of vinegar sharpened the taste.

After lunch, Christina nodded off to sleep in her rocking chair as was her habit. Gideon saw Ioana gesture to follow her into the kitchen. Out of sight should Christina wake, she put her arms around his waist and pulled him close. She stood on her toes to kiss his lips gently at first then more passionately. After a minute she leaned back and said, "Now I can say that I love you."

Gideon squeezed her hard enough to make her playfully squeal. "I love you too, Ioana."

The couple tiptoed quietly outside to avoid disturbing Christina. Ioana led Gideon to the beech tree where they had sat together before. Ioana pulled her chair close to Gideon's. "I wish tomorrow was our wedding day and our wedding night," she said without blushing.

Gideon felt his pulse quicken at her implication. "I'd like my father to marry us, if you don't mind."

"Your father is a priest?"

"No, we're Protestants. Dad is a senior pastor and preaches to more than three thousand worshipers each Sunday, and many thousands watch on the TV. He is famous in America."

Ioana shook her head slowly in wonder of such unbelievably large crowds. "Yes, you told me that before.

Having your father preside at our wedding would be an honor. How soon can he get here?"

Gideon shrugged. "I don't know." Inwardly, he dreaded the prospect of telling his parents about a sudden marriage to a woman they didn't know. *Mom will consider this a quick and rash decision. She is certain to object.*

"Well, please ask him to hurry. And your mother should come too. What are your parents' names?"

"Aaron and Madeline Dixon. My grandparents hoped for a preacher in the family. They named Dad after Moses' brother who spoke for God. Aaron means 'exalted' or 'strong.' That certainly fits Dad. Madeline comes from Mary Magdalene who first saw Jesus after his resurrection."

"Do you think Aaron and Madeline will like me?"

"Of course." To himself, Gideon added, *Eventually.*

Ioana noticed extra eagerness when Gideon then asked, "Where would you like to spend our honeymoon?"

"What is a honeymoon?" Ioana asked in return.

"You know. The first week or two after the wedding. Like a vacation. We could go to the seashore in Turkey or to Paris."

"I must continue taking care of Mama, the goats, chickens, and pigs. People are likely to need my medical help. I cannot go away."

When Gideon looked crestfallen, Ioana added in the way of recompense, "We could sleep alone at your cottage in town for a few days. I have been waiting to be with a lover for a long time. Trust me, you will not be thinking about walking by the ocean or climbing the Eifel Tower."

Having satisfied Gideon, Ioana moved onto post-nuptial arrangements. "After our in-village 'honeymoon,' you can move here to the farm. I will put Mama and Poppa's bigger bed in my room. Mama can have my smaller bed."

When Gideon didn't object, Ioana continued with practical plans. "We're far from a certified doctor here. Even if there were doctors, most rural people could not afford them. The new government does not have enough money to pay the doctors formally supported by the state. That is why virtually all doctors require monetary 'tips' from patients. Most people around here have little or no money to tip them. The people here need me. One thing good about communism was free education, if you could excel at the qualifying exams. I trained as a nurse in high school and completed three of six years of medical college. So, I do get some locally grown food and occasionally a little money for my medical services." Ioana paused a moment. "But we'll need a lot more food to feed you along with me and Mama."

"I enjoy working on the farm. My father says, 'If someone else has learned a skill, you can too.'"

Ioana became somber. "Good. You can plant larger gardens and manage more livestock. When Poppa died and left Mama with no income or food, I came home. Mama and

I ate soup with meatballs made of rats that Vlad caught until I could get the farm producing food."

Gideon leaned forward. "Have you forgotten that I have money? American money? I can buy food for us. We won't need to eat rats."

Chapter Ten

Ioana sat flabbergasted. She *had* forgotten Gideon's money. Her mind raced at the possibilities. "After we are married, would you buy some medical things for me? Antibiotics? Maybe a used bicycle?"

"You don't need to wait until then. I'll give you money for your practice and other things you need now. Would a thousand dollars be enough to start?"

Ioana felt woozy enough to faint. *A thousand American dollars? That's more money than I've ever seen. More than Mama and Poppa ever accumulated.* "We are betrothed. Would it be improper for me to ask how much money you have?"

Gideon looked embarrassed. "My missionary salary from my father's church is only fourteen hundred dollars a month."

All that money every month? Ioana marveled to herself.

Gideon continued, "But I can also reimburse ministry expenses within reason. Once we're married, my father's church may, probably will, increase my salary. And then we can consider your practice a reimbursable part of our ministry."

Ioana thought her heart would burst with joy. *I am getting married to a good man. And I had forgotten that he brought money. I will have a thousand American dollars to buy medical supplies to help people.*

She sat in rapture until Gideon asked, "Is anything the matter?"

"No, I had just anticipated us scratching out a living together on the farm." After a moment of reflection, she added, "Gideon, we can do so much good with your money!"

"I hope so," he answered. Neither spoke for several minutes as they thought about the possibilities. "What should we do with the house I rent in town?"

"You can stay there until the wedding, of course. Then you might keep it for your Bible studies and the warriors meeting," Ioana responded.

"That's a promising idea." Gideon thought another minute. "Should we talk about babies now?"

"Do not worry. They will come."

"I meant, how many children would you like to have?"

"I do not know. Right now, I am just happy to have found a good husband. More than one child, I hope. I grew up without brothers or sisters. I would like our children to have siblings. And understand this," she said, "in Romania, the husband is the head of the family. But when it comes to things like food and raising babies, the wife is the neck, and whichever way the neck turns, so does the head."

Gideon laughed and nodded assent. The shadows had lengthened in the late afternoon. Ioana rose to do the farm chores. Gideon helped under her instruction. When they finished early, Ioana pulled Gideon into the barn for more kissing.

"If you need a heart transplant, Ioana, I will donate mine," Gideon whispered in her ear.

"You think I need a heart transplant?"

"I'm trying to express how much I love you."

"Oh! American romance includes operations?" Ioana teased him.

After riding the slow and frequently stopping bus for two hours to Brasov, Gideon found that the bank would only allow him to withdraw $300 on his credit card at one time. Tellers made him take the money in Romanian leu. Sixty-eight thousand leu in mostly small denominations filled a bag.

At a public phone, he waited, dreading his parents' reaction to his engagement, for an hour while the Romanian operator connected them. At 6:00 a.m. US time, Gideon heard his father's deep voice. "Hello, Son. Sorry I missed your last call."

"Well, being in intensive care with a tumor near your heart would make talking to me difficult."

Aaron's robust laugh at the quip reassured Gideon.

"I've got some good news, Dad. Get Mom on the phone with you, please."

"I'm already on the extension, honey," said Madeline. "How are you surviving? Are you getting enough to eat?"

"I'm fine, Mom."

"So, what's the good news, Son?" demanded his father.

"I'm getting married." Silence answered Gideon. When neither of his parents spoke, Gideon tried to add details. "Her name is Ioana Nagy. She's my age, never been married, and a Christian. She's a midwife and a farmer. She takes care of her elderly mother . . ." Gideon trailed off, not knowing what else to tell his parents.

His mother spoke first. "This is too soon, Gideon. How well can you possibly know this woman? You haven't been there two months yet."

"Just wait until you meet her," insisted Gideon.

Aaron tried to be positive. "Well, you're both old enough to marry."

"Thanks, Dad. Ioana and I are hoping you'll come over and conduct the ceremony."

"Of course, I'd like to, Son. But the doctors say I can't travel for six months after the surgery."

Dismay overwhelmed Gideon. "I hadn't thought about that." He remembered Ioana's desire—one he shared—to marry quickly. "Well, I guess we could wait."

Madeline spoke again, her words coming fast. "That's a good idea. We'll come over in six months, if the doctors allow. Maybe in a year."

His father changed the subject. "How's the ministry going, Son?"

"I've started a Bible study on Sunday mornings in the house I rent. Last week, eleven attended. The Romanians are religious but don't know the Bible very well."

"Are you teaching them Scripture?"

"Yes, sir."

"Well, you're off to a good start then."

Gideon and his parents talked a while longer, mostly about his sisters and the church back home. His parents never said "congratulations" or asked more about Ioana. The phone call left him disappointed. He had hoped his parents would share his excitement.

Before catching the bus back to Horvata, Gideon searched for and purchased a simple silver engagement ring holding a tiny garnet. The thought of giving it to Ioana returned his joy.

Ioana heard a knock at her door while kneading dough to make dense brown Romanian bread.

"It's me," Gideon's voice came through the door.

"Come on in," she called. Gideon entered and stood near her. To Ioana, he seemed concerned. "How did your trip go?" she asked.

He answered with a curious American word that she knew could have various meanings. "Okay." Then he placed something on the kitchen counter. "I got this for you."

Ioana wiped her hands with a cloth and opened a little box. Inside she found the silver and garnet ring Gideon had purchased. She picked the ring up. "What is this?"

"Our custom is that a man gives a ring to his fiancée. She puts it on her fourth finger." Gideon took Ioana's left hand and slipped on the ring. "A ring on that finger signifies that she has agreed to marry. I couldn't find a gold ring with a diamond."

"Solid gold? A diamond? I would never wear that. It would draw attention to me from thieves." Nevertheless, Ioana stretched out her arm to admire the ring. She smiled. "I like it. Thank you, Gideon." She gave him a lingering kiss.

"I also collected some money for you," said Gideon and gave Ioana the bag of leu. "But the bank would only allow me to withdraw three hundred dollars' worth at one time."

Ioana squealed when she opened the bag and saw so much money. She thought about medical necessities she could immediately order through Daniela and a few trivial things to buy for Christina. She hugged her intended tightly and silently prayed, *Thank You, God.*

Then she felt embarrassed and awkwardly used her sleeve to dry her face. "One leu isn't worth much, but you've given me a lot of them," she said to distract from her embarrassment. "What exchange rate did the bank give you?" After Gideon told her the exchange rate, she added, "You could have done much better than the official government rate for American currency by exchanging on the black market. The next time you want to withdraw money you should go to the Bucharest airport currency exchange and ask for American dollars. Your currency is easier to transport too. Once we are married, we can make a trip to Bucharest together to get the dollars and buy medical supplies. That will be fun, and we will get a lot more supplies for your money."

Gideon remained silent while she started sorting the leu bills. Ioana sensed tension in him. "Is there anything the matter, Gideon?"

"My father can't come for six months because of his operation. We'll have to put off the wedding."

What! Ioana thought. *No wedding for six months! I had hoped for next week. Maybe the week after, if necessary.* "Six months will come in the middle of winter. Roads will have a lot of snow. Travel over the mountains may be impossible then."

Gideons expression revealed that he had wanted to marry quickly, also. "You're right. I really want my father to marry us, though."

"We could have a civil marriage. Sign the papers at the government office in Braşov. Then our marriage would be legal in Romania. Your father could give us the Christian ceremony when he came later."

"I want to be married before God, not some government official."

"You think God will not know and approve?" When Gideon shook his head, she added, "Please, Gideon."

"I'm disappointed too. You and I arguing won't change anything. I'd better go." Gideon hung his head and left through the door.

Ioana felt despair for the second time over a disagreement with Gideon. She couldn't help fretting and imagining the worst. *Maybe he will change his mind about me. He might meet someone better to marry in six months. Mama could die before I get married. His parents might keep delaying to prevent him from marrying a Romanian peasant woman. I could have a disfiguring accident and he would not want me.*

A knock on the door momentarily disrupted Ioana's thoughts. Opening the door, she found Claudia. "Let me call Mama—" Ioana started.

"Spirits are tormenting you, child," said Claudia in her sweet voice. Then after hearing Ioana's disappointment about the wedding and her concerns, Claudia prayed, "If there's a way, Lord, please make Ioana's wedding happen earlier."

Chapter Eleven

The sound of someone knocking on his cottage door surprised Gideon later that week. When he opened the door, Ioana entered and gave him a quick kiss.

"I'm sorry for our disagreement about the wedding," he said after their embrace.

"Good. Then we can get legally married tomorrow."

Gideon shook his head. "You know I can't do that."

She gave him a longer, more passionate kiss. "Well, then, just try imagining what you're missing."

Gideon thought, *Problem is that I can imagine.*

Ioana stepped back. "But giving you something to think about is not why I am here. I have been called to a farm outside town. A girl has been attacked. Will you collect Christina and take her to church for the mid-week service?"

"Certainly," Gideon answered while wondering what an Orthodox service might be like. He had passed the church building—by far the largest structure in Horvata—on the town square many times.

Ioana hurried away, carrying her medical bag.

The Orthodox church building formed the east side of the square and dominated the village. Plastered and whitewashed walls supported a dome with an ornate brass cross on top. Thirty feet tall, the building towered above the simple cottages, houses, and shops. Seven steps led to stout double oaken doors providing entry from the square. Windows set into the thick stone walls seemed small and narrow to Gideon compared to the ornate gothic windows favored in Western Europe's cathedrals.

After a short walk, Gideon and Christina entered the Orthodox building through the front door on its west side. Gideon looked around. He saw little of the ornate decoration he would have expected of most denominations dating from medieval times. "This is the first time I've been inside an Orthodox church."

"Oh, this is just the narthex, not part of the church," answered Christina. "It is for non-members and penitents. The church begins there." She pointed to a pair of closed doors.

Others, mostly older Romanians, joined them standing and waiting. A man with a waist-length salt-and-pepper beard and dressed in a heavy ornate robe entered through the doors they had used. A younger man dressed less ornately followed, swinging an incense burner issuing pungent smoke.

"That is Father Flavius," Christina whispered as those waiting silently parted to let the priests and some lay-brethren pass. "The young priest is Father Marcă."

Gideon watched the procession pass through the doors Christina had indicated. Those who had been waiting in the narthex followed the priests into the nave. Inside, Gideon found ornate gilded fixtures, paintings, and icons.

Christina indicated their current surroundings, "The nave is part of the church."

This is more what I anticipated, thought Gideon.

The congregation stopped and remained standing in the seatless nave. The priests passed through the templon barrier and closed the doors behind themselves.

"The sanctuary is in there," Christina whispered and pointed to the closed doors. "That is where the priests will conduct the worship. We will be able to hear them out here."

Chanting and reverent homilies could be heard coming from behind the doors. The congregation remained silent and standing as Father Flavius, in the sanctuary, conducted a liturgy in Romanian. Gideon felt irritated. *We don't even get to watch the service?* he thought.

Then Gideon looked at Christina. She stood transfixed in worship as if God Himself dwelled within the sanctuary. Despite his misgivings, Gideon had to acknowledge the service to be meaningful to Christina. He looked around at the nave and ornate decorations. *This arrangement has been modeled after the Jewish Temple in Jerusalem except that the Jews entered from the east. The decorations are designed to reflect the medieval concept of the glory of God. The services are meant to make people aspire to heaven.*

While Christina stood in reverence, Gideon edged to a position where he could peek past a curtain into the sanctuary. The art and decoration in there made the nave where they stood look shabby.

After the service, Christina exuded elation. "Wasn't that lovely? I only wish the church had services more often."

Gideon recognized that Christina's church was particularly important in her life. *I won't take that away from her. And I need to remember that eighty-six percent of Romanians profess Christ through the Orthodox church. Christina's passion for knitting to help the poor is evidence of her love for Jesus.*

* * *

Ioana took a mile-long detour to pass through the farm where Luca worked. *This girl in distress might need more healing than my medicine can offer,* she thought. Upon seeing Luca working in the hay fields, she angled to meet him.

"Good afternoon, Miss Nagy," he greeted her.

"Luca, someone has been hurt and needs our help. Would you come with me, please? You can be back at work in a few hours. I will tell your father that I asked you to help me. He will not object. I delivered your baby sister."

Glad to have a break from days of tedious raking, Luca eagerly agreed. He propped his rake against a stone wall and joined Ioana walking a winding path. "I knew you weren't a

116

real witch, Miss Nagy," the teenager babbled. "And I heard that you might marry Mr. Dixon. I like him."

Ioana chatted with the seventeen-year-old as they walked, asking about his schoolwork and future. Rattling off all sorts of teenager dreams, Luca reminded her of a half-grown puppy.

At a farmhouse a mile away, anxious parents and relatives waited. Younger children sat joylessly, knowing something horrible had happened to their older sister.

"You wait outside for now, Luca," Ioana instructed. "I will call you when I need you."

Luca, his eyes widened by apprehension, gratefully promised, "I will be here, Miss Nagy." He sat down on a convenient log.

A tearful mother guided Ioana to a bedroom where a girl lay whimpering in a fetal position under a blanket on a bed. "This is our Maria. She is a good girl."

"Let me see Maria alone, please," said Ioana. "And I'll need some warm water." The mother started crying aloud but nodded and closed the door.

"Maria, this is Ioana Nagy. I am here to help you," Ioana started.

A long silence followed. "I want to die," the girl managed.

"I know you do, child. I hope I can change that and make you better, Maria."

"Nobody can make me better."

"I am going to give you a shot that will help you relax. You will feel a little prick." The sixteen-year-old didn't answer or move. Ioana exposed skin on Maria's arm and injected a

117

mild sedative. Then Ioana sat and talked for five minutes about good things: Romanian bread still warm from baking; the crisp, cool air of fall; spring flowers.

Once the sedative had relaxed the girl, Ioana said, "I need to examine you, Maria. I will undress you now. Nobody will see you but me." Ioana slowly removed the blanket and gently pulled off Maria's soiled clothes. Ioana found bruising and a little blood around Maria's vagina. On Maria's arms and body, Ioana discovered marks from human bites that had not broken her skin. Maria whimpered a little due to soreness but didn't cry out.

"I do not see anything that needs emergency hospitalization, Maria. But it would be good for you to be seen by a doctor soon. For now, I would like to give you a warm sponge bath." Maria didn't answer. Ioana stepped outside and collected the warm water. As she wiped the girl, she asked, "Do you know who did this to you, child?"

Gradually, she coaxed the essentials from the traumatized girl. Four or more male attackers had ambushed Maria as she walked home at night from visiting a friend. She wouldn't be able to identify them because of the dark. "I heard one of them being called He Who Kills. Another man they called Bloodthirsty would not touch me. He tried to stop the others. They made fun of him. Called him 'just a wolf pup.'"

"A terrible thing has happened to you, Maria. But you can recover and have a good life."

Maria started crying. "No man will ever want me as a wife now."

"That is not true, Maria." After sponge bathing and redressing Maria in clean clothes, Ioana fully covered her with the blanket. She stepped outside.

"Luca, I need you now."

Her call startled Luca. He entered the room with arms folded from nervousness. He looked at the little figure huddled on the bed and hidden by the blanket. "What happened?"

"Some men hurt a girl. Now I need you to pray for the healing of her heart."

Luca shook his head. "I have never done that. I do not know if I can."

"I believe God can use you to heal her." Ioana folded the blanket back to reveal one of Maria's feet. "You can touch her ankle."

Ioana's proclamation of faith strengthened Luca. He gently placed his fingers on Maria's heel and prayed silently in earnest. A minute. Then two minutes. Ioana heard Luca groan quietly from the effort. Three minutes passed.

Maria stirred. Luca stopped praying and stepped back, his face contorted from the effort.

"I guess I'm lucky to be alive," said Maria. Ioana and Luca looked at each other. "I'm hungry," added Maria.

"Your mother will fix you something right away. And I will give her a pill to help you sleep after you eat. I will come back if you need me."

"Thank you," Maria answered.

Ioana collected her things and exited the bedroom, followed by Luca. Outside, Ioana told Maria's mother to feed her and gave her the sleeping pill. "Send for me immediately if Maria experiences any sharp abdominal pains, bleeding, or fever." Ioana pressed some Romanian leu Gideon had given her into the mother's hand. "This is to tip the doctors at the hospital in Braşov. Go there tomorrow and let them also examine Maria. And there's a little extra money to make the trip fun for Maria."

Ioana and Luca, who slumped from exhaustion, started walking home. After a quiet mile, Ioana said, "God worked a miracle through you today, Luca. You are a full-fledged warrior now."

"I'm afraid, Miss Nagy."

"I am too, Luca."

Ioana and the other warriors convened at Gideon's cottage on Thursday night. His encouragement and a sense of unity had enthused each of them. Ioana reported the werewolves' attack on Maria and Luca's healing of her. The others affirmed Luca, who looked embarrassed.

"I just prayed," he insisted.

Florin praised Claudia for alerting him about people needing protection from spirits.

"All I do is tell Florin. He is the one who battles them," Claudia responded.

"Aren't you praying as Florin goes out?" asked Andrei.

"Yes, she is," answered Ioana and added, "Daniela has sensed that the Caritas Investment is a way to cheat people out of their money. Our primar is promoting the scheme with former secret police."

Andrei added, "When I pass the werewolves who invaded Ioana's farm, I can sense them. I have no proof, but a man who calls himself He Who Kills is their leader. He calls up a spirit who appears as their 'spiritual protector.'"

The group sat in silence for a minute after each had spoken. Then all their eyes turned toward Gideon.

Chapter Twelve

"Let's look at some scriptures," said Gideon and opened his Bible. He described what he had heard and seen from each one and located references to their gifts in the Scripture. "I think you have these gifts. That does not mean a gift, such as faith, cannot manifest itself in diverse ways, depending on the individual." Gideon then quoted 1 Peter 4:10, "As each has received a gift, employ it for one another, as good stewards of God's varied grace."

"What is your gift, Mr. Dixon?" asked Luca.

Ioana answered for her fiancé, "Pastor Gideon has the gift of teaching. And he is going to receive the gift of me." She thrust out her left hand with the ring Gideon had given her. The others looked up at her with puzzled expressions. "Gideon and I are getting married!"

The group erupted in joy. "We expected this," Daniela whispered as she and Claudia kissed and hugged Ioana. "The official news was yours to tell, though." The men pounded Gideon on the back.

* * *

Gideon had written five letters to send to friends and family back home. When he walked into Horvata's post office, the desk clerk recognized him.

"You helped a member of my congregation get his cow out of a mud hole. You waded in to dig around the cow's legs."

Gideon looked at the medium-sized man, who was probably in his early forties. "You're a pastor?"

"The Protestant church. My name is Raphael." He gestured to his work environment. "I'm bi-vocational."

Gideon remembered a run-down church building displaying a cross on the outskirts of town. *Probably built before communism took over Romania,* he had thought. "I saw your building and knocked on the door, but nobody answered."

"I was probably here working."

Gideon smiled. "I lost a shoe in the muck trying to free that cow and had to dig it out after we freed her. I hope the cow is doing well."

"She is. And the farmer fixed the fence that let her get into trouble. He speaks highly of you."

"Would you be willing to drop in and share coffee at my home, Pastor?"

"I know your cottage. I will come by this afternoon after closing the post office."

* * *

Gideon looked forward to visiting with a Romanian pastor. He had coffee prepared and bakery treats waiting before Pastor Raphael arrived. He eagerly opened his door upon hearing knocking. "Please come in," he said, holding the door wide. "Shall we sit at the table?"

Pastor Raphael glanced around the room. "Yes, thank you."

Gideon found his guest to be of the no-nonsense type. Even before tasting the coffee, Pastor Raphael demanded, "Why are you here in Romania?"

"I'm here to tell people about God."

"So I have heard. Then say, 'Jesus is Lord.'"

"Jesus is Lord."

"Has Jesus come in the flesh?"

"Yes. His earthly body was crucified, died, and was resurrected after three days."

"Where is Jesus now?"

"At the right hand of God."

Pastor Raphael visibly relaxed after Gideon passed the biblical tests of a believer. "Thank you." He reached for his coffee. "How is your ministry going?"

"Slowly," Gideon answered. "Romanians already attend church and are understandably leery of a newcomer."

"I heard you found a Romanian, Ioana Nagy, to be your bride."

125

"Yes. I've never met anyone like her."

"Neither have I," quipped Pastor Raphael. After both men laughed, he added, "Miss Nagy attends the Orthodox church with her mother. And she certainly does a lot of good. I am glad she attends your Bible study. You *have* stolen one congregant from me."

"Who?"

"A teenager named Luca used to attend our services with his parents. He mostly dozed through my sermons, though. Although I would prefer Luca attend church with his family, I am glad you have him voluntarily attending a Bible study."

"Have any others from your congregation stopped attending services?"

"No, just Luca."

"Then we're cooperating to reach the community."

"Starting now, we are."

"What about the Orthodox church? Would they be willing to work with us too?" asked Gidon.

"The head priest, Father Flavius, is completely traditional and considers Protestants to be a cult and enemies of the true church. He aspires to advancement within the Orthodox hierarchy. He cozied up with the communists after being assigned here and asked them to shut down any non-Orthodox groups. He called anybody in my congregation a cultist and said they couldn't be loyal Romanians."

"What did the communists do?"

"Policemen interrupted our services sometimes, claiming to look for troublemakers. They just wanted to scare worshipers away by intimidation. Under communism, the government controlled all the jobs. They denied decent jobs to anybody accused of being cultists. I worked as a manual laborer on a government farm. My wife, who was always frail, took care of farm workers' children. But doing so allowed her to be with our son. The new government gave me the job I have now at the post office."

Raphael paused a moment and took a deep swallow of coffee. Gideon sensed he had more to say and waited.

"Telling people about Jesus—Father Flavius and the communists called it proselytizing—was strictly illegal before the revolution. My wife and I refused to compromise our beliefs, though. I've been arrested and interrogated three times." Raphael pulled up his sleeves to show burn marks.

Gideon sat back, aghast. "How did you and your congregants survive?"

"A lot dropped out of church and wouldn't even acknowledge knowing me publicly. We met secretly and prayed with those who wanted to hold onto their faith. Many of those who had quit came back to services after the revolution."

Raphael paused again, swallowed more coffee, then looked Gideon in the eye. "If I wouldn't yield to communist persecution, I certainly won't compromise now."

"You mentioned your wife. Does she work outside your home?"

"Malnutrition, fear for me and our son, and ailments caught from the children wore her down. She contracted some sort of viral respiratory disease before the revolution and died of pneumonia."

"Where is your son now?"

Raphael brightened at the mention of his son. "He enlisted in the new Romanian army. The army is teaching him how to use the small new computers Westerners call 'personal computers.' He thinks that after his five-year commitment is finished, he'll be able to get a good job and start a family."

"That's wonderful."

Pastor Raphael nodded. "You had asked me about cooperating with the Orthodox. I wouldn't expect any cooperation from Father Flavius. But the new young novice priest, Father Marcă, is rather gregarious and may be open to cooperation. I've heard he is sympathetic to a reform movement among the Orthodox. They call themselves 'The Lord's Army.'"

"I will try to meet Father Marcă."

"You are young, and he is young. Maybe the two of you can convince more of Horvata's young people to follow Christ."

"I would like that. And I hope you and I can be friends."

"We already are, Gideon."

Sofia arranged hay and spread her blanket to make a place to sleep in a barn loft. She longed for a bath after hoeing gardens all morning and shoveling cow droppings in a dairy barn that afternoon. Her payment had been a filling meal of tripe soup and plain brown bread to eat alongside the hired men and a roof to sleep under. Already Sofia looked forward to breakfast. More bread, a little butter, a cup of coffee, maybe an egg. She remembered her life not long before in a government-sponsored orphanage. Hot soup with bread, oat porridge, cabbage, mashed rutabagas, and occasionally a sliver of pork. Not glamorous food, but regular.

Once she turned sixteen, the orphanage had sent Sofia out to make her own living. She dreamed of finding a job as a live-in housekeeper. Hopefully she would do so before winter arrived. That elevated status might allow her to find a husband.

She had seen Ioana passing by earlier that day. *People say she is a witch,* Sofia thought. But she didn't care about that. Ioana was beautiful, well fed, and confident. Sofia longed to be like her. She had even heard that a rich American would marry her idol, Ioana.

Ioana woke with a start. She knew something was wrong. She listened to the silence. She sniffed. Her nose detected nothing but the normal odors of a farm—manure, mildewing hay, and mud. A momentary shadow passed over the moonlit spot in the floor. *Something is out there,* she realized.

Ioana quietly slipped out of her bed. *Is it werewolves again? No. This is too quiet.* She clasped the fireplace poker as she had during the werewolf attack and looked out the window. Nothing. She tiptoed on bare feet to check on Christina. Her mother slept blissfully, albeit not quietly, due to a gentle snore. Vlad had left his place at Christina's feet and peered out from under the bed. Ioana moved into a shadowed corner to watch the windows from the darkness.

There! Something paused by another window. Seconds later, a dark face looked in. Ioana froze in horror and held her breath. Due to the moonlight behind the face, Ioana could not clearly see features. She heard the window issue an almost undetectable squeak. Someone had tried to lift the sash. She felt grateful that window had been stuck for years.

The face moved away from the window. Ioana breathed again. Then she saw the front door handle turning back and forth. The door yielded millimeters until stopped by an old slide bolt. The wooden door creaked as the intruder pushed, hoping to force out the screws holding the slide bolt in place. Ioana tightened her grip on the poker. She willed her legs to move forward in the dark where she could strike if the slide bolt screws yielded. The door shifted another millimeter inward, but the screws held.

The menacing figure circled the cottage, looking for any entry point. The night visitor found the coal chute used when Ioana's grandparents had been able to afford coal. The cast iron chute flap slowly swung inwards with a squeak. A hand explored the opening as its owner considered trying to wriggle through.

Chapter Thirteen

"Ioana, are you awake?" A clear male voice spoke from the farmyard. The broken silence startled Ioana. The chute flap banged down. The would-be intruder fled on soft steps.

Ioana unlocked and opened the front door. "Yes, I am awake, Gideon."

Gideon paused a few seconds to catch his breath from running. He approached the cottage entrance. "You're alright, then?"

"Yes, Christina and I are safe. Why are you here?"

"Claudia came to my cottage in the night. She scared me knocking on the door."

"Why did Claudia come to you?"

"She said that you needed help. Something about a spirit-incited vampire."

Ioana nodded. "Claudia was right. Something tried to enter the house."

"What was it? Was there a bat at the window?"

"Come on in, my intended. I will make you coffee and

tell you about real vampires." Ioana put water in a kettle and lit a propane flame underneath.

Gideon reached for a light switch. "Hold it," Ioana insisted. "If we turn on a light inside, anything outside can see us, but we won't be able to see it."

Gideon settled into a chair. In the dark, he instinctively lowered his voice to a whisper. "So, tell me about vampires."

"Real vampires are not like the cinema version any more than real werewolves. The Irish author Bram Stoker depicted vampires as blood suckers who enter a young woman's bedroom as a bat and bite her neck to suck blood. Romanian vampires are even scarier than that because they are human beings among us. Evil spirits influence them to prey on the weak. Usually solitary or loners, real vampires take the life force of others: money, innocence, health, even lives. Satan is the father of liars. Spirit-inspired vampires can control people through lies. They also creep around in the night and do harm where no one can see."

Gideon shuddered. "I should stay here with you tonight."

Ioana mischievously smiled at Gideon in the near darkness. "You would like that, would you not?" Her voice indicated her to be teasing. "Not until we are married."

Gideon sighed. "I didn't mean that."

Ioana smiled. "I know you did not. Maybe I just hoped you did."

"I'll sleep on the floor."

Ioana turned serious. "I was so afraid, Gideon. Please do stay. But sleep in my bed. I will go sleep with Mama."

* * *

Gideon awoke early after sleeping in Ioana's bed. Her small room had been pitch-black the previous night. Morning light revealed a young woman's bedroom like his sisters' rooms before they married and left home. He saw stuffed animals, posters of inspirational women, some childhood toys, a picture of Ioana's mother and father, functional clothes hung on a rod suspended from the ceiling with two chains, and a few cosmetics on an old beat-up dresser with a mirror. A plastic zippered clothes bag protected Ioana's few nicer clothes. A sweet female odor permeated the air. Unlike his sisters' rooms, Ioana's room also contained medical supplies. A simple canvas bag waited to convey items necessary for a call.

He smelled coffee. Gideon dressed in the outer clothes he had taken off to sleep and headed for the kitchen. Christina waited for him there.

"Ioana made coffee for you, and porridge is left from last night."

"Where is Ioana?"

"She always starts work early. You will probably find her in the barn or garden."

Gideon gulped a couple of swallows of lukewarm coffee and headed to find Ioana. She had just finished milking the nanny goats and had put them out to pasture.

"What can I do to help?" he asked.

"Collect the chicken eggs. Be careful of the big red hen. She will defend her nest."

Gideon did find a large reddish hen settled in one of several nest boxes. He slowly slid his hand forward to feel for eggs under her. Just as his fingertips touched feathers, he felt a sharp pain in his wrist. Jerking his hand back, he saw a drop of blood oozing from where the chicken had pecked. He looked at the hen's sharp beak as she stared at him through one eye with her head turned sideways. The other hens clucked and made a ruckus.

He looked around for a prod and found an ancient pitchfork leaning against the goat enclosure. His wrist smarting, Gideon pictured himself sticking the vicious bird through. *Ioana wouldn't like that,* he realized. *Just frighten the chicken off the nest.* He approached with the pitchfork, prepared to use the prongs to push the hen away. *Let her peck this.*

But rather than attack the pitchfork, the hen flew up toward Gideon's face with her wings flapping and clawed feet extended. Gideon retreated. Looking back, he could see the hen standing defiantly over her egg and two others, probably laid by other chickens.

Ioana's voice came from behind him. "Make egg collecting easy on yourself." Gideon turned to see her scatter a handful of cracked corn on the ground outside the barn. All the chickens, including the big red hen, scrambled to gobble their share. More than a dozen eggs remained exposed. Gideon hurried to collect them.

Ioana poured the warm goat milk into a wooden churn. She sat down on a stool to separate the fat into butter.

A pre-teen boy suddenly arrived out of breath. "Miss Nagy, Mama has started labor. Poppa sent me."

Ioana hung her head for a moment and sighed deeply. Then she rose and said, "Run back and tell your father that I am coming, Alexandru. Ask him to make your mother comfortable and get hot water ready."

"Yes, ma'am. The water is boiling already," the boy replied before turning and dashing away.

Ioana looked at Gideon, shrugged, and gave a half smile. "I've got to go."

"I know you do. I'll churn the milk and feed the pigs the residual."

"Thank you. We are nearly out of cracked corn for the chickens but have over a hundred eggs saved up. Could you carry the eggs to the village? Sixty should get a bag of corn at the feed store. Christina knows where. The remaining eggs are our profit. Take them to the butcher and exchange them for beef to make meatballs we'll have in soup. The butcher should be glad to get rid of his older meat. I delivered his fourth child. Tell him I sent you, and he will treat us honestly."

Ioana turned to go. "Wait a second, Ioana, please," begged Gideon. "I thought a lot last night before falling asleep." Ioana stood waiting. "You need protection at night. I'll ask Pastor Raphael to marry us immediately."

Ioana visibly perked up. "What about your father presiding?"

"I'll get him to bless our union later."

"Thank you, Gideon." Ioana approached Gideon and gave him a long, affectionate kiss. After breaking away, she added, "Mama will want her church's blessing for us too."

"Sure. Why not?"

Gideon watched Ioana hurry to the house and then run down the road in the direction the boy had gone carrying her canvas medical bag. He sat down and started churning. Two pigs and Vlad the cat arrived for their share of the buttermilk.

*　*　*

Immediacy aside, the wedding preparations took a week. Gideon let Ioana and Christina decide on a traditional country Romanian wedding. In a complicated arrangement between herself, the butcher, the market, and a dressmaker, Ioana traded one of her two pigs to obtain for herself a wedding dress and to give Gideon a traditional linen shirt for a wedding present.

Gideon traveled to Braşov to phone his parents about his impending marriage.

"For it is better to marry than to burn," his father quoted the King James Bible. "God will recognize your union without me."

"Couldn't you wait a little longer to be sure?" his mother implored.

Gideon decided not to talk about the threats to Ioana. "You heard Dad," he replied. "But, Mom, trust me. You're going to love Ioana."

"I'll have no choice," his mother answered. "I'm just concerned that you're moving too fast. And maybe I'm a little jealous about sharing my only son with another woman. A woman I don't even know."

After telling about Ioana's midwifery, work habits, and care for her mother, Gideon added, "She's a very dedicated Christian. God uses her to help people."

"You wouldn't pick any other," his father affirmed.

After the call home, Gideon searched the town until he found and purchased two gold wedding bands. For Ioana's wedding gift, he chose a used straight-drive bicycle with a large front basket and heavy tires.

Gideon rode the bicycle to the farm from the bus stop in Horvata. Ioana could not suppress her joy when she saw the gift. "Thank you, Gideon!" Then the gold bands made her speechless.

"You wear this with your engagement ring after the wedding," Gideon explained.

"No, I'll keep both hidden safely somewhere." She grabbed Gideon around the neck and squeezed him as hard as she could. Tears of joy ran down her cheeks.

Embarrassed at her tears, Ioana teased, "Women in the town say that I'm a fairy witch who cast a love spell on you. In Romania, fairies are supposed to have seductive power over men."

Gideon played along. "How do you break a love spell?"

"You think my no-nonsense answer about practicality and respect coming before love bewitched you?"

"No, but your beauty did." Gideon paused. "Do people still think you're a witch?"

"Yes, but most think I am a good witch. They are wondering if getting married will break the love spell."

"Not for me," Gideon predicted.

On Friday, their wedding day, Gideon and Ioana completed the farm chores together before dawn then caught the earliest bus to register their union at the government offices in Braşov. After a long wait standing in line, they reported their names, answered questions, and signed papers. The process reminded Gideon of getting a driver's license except without the eye test. Outside the government offices, Ioana gave Gideon a passionate kiss.

"We are legally married now," she said.

"Should we run off somewhere together?"

"We had better not. A lot of people will be waiting for us in Horvata."

Returning to Horvata, Gideon and Ioana found nearly a hundred villagers, most dressed in colorful Romanian costumes, waiting near the bus stop. The crowd congregated, cheered, clapped, and rattled cow bells as the newlyweds descended the bus steps. The bus driver recognized the moment and added to the din with the bus horn.

Christina and Daniela came with two zippered bags of clothes. From one bag, Ioana withdrew the traditional Romanian shirt she had purchased with one of her pigs. The pullover white linen garment had buttons halfway down the front. Blue and ruby-red yarn embroidered the collar, cuffs, and around the buttons. Before all, Ioana presented Gideon with the traditional costume as a wedding present.

"Please wear this," she whispered.

The crowd roared with approval when Gideon immediately pulled off his American shirt and replaced it with Ioana's gift. They roared twice as loud when Ioana shouted, "Now you are twice as handsome as before," and roughly kissed him. More villagers hurried to join the excitement.

Gideon feigned a grab for Ioana as Daniela pulled her away to change into wedding clothes. Men restrained him. Andrei bellowed above the tumult, "Wait until later, brother!" The men laughed raucously.

As all the women followed Ioana to Daniela's shop, the men started chanting, "Later! Later! Later!" Gideon saw a burly man distributing bottles of liquor. As bottles started passing hands, the men grew more boisterous. They took turns reciting ribald stories, each teller rewarded with a laugh and a turn at a bottle.

Someone pressed a bottle into Gideon's hand. Every male eye present watched as he sipped the bottle and coughed as the alcohol burned his throat. The men laughed good-naturedly. "Is Romanian nectar too strong for an American?" Florin called out. The men laughed louder.

Gideon wiped his eyes. "It just takes a little getting used to." The men laughed again. Then Gideon tipped the bottle back and swallowed a big swig. The men roared approval. After bending over choking, Gidon's voice sounded like a croak. "I just hope I can live until the 'later.'" The men shouted affirmation.

Andrei and the man who had distributed the liquor bottles lifted Gideon to their shoulders and bounced him around the town square. Men reached out to pound Gideon's back and shake his hand while chanting "Later! Later! Later!"

Florin captured everything on a video recorder.

Chapter Fourteen

Women returning to the square drew the men's attention. Andrei and the other man carrying Gideon placed him on his feet in front of the females. Everyone recognized a solemn moment and became silent. The women parted to reveal Ioana in a collarbone-to-ankle white dress with ruby red embroidery matching Gideon's shirt. A circlet of flowers adorned her hair, which had been piled stylishly on her head. Ioana's elegant, thin neck extended upwards to highlight her radiant face. She was wearing red lipstick but only a trace of other makeup. She carried a bouquet of white roses. Her beauty held every man's gaze. Gideon involuntarily gasped and stood awestruck.

Ioana walked to Gideon and smiled. "I am for you, forever," she said in a clear voice all could hear.

"I don't deserve you," he answered.

"You just keep reminding yourself of that," she returned. The onlookers laughed then cheered and clapped.

Ioana held Gideon's arm as they led a procession of merrymakers through the village of Horvata to the Orthodox church. The celebrants silently followed the couple inside. Christina waited in the nave at a curtain between the nave and sanctuary.

"Your father would be so proud," Christina said to her daughter.

The young priest, Father Marcă, met them at the curtain and from the sanctuary side performed a brief ceremony and conveyed the church's blessing.

"Will you come to the celebration, please, Father?" asked Ioana.

"I will be there," the friendly young man promised. "Best part of being a priest."

The onlookers in the church parted and fell in behind as Gideon and Ioana passed back through the nave and narthex to the street. They led the procession to Pastor Raphael's church. Well-wishers filled the plain meeting room where Pastor Raphael performed a short Protestant ceremony.

The newlyweds walked together down the center aisle. At the church's exit, a bucket filled with water waited. Gideon and Ioana each placed a foot on the bucket rim. Gideon counted, "One, two, three." On three, they pushed the bucket over, spilling the water. A cheer from the crowd affirmed them.

Ioana recited a traditional Romanian saying, "That all the bad things may be washed away, and all the good things may come together." Children collected small amounts of money from attendees as wedding gifts to the newlyweds.

In the town square, women had brought food—plenty of food—and piled it on the tables used on market days. Gideon saw cabbage rolls, grilled minced meat, a half dozen types of soup, innumerable sweetbreads, a form of Romanian haggis, beef loaf, fried cheese, and many dishes he didn't recognize.

Others had brought alcoholic drinks. Homemade wine and beer waited on the tables. More potent bottles of *țuică,* distilled liquor made from plums, circulated among the men. Gideon found places already set for himself and Ioana at the table brought from his house. Daniela, who had taken charge of the dinner arrangements, poured wine for each of them into a goblet loaned by the butcher.

"The groom customarily makes the first toast," Daniela whispered.

Gideon found himself uncharacteristically buoyant due to the liquor consumed earlier on an empty stomach. *If my parents could see me now,* he thought. He eyed the goblet full of dark red wine, stood, picked his drink up, and addressed all present. "When coming from America, I never anticipated that the first Romanian wedding I attended would be my own." He paused as the guests laughed loudly. "I toast the people of Horvata who have given me their best as a bride and are allowing me to become a Romanian."

Murmurs of approval answered him as everybody held up vessels of wine. Gideon looked at his wine again. *Wine isn't as strong as distilled liquor,* he told himself. *Just get it over with.* Then he tilted the goblet back and drank all the wine it contained.

The crowd gasped. "He must really like it," someone cried. A chorus of voices demanded, "Pour him another."

Sitting next to Gideon, Ioana stifled her laughter. "You're supposed to sip it," she whispered.

"Sorry," he answered while looking at another full goblet someone had placed in front of him. "Where did all the food and drinks come from?"

Ioana sipped her wine in response to Pastor Raphael's toast to the bride's mother, Christina, seated beside her. "People in Horvata do not have much, if any, money to buy gifts. They brought homemade food and drinks as our wedding presents," she explained.

Around the town square, scores of people ate, drank, and exchanged stories. Loudspeakers played recorded music that ranged from sweet to boisterous. Gideon recognized the tune to James Taylor's recording of *How Sweet It Is (To Be Loved by You)*. The guests sang to popular tunes. Pastor Raphael and Father Marcă sat together laughing, eating, and singing.

As the sun set, strings of lights suspended above the square provided a golden glow to the festivities. Three women started a hora dance when a medley of lively rhythmic tunes began. The line grew to include half the guests snaking around the square.

Gideon spoke above the tumult. "I thought the hora was Jewish."

"The dance is part of traditional Romania. Maybe the Jews learned it from us," Ioana answered.

Gideon sat mesmerized, watching the festivities in the warm summer night. He also felt a bit woozy from the unaccustomed alcohol. "Thank you, Ioana, for giving me this wonderful experience."

"You are welcome, husband of mine. Remember that I would not be here either without you. I love you so much, Gideon. We can build a good life together."

Claudia's approach cut off Gideon's response. "Ioana and I prayed for your wedding to come quickly. God can use anything for good. He used werewolves and a vampire to hasten this moment."

"I'm glad He did," answered Gideon and took a reasonable sip of wine.

As Claudia and Ioana continued to talk, Gideon watched people enjoying themselves around the square. He saw a skinny teenage girl, poorly dressed, alone, and staring at Ioana. The girl focused so intensely that she didn't notice Gideon looking at her. *Is she a threat to my wife?* he wondered. *I should walk around anyway.*

Other women joined Claudia, congratulating Ioana. None noticed Gideon slipping away. Shaking hands and declining drinks slowed him down. Nevertheless, he circled behind the still-staring teenage girl.

"Good evening," he said to get her attention.

The girl turned and visibly started. "I am sorry, sir. I only ate a little."

145

Gideon smiled. "Eat all you want. I noticed you watching my wife, Ioana."

"Ioana is so wonderful. I wish that I could be like her."

Perceiving no danger to his bride, Gidon asked, "How do you know Ioana?"

"I only have seen her in the village. She doesn't know me."

"Oh. Well, would you like to meet her?"

"No, I could never."

"Ioana won't mind. Come on. I'll introduce you." When the girl's face expressed fear and her eyes looked for ways to escape, Gideon said, "You don't have to meet Ioana." The girl relaxed. "Are your parents here?"

"I don't have any parents."

"Where do you live?" When the girl shrugged, Gideon guessed she was homeless. He looked at her emaciated body. "We have plenty of food. Take some with you."

The girl's eyes widened. "I should not."

"Why not? I'll help you. Just follow me." Gideon dodged the ever-twisting hora line to pick up an empty container and led the girl to the food tables. "What would you like?"

"Anything."

Gradually he coaxed the girl to make nutritious and tasty choices. "What's your name?" he asked while loading the container with enough food to last for days.

"Sofia."

"Well, Sofia, some of the people here, including Ioana, meet on Sundays. I'd like to invite you—"

146

A powerful bearhug crushed Gideon and cut his words off. He turned his head to see inebriated Andrei squeezing him. The dog, Dragon, stood by his master. Gideon could smell alcohol in Andrei's breath close to his ear.

"Congratulations, Pastor. The Bible verses you had me memorize are keeping the spirits away."

Gideon needed a couple of minutes to extract himself from the big man's powerful arms. Thanking and encouraging Andrei took more minutes. By the time he turned back to Sofia, the girl had disappeared along with the container of food.

The festivities lasted late into the night. Gideon wished the party would end and guests would depart, allowing him and Ioana to go to the cottage. Eventually, the crowd thinned. Guests spoke to the newlyweds as they departed, saying, "House of stone."

"That means 'May you have a long and trouble-resistant marriage,'" Ioana explained.

At about 2:30 a.m., the few remaining guests noisily escorted Ioana and Gideon to his rented cottage. Andrei led the men chanting, "Later is now. Later is now."

Finally, Gideon and Ioana experienced the later.

Gideon woke with an aching head—his first ever hangover. He found no Ioana. A note she left explained.

Had work to do. All my love. Ioana
PS Last night we figured out what to do together.
Now that we know how, tonight will be even better.

Gideon's memories of the wedding day and night overwhelmed him. Images flashed into his throbbing head. He could hardly believe all that had happened. Then he remembered, *Florin recorded everything at the wedding. Should I send a copy of the video to Mom and Dad? At least they won't understand the Romanian words.*

After strong coffee, he emerged from the cottage. Evidence of the night's celebration remained in the town square. Pigeons and crows fed on spilled food. Women cleaning up the tables teased him.

"Ioana cast a spell on you, Mr. American."

"Every man should hope to be so bewitched."

The women grinned and nodded until one asked, "How did you enjoy the 'later'?"

Parts of the night remained hazy to Gideon. But he answered, "Wonderful."

"It will be better when you're not drunk," one returned. The women cackled merrily.

One woman became serious. "You got yourself a good one in Ioana, young man. None better. She is already at work taking care of her mother and raising food for you. If you are smart, you will get out to her farm and help her. She will remember that always." All the women nodded.

148

Gideon hurried to the farm where he found Ioana catching up on chores. He joined her by starting to shovel out the goat droppings in the barn. About sunset, Ioana led him back to their cottage in the village.

Chapter Fifteen

The mother should have had antibiotics as a precaution against infection, Ioana thought as she rode her bicycle home after delivering a baby. Her payment, a short string of last winter's hard, dried sausages, rode in the basket in front of her. *Maybe Gideon is ready for our trip to Bucharest.*

Gideon couldn't be found at his rented cottage. He had started to call it "the town-cottage" after he moved to the "farm-house." Ioana located him at the farm holding a burlap bag in an old apple tree her grandfather had planted decades earlier.

Christina stood nearby saying, "If you could climb a little higher, you would reach more fruit." Two bags of picked apples waited by her feet. "I will make us some apple sauces for next winter," Christina promised.

Mama means that her daughter will make the sauces, thought Ioana. She couldn't help but smile at Gideon's forbearance, as he, exhorted by Christina, edged a little higher and strained to reach an apple. A branch cracked. Gideon retreated and hugged the main trunk. His face showed alarm.

"You already have enough apples for sauces," Ioana called. "You are too heavy for the tree. Better come on down."

Gideon gratefully descended, bringing with him the partially filled third bag. When his feet touched the ground, he asked, "What about the apples remaining?"

"The pig or goats will get them. They can hear the thump of a falling apple from a long distance. They will race to see which one gets to eat it."

Gideon picked up the bags to carry to the root cellar. "How did the delivery go?"

"No problems. Healthy baby boy. The mother's third delivery. The father could not conceal his joy for a son after two girls."

"I'll be happy for sons or daughters."

"I know you will. But I had no antibiotics to give the mother to prevent infection. Are you ready to make the trip to Bucharest we had discussed? We would get American dollars and medical supplies."

"Sure. But what about the farm and your mother? I could stay here and care for them while you went," Gideon offered.

"The currency exchange at the airport will require you presenting your passport. We both need to go. I still have some of the leu you gave me earlier. We could hire someone to stay here."

"Who could you hire?"

"Luca. He is a farm boy and would be delighted to get some cash. He helped me on that difficult medical call. I trust him. We can pay his mother to cook meals for him and Mama."

"Okay. When should we go?"

"Two days from now, maybe? We can stay there overnight. I have friends who would give us a place to sleep."

"How about staying in a hotel?"

Ioana answered with a delighted smile and mimicked Gideon's American speech. "Okay."

* * *

Gideon and Ioana rode the bus on the winding road through the Carpathian Mountains. The older bus struggled up steep inclines. Then on the descents, the bus appeared to be ready to pitch over the precipices alongside the narrow road. Gideon remembered the magical journey he had enjoyed initially traveling to Horvata. The land had appeared enchanted then. Now having seen and experienced what he had, the forested mountains seemed more mysterious and dangerous.

"Our forests have bears and wolves," claimed Ioana. Her words made the mountains sound more exotic and special to Gideon. "Not many wolves remain in the mountains anymore but plenty of bears. They sometimes raid towns looking for food."

The bus stopped near the train station in Braşov. Ioana obviously felt at ease. "This is how I traveled to medical school," she explained. Together they walked the short distance to the train station. Gideon dragged his wheeled suitcase packed with their overnight things. At the station, a posted announcement reported a four-hour delay of their train.

"This is terrible," Ioana uncharacteristically complained in her eagerness to get to Bucharest.

Gideon looked at a posted map. "We're not far from Braşov's town center. Let's look around."

"What for? It is just an old town."

"But Braşov appears quite charming to me," Gideon appealed.

The town's medieval center lay nestled in a valley between forested hills. The newly married couple followed narrow streets leading to a cobblestoned triangle formed by old three-story buildings. A cathedral-sized Lutheran church stood in the triangle's center and reflected Braşov's Germanic heritage. After entering, they saw thick, clear lead glass filling pre-gothic windows with Roman arches. A massive pipe organ towered over the pews.

Gideon picked up a pamphlet available for visitors to read and shared, "This is called The Black Church because of scars left by fires. It was built in 1440 as Catholic St. Mary's. The Reformation changed the denomination to Protestant in 1542. They still conduct services in German here."

"That *is* interesting," Ioana agreed.

After visiting the church, Gideon located Braşov's medieval Saxon walls and bastions, which had once protected the residents. Gideon patted the cold stone. "These walls have been here longer than my country has existed," he marveled. "They're part of your heritage."

Ioana looked around. "I never noticed them before. They do give me an appreciation that we Romanians have endured many centuries of troubles. Every nationality that contributed to modern Romania has had challenges."

Gideon pointed to a newly opened ice-cream shop. "Let's have a treat." Inside the shop a dozen flavors were on display. "What flavor would you like?"

"I don't know. Homemade ice cream is usually flavored with honey or local fruits."

"Then try the chocolate mint."

Ioana's eyes widened as she tasted that variety. "This is fun, Gideon. I never did any traveling for pleasure or sightseeing before."

"We'll have lots of opportunities together, sweetheart. But missing our train would spoil our memory. Let's get back to the station."

Masses of travelers waited for the train to arrive. When it arrived, those attempting to board obstructed those trying to exit.

"Come on," Ioana urged him and pushed against the outward flow. "We won't get a seat otherwise."

Gideon felt reluctant to force his way and regretted not buying first-class tickets. But Ioana had bought the second-class tickets speaking Romanian too fast for him to follow. As the last arriving passengers exited, he managed to step just inside the train's sliding doors. There he found Ioana seated but surrounded by others standing. She shrugged then gave up her seat to a young Romani woman carrying a baby.

"I'll stand next to you," she said. The bodies of other standing passengers crushed them together as the train, built in the 1950s, jerked to a start.

The September midday had already warmed to ninety degrees. Passengers by the windows opened them to provide air for all. Some near the windows hung their heads outside to escape the stifling heat of the packed travelers.

Gideon leaned over to watch the passing countryside through the windows. Level tracks to Bucharest passed through rich produce fields. Teams of men and women hand-harvested dried ears of corn, grapes, summer potatoes, cabbage, and rutabagas. Decrepit machine harvesters cut fields of wheat. Farmworkers raked the straw into long rows to dry before heaping it onto horse-drawn wagons. Large, black ravens poked around the cleared ground, looking for grasshoppers.

As the train approached Bucharest, Gideon saw a large, insulated pipeline entering the city. "What's that for?" he asked and pointed.

"That is steam for heating flats." Ioana pointed. "Like those." The train passed a neighborhood with dozens of closely packed, wide, shabby eight-story buildings that looked like 1960s tenements in New York or Chicago. Gideon almost imperceptibly shook his head. Noticing, Ioana added, "The individual apartments are nicer on the inside."

"I'm just glad we live in Horvata," he said.

"Me too."

Buildings in the city's center looked similarly dilapidated. Gideon had read that the city of Bucharest had once been as stylish and beautiful as any in Europe. But the elegant buildings had decayed during decades of neglect. Without thinking, Gideon blurted out, "This is like Europe in a nightmare."

"What do you expect after a devastating war followed by forty-four years of communism?" returned Ioana. "That was the nightmare. Ask anybody."

Ioana led the way to the airport by city bus. At the currency exchange, Gideon used his credit card and passport to collect a thousand American dollars minus a sixty-dollar fee. When Gideon fumed about the fee, Ioana said, "Do not worry. We will more than make up for that fee by having your dollars rather than leu. Carry the money inside your clothes so pickpockets will not know you have so much."

"Will we exchange the dollars on the black market?" he asked.

Ioana shrugged. "Maybe. Or simply use dollars to pay at black market exchange rates." Her voice revealed disappointment when she said, "The medical supply store is closed now. Because of the train delay, we will have to wait until tomorrow."

"We had fun in Braşov, though. Where is the hotel?"

"Near the former communist headquarters. There is a guest house from the communist days. Officials from around Romania used to stay there when in Bucharest. Now the government rents rooms to anyone with money."

Gideon expected the communist guest house to be luxurious. Cut glass and heavy gold-painted fixtures decorated the lobby. But the guest house also had the neglected air that permeated all of Bucharest. The Spartan room they rented for fifteen dollars contained two cot-like beds, an old-fashioned radiant-steam heater, and minimal bathroom fixtures. Downstairs, a former dining room turned into a public restaurant offered a meal of thin onion soup, boiled potatoes with cabbage, a slice of greasy fried pork, and stale bread.

"I almost feel sorry for the communist officials," said Gideon about the food and room.

"Do not bother. This is much better than non-party members ever had during communism. Better than most people live even now."

Chapter Sixteen

Ioana could hardly suppress giddiness while buying medical supplies the following morning. The antibiotics especially excited her. "We can treat so many people with these: women after childbirth, those with injuries, children with strep throat."

"Will you need a prescription?" asked Gideon.

"Why?"

"In America, you need a licensed doctor to sign for most medicinal drugs."

"Not in Romania. Not yet, anyway. But even if we did, one of the doctor teachers who knows me from medical school would authorize antibiotics for me to use in Horvata."

An hour later, Gideon carried two heavy bags of medical supplies while Ioana dragged the suitcase and carried a third bag containing her treasured antibiotics. "Do we have time for lunch before catching the train to Braşov?" he asked.

"We have enough time. What type of food would you like?"

Gideon grinned sheepishly. "I could use some American food."

"Sounds like fun. Where?"

"I saw a sign for a new McDonald's in Bucharest."

Ioana's eyes widened in anticipation. "I have heard about the place called McDonald's. What you Americans call 'fast food.' Soft bread with minced beef and fried potatoes."

"That's right. Follow me."

After a fifteen-minute walk, Ioana stared at a bewildering menu over the heads of young Romanians taking orders at four cash registers.

"You can choose anything you like," Gideon offered.

"There are so many choices."

"You'd probably like the Big Mac."

"Okay, the Big Mac. What about the fried potatoes?"

"We'll take two Big Mac combo meals," Gideon told the young woman waiting for their decision. After she rang up the order, Gideon paid her eight dollars in leu, took the receipt, and stepped back. The young woman taking orders looked for the next customer.

Ioana cringed at the cost but didn't complain. "Where is our food?" she asked.

Gideon pointed to the order number on the receipt. "They'll call our number."

Two minutes later, a young man slid a red plastic tray across the counter and called, "Number eighty-two."

"That's us." Gideon stepped forward to pick up the tray. He looked around at tables crowded with customers eating and talking. "We'll probably find more seating upstairs." He pointed to a wide flight of stairs. "If you'll carry the tray, I'll bring the bags."

"I can also manage the antibiotics," Ioana answered and put that bag's strap over her head and shoulder. She then followed Gideon up the stairs to find seating in a less crowded area. She put the tray on a table and picked up one of the empty paper cups. "They forgot to give us our drinks."

"The drinks are at a self-dispenser downstairs. I'll get them while you watch our bags. Coca-Cola alright for you?"

"Sure." When Gideon hurried away, Ioana looked around to see large windows looking over a Bucharest street, a statue of a smiling clown, and well-dressed Romanians enjoying themselves. *This is a strange and different world for me. This is a glimpse of Gideon's world. Thank you for allowing me to experience new things, God.*

Gideon returned holding two iced drinks, straws, and packets of ketchup, mustard, salt, and pepper. After a short prayer, Ioana tasted her first American hamburger and French fries. *This is wonderful,* she thought. She sipped her Coke through a plastic straw. "Thank you for bringing me here, Gideon. You are going to spoil me."

"Nothing could spoil you, sweetheart. I do hope to make you happy."

* * *

Ioana approached the ticket window at the Bucharest central train station the following morning.

"Let me buy the tickets for this trip," Gideon suggested.

She stepped aside and gestured for her husband of a week to proceed. To her surprise, he returned with tickets for first-class reserved seats. Part of Ioana felt elated at the unexpected privilege. Another part felt guilty for spending the extra money.

They passed a large crowd struggling to enter the second-class cars and boarded the first-class coach at leisure. Sensing Ioana's discomfiture, Gideon pointed toward the tumult of second-class passengers pushing onto the train. "Would you want to try boarding back there with our suitcase and your medical supplies?"

"No, I think not."

They found their seats in a compartment for four. Gideon placed the three bags of medical supplies and suitcase in the compartment's empty seats.

"Won't someone sit there?" Ioana asked.

Gideon shook his head. "I paid for all four seats. We'll be able to talk freely. I have questions."

"How much did the tickets cost?"

"Twelve American dollars for the compartment."

The amount staggered Ioana. She remembered scratching out a meager living on the farm for herself and Christina without seeing that much cash during a year. She looked at the bags carrying over six hundred dollars' worth of medicines and supplies she needed. *You're living a different life now,* she told herself. *You have a husband who loves you now. Let him be nice to you. Enjoy the moment.* She settled into her seat and linked her arm through Gideon's. "Thank you, Gideon." To herself, she added, *and God.*

"You're welcome, sweetheart."

The train jolted into motion. They had not left the city when Gideon began, "Andrei can identify individuals influenced by spirits. He thinks the vampire intruder at your farm was Primar Serban. What is a primar?"

"You might call Primar Serban an elected mayor over our comună, which includes three villages. He was a communist before the revolution. Most people think the election run by his former comrades was rigged. Nobody I know voted for him. But what can we do about it?"

"Does he have much power?"

"Road signs and repair. Collecting taxes. Representing our comună to the government. The primary power is Prefect Lazar in Braşov. The constitution created after the revolution kept that office. Prefects are appointed to run a judeţe—you might say a county—on behalf of the federal government of Romania. Our prefect controlled this judeţe under communism too. He likely bribed someone to stay in his position. The police and all the government workers in our judeţe report to him."

"What job did Primar Serban have under communism?"

"He ran the collective farm. When the communists took over after the Second World War, they seized all the land, including the farm that had belonged to Poppa's family for generations. They put all the confiscated farms into one big

163

farm owned by the communist government. Poppa, like everyone, worked for the government on the big farm. Mama did too. The collective farms never produced well because everybody did as little work as possible. People said, 'As long as the government pretends to pay us, we will pretend to work.' But Mama and Poppa usually had food for themselves and later for me."

"How big is your farm now?"

"Our farm," Ioana corrected her husband. "Just over forty-eight hectares."

Gideon computed in his head. *About a hundred and twenty acres.* "And how did you get the farm back from the government?"

"Poppa had kept the papers from before the war saying that his family owned the land. After the revolution, the new government returned ownership of the land and buildings to Romanians who could prove pre-communism ownership. But Poppa was over eighty years old and died before he could make the land productive. I came home then. I told you that Mama and I ate rats." Ioana's voice choked a little at the unpleasant memory.

Gideon took her hand and squeezed, then changed his line of questioning. "Florin tells me that former communists are still in the government. I thought this was a democracy now."

"We do vote now. And former communists can run for office. But we used to have a king and queen like England."

"That was Mihai, right? Florin told me he ousted the fascist military government in 1944 but abdicated the throne and went to Switzerland after the war."

Ioana's tone of voice revealed regret. "Mihai had no choice. He opposed Ceauşescu's takeover after the war. The communists forced him to leave Romania. He and his wife, Ana, visited our new Romania last year to great acclamation. They are poised and dignified like a king and queen should be. Romanians love them."

"But why are some former communists still in positions of authority?"

"The major cities are run by elected non-communists. In towns and rural areas, former communists sometimes retained control because they knew how things operated. Some are not so bad. Most are corrupt."

"Why would Primar Serban have targeted you when he came at night to the farm?"

"I commandeered his car recently after an accident. Plus, I have a history of exposing evildoers, probably his cronies. Claudia thinks spirits motivate him to do something bad involving cheating people out of money. It's called the Caritas Investment. He promises big results investing people's savings. But they pay the first investors well with money from new investors. That gets others to give the promoters more money."

"In America, we call that racket a Ponzi scheme."

"I do not know what to call it. I only know that spirits guide vampires to take what people need to live."

"Everything is about spirits to you, isn't it? What about everybody's natural tendency to be selfish? To not care for God or other people?"

Ioana shrugged. "Yes, everybody is bad at times. However, a few people are evil. In Romania, we are more aware of spirits than most other places. We have known about them since Roman times. Romanians have suffered much from wicked men. Vile atrocities committed by Vlad, the Nazis, and later the communists can only be explained by hateful spirits. These spirits are still influencing men and women to do evil. You will soon see the results."

Chapter Seventeen

The senior priest at Horvata's Orthodox church had a secret—multiple secrets, in truth. *God doesn't expect perfection of his chosen representatives,* Father Flavius assured himself. *King David—a man after God's heart—took what he wanted. Because God knows the future when He chooses priests, any so-called wrong they might commit has already been allowed by Him. God gives leeway to those priests completely faithful to the Orthodox church—the only true church representing God. And who else among God's Orthodox priests has a private messenger from God as an adviser, like I do?*

Father Flavius looked at a fifteenth-century painting of devils and the souls they tormented. His mentor had located the painting and influenced its owner to donate it to the church. He pulled the window curtains, giving himself complete privacy in the residence the church provided. He lit a single candle then turned off the electric lights. "Come, Enlightened One. I welcome your counsel," he whispered to summon his mentor. As usual, nothing happened in response to the initial invitation. "Come, Enlightened One. I welcome your counsel," Flavius repeated in a normal voice. Green glimmers of light began flashing around the room. The air became chilly. Flavius elevated his voice to finish, "Come, Enlightened One. I welcome your counsel." The glimmers of greenish light outlined a dark man-like shadow.

Flavius bowed his head in respect. "Attendance at church services and donations have increased since our last meeting."

A deep, hollow voice from the shadow reverberated in the room. "Your request for me to visit the thoughts and dreams of the reluctant ones has worked. Your sheep have developed fear of the consequences of disloyalty to the church. Our all-powerful master has noted your devotion."

Flavius bowed his head again and felt a surge of confidence. "May I place another request?"

"Certainly, faithful one."

"I am allowed a wife but have remained married to the church to better serve. Yet I have physical needs that might distract me from my duties. Do the Holy Scriptures not record Moses telling the warriors of Israel to take the virgin girls for themselves in Numbers 31:18? I am a warrior of the church."

"Have I not provided for your frequent needs in the past?"

"Of course. And I ask you to do so again in a manner that could not be misconstrued by the unenlightened or cause doubt in the church."

The spirit remained silent for a minute before responding, "A girl, as young as the others you have taken, works for food and a pile of hay to sleep on in the village. Her name is Sofia. She has no friends or family. She longs for a position as a live-in housekeeper. Send for her and tell her that you have supernaturally sensed her need. Promise her you will care for her and give her a future. She will trust in you with all she is."

Flavius smiled at the spirit's indulgence. "Thank you, Enlightened One."

"Now I have instructions for you," the hollow voice continued. "A threat to your church has arrived in the village. An American cultist named Gideon seeks to draw Romanians away from your congregation. He has allied himself with others who oppose our work, especially the witch-woman Ioana and the Protestant cultist Raphael. You must discredit the American and his followers. The witch-woman is a key to eliminating the threat. You and our allies should terrorize her. Force the cultist Gideon out of Romania by threats to his wife. She would go with him. The other so-called spiritual warriors opposing us will scatter and hide."

"I understand, my lord," Flavius answered. He waited until the man-like shadow and greenish light grew smaller and disappeared. *I'll send Marcă to fetch Sofia tomorrow,* he promised himself.

* * *

The non-warriors left Gideon's cottage after Bible study on Sunday. The warriors had developed the habit of lingering afterwards. Gideon waited for them to speak.

Daniela could hardly wait to report at the informal meeting. "I'm hearing a lot of nasty talk at the market. Malicious rumors about some of you are being circulated in the community."

"What sort of rumors?" asked Florin.

Daniela turned to face Florin. "About you, they are saying that you stole some tools from your last job. And that you like men rather than women."

"My wife died in the revolution while trying to help some wounded," Florin returned with indignation.

"What about the tools?"

Florin hung his head. "I did take some tools in Timişoara as partial payment for three months in back pay. But the other is an outright lie."

Ioana used her hand to indicate herself and Gideon. "What are people saying about us?"

"More accusations of witchery for you. Anything bad happening to someone in the village is blamed on curses you cast. They also say the Devil speaks to you. Because you married Pastor Gideon—whom they call a cultist—they say you are using magic to lure people away from God's true church."

Ioana shook her head. "I do receive occasional premonitions. But I've never made a spell or tried to use magic. Even when Mama and I ate rats to avoid starvation, I refused to attempt placing curses on people in exchange for money. And they say Gideon is a cultist?"

"Yes. He supposedly takes orders from Satan through you." Daniela hesitated before continuing, "The rumors say Pastor Gideon was a failure in America. That he didn't lead a church but stocked shelves in a store. Then he joined a cult and brought it to Romania."

Gideon inhaled deeply. "I see a pattern. They take a little truth and mix it with monstrous lies. I did stock store shelves in America. But I didn't join any cult, and I certainly don't take orders from Satan through Ioana." He paused in thought as the others waited. "I wonder how they knew about me stocking shelves?"

"Evil spirits know secrets. The spirits tell their followers what to believe," suggested Claudia.

Gideon nodded. "But who listens to the spirits that know secrets?"

"Vampires," said Andrei. "Father Flavius and Primar Serban spread rumors, trying to take away dignity and respect from those they accuse. The priest even leads prayers in worship imploring God to curse the foreign cultists and witches. Everybody knows who he means."

Gideon looked around. "Anybody else experiencing persecution?"

"Our shop has had two broken windows," reported Daniela.

"A group of men chased me after I cared for your farm. I could not see them in the dark," said Luca. "I hid behind a hedge."

"Those are would-be werewolves," said Andrei. "They've been howling outside my cottage several nights. Dragon mimics their howling."

Words trailed off. Each person considered the threats and dangers to themselves and the others. Gideon broke the silence. "Jesus delivered the greatest sermon ever on a mountain. Among other things He said, 'Blessed are you when men revile you and persecute you and utter all kinds of evil against you falsely on my account.'"

Gideon smiled and made eye contact with each of the warriors. "Today we don't feel blessed, do we?" A few hesitant laughs and shaken heads answered him. "But the persecution demonstrates that we are doing Christ's work. And in this we are blessed. Apostle Paul suffered greatly for his faith. He wrote a letter for everyone to read. In Philippians 1:27, he says, 'Only let your manner of life be worthy of the gospel of Christ, so that whether I come and see you or am absent, I may hear of you that you stand firm in one spirit, with one mind striving side by side for the faith of the gospel.'"

Gideon bowed his head to pray. "Father in heaven, we ask that you allow us to stand firm together. Help us resist the works of Satan. And we thank you for allowing us to be part of your work. Amen." A chorus of cautious amens joined his.

* * *

Ioana examined the eight-year-old boy's throat. She could see inflamed tonsils. The condition had persisted for over a year. Three previous times she had provided scarce antibiotics for him. The condition always returned after a couple of months.

"Does he eat?" she asked the worried mother. "He looks abnormally thin."

"Whenever medicine made him better, he ate like a pig," the mother asserted. "But when the soreness returns . . . hardly anything, not even soup or milk."

Ioana hesitated as she thought, *Tonsils are part of our immune system. But if they are preventing the child from eating, it is better to take them out.* "I need to take out his tonsils. Not eating weakens his body, which will make recovery almost impossible."

"If you think that's best, Ioana."

Ioana took a pill out of her bag and gave it to the boy. "I know swallowing hurts, Ionuț but this is the first step to getting better. Take a little milk with the pill," she added and handed him a cup.

Ionuț looked at his mother, who reached out to pat her son's arm. "We will have ice cream," she promised. The boy's father, silent with concern, nodded. The boy grimaced with pain when he swallowed the pill.

Ioana explained to the parents, "The pill will make him drowsy. Then the procedure will only take a few minutes.

173

Afterwards he will need soups and soft food for about a week. Milk with cream would be good. He should eat normally after the soreness fades."

A half hour later Ioana removed the tonsils one layer at a time. She remembered her teacher in medical school describing the procedure as being "like peeling an onion." Afterwards she swabbed the blood oozing out until bleeding stopped after a few minutes.

"Let him sleep now. Be ready with the ice cream when he wakes. Make him take these antibiotics for ten days to prevent infection." Ioana smiled. "Tell Ionuţ to share the ice cream with his sister."

Ioana departed with a butchered rabbit in her bicycle basket for her services. *Gideon provided those antibiotics,* she remembered. She continued thinking about her husband. *You are fortunate to have such a good man.*

She noticed a couple of male figures hiding in some brush alongside the road as she descended a long hill. *They mean to ambush me.* She remembered the assaulted girl, Maria. *My only chance is to beat them on the bicycle.* She started pumping frantically.

Seeing Ioana increasing her speed to elude them, the men reacted. They darted out of the bushes toward the road. Howls announced them to be werewolves.

Two men managed to get onto the road just as Ioana swerved around them at a reckless speed. "Cut her off on the other side of the loop," one man yelled.

Chapter Eighteen

The downhill road looped in a horseshoe shape as it descended a large hill. Four men ran downhill across a pasture to intercept Ioana as she followed the road. "Awooooo! Awooooo! Awooooo!" the would-be werewolves cried as they reveled in the chase.

Ioana had to slow down to negotiate the curve before continuing downhill. She could see her pursuers converging on an intersection point. She resumed pumping madly. Her legs ached. One man outran the others and reached the road just before she approached. He extended a hand to grab her. She took one hand off the bike handlebars to fend the man's hand aside. Pushing against him nearly threw her off balance, but the centrifugal force of the bike's wheels righted her, and she flashed by the pack. Wolf howls chased her as she sped away. *Thank God for the bicycle Gideon gave me,* she thought.

* * *

November intensified activities in rural Romania. Farmers harvested crops, slaughtered livestock raised over the summer, made apple cider, stacked hay, and split firewood for the snowy months ahead. Homeowners stripped gardens of the last vegetables. Hunters brought wild boar, venison, and even bear meat to the market. Everybody collected and stored Carpathian walnuts. Gideon purchased wagonloads of hay for Ioana's goats and bags of cracked corn for her chickens.

The early morning air felt crisp and added forewarning of colder weather coming. Odors of wood smoke permeated the village as cottages and houses stoked up brick stoves. Woodcutters hauled hand-cut firewood to customers using horse-drawn and bell-laden wagons. Haystacks and pumpkins dotted the fields. Oaks turned red, and golden beech trees contrasted with dark green fir trees. The activities and colorful landscapes reminded Gideon of nineteenth-century farm scenes of Ohio or Vermont.

A chill wind brought the first snow flurry. Ioana showed Gideon their built-in brick stove with a small cast-iron door. "Much more snow will come," she hinted. She then indicated a larger door above the firebox. "This is for baking and roasting all winter."

Christina clapped her hands when Gideon led one of the woodcutters to the farm with a heavy load of four-foot-long split beech logs seasoned over the summer. Ioana showed him how to push the long sections through the iron door of the stove to create slow-burning warmth all day. Christina seemed so overjoyed by the steady heat that Gideon asked, "Why is your mother so excited?"

"We couldn't afford to buy firewood last winter or the years before."

"How did you stay warm?"

"In the worst weather, we shivered and stayed in one bed with all the covers we owned covering us. Vlad joined us under the blankets. In good weather, I collected branches from the forest to cook and give us a little heat."

As the fall turned to winter, persecution of the warriors decreased. Like everybody, vampires and werewolves stayed sheltered. The rumors and gossip had become old news. A sense of peace settled over Horvata. "Spirits don't like cold weather," reported several of the warriors. Gideon suspected that colder weather deterred the people rather than the spirits but made no contradictory comment.

* * *

"What am I supposed to do with these?" asked Ioana, staring at three lean-looking turkeys Gideon had brought home.

"We can eat them."

"Oh, we will eat them. Better than rat soup . . . probably. But why turkeys?"

"They're for Thanksgiving later this week," answered Gideon. "I found them on a farm during a walk."

"We do not celebrate American Thanksgiving in Romania."

"I know. But I thought it might be fun."

"Why did you buy *three* turkeys? A big stupid bird that cooks tough and dry. Goose would be better."

"They're tough and dry in America too. Most people eat them only once a year." Gideon paused a moment before revealing his true purpose. "We could invite some guests to dinner. Let them experience a different holiday."

"How many people are you inviting?"

"Everybody."

"Everybody in Horvata?"

"No, just the warriors and those in the Bible study . . . and Pastor Raphael. His wife died and his son is in the Romanian army. I thought about inviting Father Marcă too. He has no family here and he certainly enjoyed our wedding celebration."

Ioana sighed. "Well, you can kill, pluck, and clean these birds. Don't forget to save the hearts, gizzards, and livers. Give the entrails to the pig."

"Sure." Gideon grimaced then picked up the trussed birds and headed toward the barn to start the messy task.

"Don't forget to scald them before plucking," Ioana called after him.

"How do you scald a turkey?"

Ioana felt compassion for her thoughtful, but unskilled, husband. *I can do this much easier than he can,* she realized. "Never mind. I'll prepare the turkeys for cooking. But we will

178

need to serve our guests some wine with the dinner. Would you go buy some?"

"Where?"

"Ask for Eugen, the blacksmith in the village."

Ioana could see Gideon's relief at being excused from fowl-cleaning duty. "Thank you, sweetheart," he said.

"You are welcome, lover. Your Thanksgiving celebration could be fun."

Everybody Gideon asked in the village knew Eugen and directed him to a smithy on the outskirts of Horvata. The workshop and an adjoining storeroom dated from the late 1800s. He smelled burnt charcoal, scorched iron, and alcohol as he approached the run-down buildings.

"Come on in," a gruff voice answered Gideon's knock on the workshop door. Inside, he found a man welding a piece of steel plate onto an old car axle for use on a horse-drawn wagon. A sun-bright-white electric arc melted the axle surface, plate, and welding rod to fuse them together. Acrid smoke from the burning flux permeated the room. Gideon saw a burly man in a leather apron but couldn't see his face under the welding shield.

"Don't stare at the arc," the gruff voice ordered. "It could burn your eyes."

Gideon looked away until a minute later the arc of light disappeared. The welder leaned back and removed the shield.

Gideon recognized him as the man he had seen distributing spirits at the wedding celebration. "Are you Eugen the blacksmith?"

"I am a metalworker. I forge iron, do some grinding, and welding." Eugen removed the heavy leather gloves he had worn while welding. "You are the American missionary whose wedding I attended. I carried you on my shoulder. How was the 'later'?"

Gideon laughed. "Wonderful."

"I heard rumors about you being a cultist. I don't believe them, though. Your new wife does what I think an angel would do. Ioana helps whoever needs help. She saved my daughter's life by performing an operation during her baby delivery. Saved my only grandson too." Eugen extended his hand.

Gideon stepped forward and clasped the proffered hand. "Glad to meet you, Eugen. You brought some strong drink to our celebration. Your contribution made our wedding celebration . . . more festive and . . . less rememberable."

Eugen laughed heartily. "You have got a witty tongue, young man. I like you."

"I like you too, Eugen."

"So, why have you come to my workshop today?"

"Ioana sent me to you to buy wine for about twenty guests for our Thanksgiving dinner."

"The American holiday?" After Gideon nodded, Eugen said, "My other occupation is making wine and schnaps. Come this way."

In the adjoining storeroom, fumes of alcohol nearly made Gideon lightheaded. He saw vats of fermenting fruit mash. "Are you making wine in these?"

"No, winemaking is finished for the year other than regularly turning the bottles. These are the pulps from winemaking that I'm fermenting. Later I will distill them to make a liquor with high alcohol content, what the Germans call schnaps. I think the word in English is 'brandy.' In Romania, schnaps made from plums is *ţuică*." Eugen pointed to shelves where more than a hundred corked bottles of wine matured. "There is the wine."

"I don't understand the difference," said Gideon.

"Let me give you an example. You take wine grapes, remove them from their stems, and press them to collect their juice. That juice you ferment into wine with about twelve percent alcohol. But the grape pulp remains as a byproduct. That I ferment by itself, then distill, and collect the alcohol that boils off at a lower temperature than water. The resulting schnaps is about sixty percent alcohol. Pigs eat the fermented pulp after distillation. You should see a drunk pig sometime. The same process works for any fruit with sugar. I make grape, apple, and plum wines and then schnaps from their pulps."

Gideon laughed. "I would like to see a drunk pig." Then he added, "You must have a still?"

"Of course." Eugen led Gideon outside to see a copper boiler and condensation using a car radiator under a wall-less roof. "So, do you want wine or schnaps?"

"Wine will do, thank you. What wine would go with turkey?"

"From what I understand of your Thanksgiving, any wine. And with the tough turkey bird, maybe the schnaps would be better."

Gideon laughed again. "I'll take five bottles of your best wine." Gideon handed Eugen fifty dollars. "Is this enough?"

Eugen's eyes widened at the cash. "People in Horvata rarely pay with money. And never in American currency. But I do need money to pay for metalworking supplies." He tried to return most of Gideon's dollars. "This is enough for twenty-five bottles of my wine."

"Did people pay you for the drinks you supplied at our wedding?"

"No. Almost nobody paid."

"Then give me five bottles of wine and apply the rest to what you're owed. You did help make our celebration enjoyable for our guests."

Eugen stood still in surprise. "I will pick out my very best wines, Gideon."

On an impulse, Gideon proposed another idea. "Would you bring them? And stay for dinner, yourself? You could bring your family."

"I have no family, except the daughter Ioana saved."

"So, you'll come?"

"I will."

Chapter Nineteen

Dinner guests, eager to experience an American Thanksgiving, filled the town-cottage. Despite her initial misgivings, Ioana had developed enthusiasm for the holiday and decorated the cottage with candles. She created table centerpieces with nuts and apples. She baked only one turkey golden brown to carve like she had seen in pictures. She boiled the other two birds and giblets in a large stockpot to make spicy soup. Their tenderized meat she used in place of red meat in zesty Romanian recipes.

Ioana, along with help from the knitting widows, had worked for two days making pumpkin pies, green bean casseroles topped with oil-fried onions, macaroni with goat cheese, and baked sweet potatoes served with goat butter. "I mixed finely ground cornmeal with some wheat flour to make American cornbread," she explained to the female guests. "Eggs make the texture firm rather than crumbly. The cornbread tastes better with a lot of butter."

Daniela's husband surprised all by producing three imported cans of jellied cranberry sauce. "I ordered them from a foreign foods store in Budapest," he explained.

Eugen showed up with eight bottles of his finest wines. He let guests who wanted to drink wine taste samples and then choose their favorite. He placed the bottles on the tables and sat down alongside Florin and Andrei.

Pastor Raphael and Father Marcă came and sat together as they had at the wedding celebration.

Gideon called everybody's attention before the meal began. "Rather than have formal prayer, let us express gratitude to God by naming something for which we are grateful."

Nobody wanted to go first until Christina said, "At my age, I'm grateful to be alive." After laughter from those assembled, she added, "I'm grateful for my daughter and that God gave her such a wonderful husband."

"Mama is not as grateful for Gideon as I am," Ioana asserted to another round of laughs.

Then everybody shared something. Most guests contributed along the themes of health and gratitude for each other. When the praises slowed, Andrei asked, "What about you, Pastor?"

"I'm grateful for the opportunity to live in Romania and know each of you. Your faith makes mine stronger." Gideon paused for some light *oohs*, before adding, "And a wonderful wife." The group applauded.

Everybody tried the carved turkey, but obviously preferred Ioana's turkey à la Romania dishes. All enjoyed the traditional American foods as well.

"How did Thanksgiving get started in America?" asked Luca.

"Religious dissidents from England called Pilgrims moved to the unsettled wilderness of North America. They saw God as being more personal than public. The Pilgrims wanted freedom to worship God the way they chose rather than attend the Church of England.

"But they were city-folk rather than farmers or hunters. More than half of them died due to malnutrition and disease the first winter. The next summer the Indians, people who already lived in what became America, showed the Pilgrims how to raise vegetables and forage from the land. After their first harvest, the Pilgrims had a celebratory dinner to thank God. That was the first Thanksgiving. The Pilgrims invited the Indians as guests, who brought wild turkeys to be part of that meal. A meal of thanksgiving, usually with turkey, at the end of harvest season became a custom in America." Gideon paused. "After eating a large meal, most American men watch football on television."

"Do you mean football with your feet like we play in Romania? Or American football where the players are armored, carry an oblong ball with their hands, and smash each other?" asked Florin. Everybody laughed.

"I meant the smash-style football," Gideon answered. "The watching men can also be thankful they aren't playing." Everybody laughed again.

After the meal nobody seemed anxious to leave. "Tell us a story, please, Mr. Dixon," asked Luca.

So Gideon told and acted out the stories of Daniel thanking God while in Babylonian captivity, David thanking God after escaping from his enemies, and Paul thanking God when shipwrecked. Pastor Raphael and Father Marcă each spoke briefly afterwards, sharing scriptures that valued thankfulness.

Winter unlike any Gideon had experienced in America's South set in after Thanksgiving. A foot of snow fell, then another foot, and more kept coming. Without snowplows for the road, the village became isolated for days at a time. Temperatures fell below zero Fahrenheit during the long nights. Romanian cottages with brick or ceramic fireplaces and firewood remained warm and cozy.

People ventured out only when necessary. Farmers took care of their animals. Children went to school when weather allowed. With the roads all but impassable, horse-drawn sleds became the favored means of transporting everything. Ioana and Gideon hitched rides on them to make critical medical calls.

Ioana had her remaining pig butchered, then she purchased four suckling pigs to begin raising for the following year. The piglets received table scraps and the whey from Ioana's cheese making. The noisy little pigs grew rapidly.

Eating the hay Gideon had purchased that fall, the goats continued to produce plenty of milk. Butter and cheese started to accumulate in the root cellar. Ioana's chickens, eating the cracked corn Gideon had bought, continued to lay eggs. Remembering the hard winters that she and Christina had endured, Ioana shared her farm's productivity with widows and infirm residents in Horvata.

Despite the wintertime decline of spiritual warfare, growing prosperity of his family, and marital satisfaction, Gideon mentally struggled. *How can I explain this ministry to my father and his church? Are we a home church or a Bible study? We don't really conduct worship.* Gideon enjoyed frequent theological discussions over coffee with Pastor Raphael. The senior man sometimes chided Gideon about keeping people out of church on Sundays by hosting his Bible study at the same time.

"We are gathering believers together as Apostle Paul suggests," Gideon would answer.

"True," Pastor Raphael would admit.

Still, the issue of explaining his ministry to his sponsors back in America remained. *They wouldn't understand the strategic value of the few warriors. Romanians are still careful of their identity after years of communist oppression and secret police. Even if I had a large group, most would be reluctant to be photographed.*

187

Gideon looked around the town-cottage, which he still rented. The regular Bible study group had grown to eighteen including Eugen. But they only met on Sunday mornings. Aside from coffee discussions with Pastor Raphael and the odd private meeting, the space went unused otherwise.

How can we make the most of this space? Gideon pondered. He remembered Pastor Raphael's desire that he try to interest Horvata's younger people. *What would interest people? Especially younger people?* Then an idea came to him: *English language classes! We might get a good response. There's not much to do in the wintertime here, and most Romanians think knowing English could be valuable with the country hoping to join NATO and the European Union.*

Ioana enthusiastically agreed, but stated, "Because of my medical practice, I won't be able to attend every class." She suggested enlisting Gideon's Bible study participants to spread the word around town that English classes would begin on Friday night.

The following Friday, Ioana baked cookies and made coffee and sweet lemonade with a concentrate Daniela had recommended.

A dozen quiet and respectful young adults arrived for the first class. The party-like atmosphere Ioana created soon filled the town-cottage with noise. Gideon began teaching the participants with simple statements. "My name is . . ." "What is your name?" "I like cookies." "Where is the train station?"

The pupils practiced with each other. Then he asked, "What would you like to say in English?" This created great merriment as the young adults proposed ridiculous things to say.

"I haven't slept for three days, because that would be too long."

"If you need me, I'll be inside until spring."

"Our president has decided to move Romania to the South Pacific."

"Winter will be cancelled next year."

The merriment multiplied when Gideon had them stand to try repeating the English versions of their quips.

Subsequent classes started with a short lecture about English grammar and sentence structure with handout sheets, then proceeded to exercises. A popular aspect of the classes involved Gideon telling one of Jesus' shorter parables in English, which the pupils could follow in the Romanian Bible. Then students would try to retell the story in English themselves, usually generating uproarious laughter and applause. The class rapidly grew to twenty-six, including the warrior Luca. The young adults started calling themselves The English Club. Many of The English Club joined Luca in attending the Sunday Bible study just to enjoy more of Gideon's animated stories. Maria, the girl Luca had helped heal, became an enthusiastic English student. Although both knew Ioana, neither Luca nor Maria recognized each other.

Gideon still wished to offer some aspects of worship on Sundays. "Singing is part of worship," suggested Ioana.

"How would we provide music?"

"Florin can play a guitar. Ask him."

189

Soon a few contemporary praise songs opened the Bible study. The young attendees from The English Club loved singing and added a lot of energy to the gatherings.

* * *

Pastor Raphael had heard slanderous allegations in the village against some participants in Gideon's Bible study group and discounted them as untrue. But curiosity made him wonder, *Why have those people been viciously targeted by Father Flavius and others? How are they considered a threat?*

One afternoon he saw Luca walking ahead of him on Horvata's main street. "Luca!" he called while catching up. *Maybe I can learn something about Gideon's group.*

The teenager turned and smiled. "Pastor Raphael!"

"I miss seeing you with your parents on Sunday mornings, Luca."

"Well, I am attending Bible study with Mr. Dixon and Miss Ioana. I mean Mrs. Dixon. I like Mr. Dixon's Bible stories. I'm part of his English classes too."

"I thought their wedding celebration was exciting."

"The best. And I have been making some money caring for their farm."

"So I heard. What stories does Gideon tell?"

"Stories from the Bible. He makes the old stories exciting. The warriors love them. The stories give us courage."

Pastor Raphael nodded while wondering, *Who are the warriors? Luca considers himself among them.* "We warriors need courage, Luca." Pastor Raphael lowered his voice and spoke in a confidential tone. "I need courage myself. What causes the other warriors to need courage?"

"The spirits are evil liars. They have been persecuting us. Saying hurtful and untrue things. Florin has seen his business decline because rumors make people mistrust him."

"Why would spirits target Florin?"

"Because he can force the spirits to leave people alone. He can even cast them out of those who are possessed."

What? thought Pastor Raphael. But rather than react he asked, "How else are spirits persecuting the warriors?"

"They have incited people acting like vampires and werewolves against us, especially against Mrs. Dixon."

"Why is Ioana especially threatened?"

"Because she knows what the spirits and those they deceive are doing. Mr. Dixon thinks she is a prophetess. Once, Ioana took me with her to help heal a girl who had been attacked by werewolves."

"You healed a girl?"

"No, God healed her when I prayed. Mr. Dixon helps us understand that our powers are only because of God. But he thinks God uses me sometimes to heal."

"He's very right that God does the work, Luca." *I thought something was going on at that study. Sounds like God is bestowing some supernatural gifts.* "What do the other warriors do, Luca?"

Pastor Raphael listened intently as Luca named the warriors and described gifts of discernment, wisdom, and foreknowledge.

* * *

Sofia had felt deeply honored when the young priest Father Marcă came to find her on behalf of his senior. He had explained that Father Flavius wanted to help her situation by making her his housekeeper. She would have plenty of food and a warm place during the coming winter. She had agreed with deep gratitude.

Father Flavius coming to her bed in the night surprised Sofia. But she realized that she knew nothing about the ways of priests. *If he is a priest, he must be doing right. I think Father Flavius loves me. Even if our ages are so different, maybe he will marry me.*

Chapter Twenty

Blue skies and crisp, dry air followed a gentle two-day snowfall. Ioana walked arm in arm with her husband along a trail at the edge of a steep, snow-covered pasture. Village children and young adults played by riding an assortment of inner tubes, sheets of plastic, pieces of cardboard, one broad shovel, and a sturdy homemade toboggan down the steep slope.

"Hey, Mr. and Mrs. Dixon," called Luca. "Would you like a ride?" He indicated the toboggan. A dozen young adults, mostly from The English Club, urged them to try.

"Sure!" Gideon shouted back and headed for the toboggan. "Come on, Ioana."

She pulled him back and hissed, "Wait a minute! We are adults now. Snow riding is for children."

"Wouldn't you like to be younger again, just for a few minutes?"

"My childhood was not so pleasant," she answered. She noticed the young peoples' amusement to see their English teacher arguing with his wife.

"All the more reason for grabbing a little piece back." Gideon took her hand and led her to where Luca waited. Maria dusted snow off the toboggan and pointed it downhill.

Ioana remembered a few occasions of snow play as a child. *This might be fun,* she acknowledged to herself. Gideon had already seated himself on the toboggan with his legs extended before him. His hands held onto a rope. Ioana sat down behind him and wrapped her arms around his waist.

"How do you steer?" Ioana heard her husband ask Luca.

"Wait! You have never ridden a toboggan before?" she asked.

"Nope. Didn't snow often where I grew up and not much when it did."

"Just try to hang on," said Luca and then started them downhill with a mighty shove.

Before Ioana could scream, much less get off, the toboggan accelerated to a terrifying pace. Snow crystals flying up blinded her. The toboggan went over a slight dip and bounced. Dimly, Ioana perceived evergreen trees looming ahead. *Trees have trunks,* she realized.

"Abandon ship!" Gideon yelled and threw himself to the side, taking Ioana with him. Together they tumbled into a mixture of arms, legs, and snow. The unburdened toboggan ricocheted off a tree trunk and stopped.

Gideon came up laughing hysterically. "Wow! That was great!" he cried in English without thinking. Up the slope, Ioana heard cheers and applause from the young people. "Best ride all day!" called Luca. Ioana started laughing herself as she brushed snow off.

Gideon ran up the hill, pulling the toboggan and laughing. Ioana followed at a slower pace. Before she reached the top, Gideon zipped by her riding an old inner tube.

As Ioana tried to remove the snow that had gotten inside her clothes, she enjoyed watching her young husband relish a new experience. She knew many of the kids attended his classes and looked up to Gideon. She noticed the girl, Maria, who had been injured by werewolves, glancing at Luca. He offered to share a toboggan ride with her, which Maria readily accepted.

On Maria's return from the trip downhill, Ioana spoke to her. "Luca is a nice young man, isn't he?"

Despite rosy cheeks from the cold, Maria blushed. "Yes, he is. I think he likes me."

"I think so too. And you are a nice girl for any young man to like." Ioana paused. "Luca came to your house once and prayed for you."

"You mean when . . ." Maria didn't finish.

"Yes. And after he prayed, your heart felt much better."

"Did Luca . . . see me? Does he know who I am?"

"No and no. You were completely covered by a blanket when he came in except for one foot. But he will remember the house where you live. You won't keep that secret forever."

"Thank you, Mrs. Dixon. Let me tell Luca, please, if he needs to know. And when I am ready."

"Certainly, Maria."

Ioana saw Luca position the toboggan and glance around for Maria. At his gesture, Maria hurried to join him and shrieked with joy as they raced downhill. *Thank you, God,* Ioana prayed.

* * *

Thirty people had crammed into the town-cottage for Sunday Bible study the previous morning. *We need more space to meet,* Gideon told himself as he walked down Horvata's main street on Monday. *Are we a church or a Bible study?* he asked himself for the hundredth time. And he knew some Romanians were torn between attending Gideon's meetings and their traditional church.

A familiar voice startled him. "You need a larger meeting space," said Pastor Raphael.

Gideon turned and smiled. "Last summer I wouldn't have believed that possible."

"Some from my church would like to attend your meetings but want to have more traditional services on Sunday."

Gideon nodded. "Some in my group would benefit from attending services on Sunday too."

"I have got a partnership to propose," continued Pastor Raphael. "You could meet in our building on Saturdays."

Gideon felt like God had answered his question. *Your group is a Bible study, not a church.* He held out his hand to shake an agreement. "We accept. Thank you, Pastor Raphael."

"I understand that some members of your group are rather special," said Pastor Raphael as they shook.

"Everyone is special to God."

"Of course. But you know what I mean," Pastor Raphael answered.

"Yes, I do. But we have enough opposition already without giving people something else to question. Could we not publicize the magic-like spiritual gifts and our battle against evil spirits unless God reveals them? Some people might not understand."

"I think that would be wise."

The odor of a home-raised ham roasting for dinner filled the farm-house on Christmas Eve. Ioana looked at the small fir tree Gideon had cut, brought inside to the main room, then decorated with a short string of colored lights and a few plastic ornaments. A delightful fir smell mixed with the ham odor. The lighted tree had obviously entranced Christina. Gideon had started her mother stringing popcorn to place on the tree.

Some of Gideon's American traditions are charming, Ioana admitted to herself.

Gideon had left early for a special Saturday Bible study program at Pastor Raphael's church. Ioana and Christina followed a little later. Ioana walked slowly holding her mother's arm to prevent a fall on Horvata's icy streets. Outside the church entrance, a live nativity scene with Luca and Maria as Joseph and Mary greeted the guests. Inside, Ioana found a sense of excitement and anticipation for an unprecedented Christmas program.

A hundred and four individuals plus some young children attended from the Bible study, English classes, and Pastor Raphael's congregation. Father Marcă and several from the Orthodox church also came. Ioana heard Father Marcă say to her husband, "I heard you are encouraging people from your Bible study to attend churches of their choice on Sundays."

"I thought it the right thing to do," Gideon replied.

"I agree," answered the young priest.

The program began with Pastor Raphael welcoming everybody. Florin played the guitar and led several Christmas carols. Two women and a man sang beautiful *a cappella* solos. Gideon and Ioana told the story of Jesus' birth from the perspective of Joseph and Mary. They injected some fictional and humorous dialogue between the couple that made the crowd roar with laughter. The attendees then sang a *colindă*, a traditional Romanian carol based on the nativity. On an impulse, Gideon asked Father Marcă to close the program with a prayer and a blessing. The priest seemed surprised but delivered a beautiful prayer thanking God for Jesus and asking His blessing for the coming year on all attending.

"Please stay for refreshments," Daniela hollered after Father Marcă concluded. She and her husband then served baked goods and coffee as well as fruit punch and frosted cookies for the children.

Ioana looked at the participants exchanging greetings and mingling. *I wish Gideon's father could see this.*

Christmas Day dawned with fog typical of winter in Eastern Europe. Under the tree several presents had been placed. Ioana and Christina tried to contain their excitement while waiting for Gideon to distribute the packages. Various pieces of useful clothing exchanged hands, including a sturdy farmer's work suit from Ioana to Gideon. Christina gave knit mittens to Gideon and her daughter. After those exchanges, two large brightly wrapped items remained. Ioana opened a heavy box to find a microwave oven. She hugged Gideon's neck and rushed to the kitchen with her gift to try warming some dessert pastries.

Gideon's gift to Christina puzzled the older woman. "A blanket? I have blankets already."

Ioana heard her mother from the kitchen above the hum of the microwave and returned to stand by the Christmas tree. "No, Mama. Don't you see the cord? Gideon has found you an electric blanket with a thermostat. You can be as warm as you like every night." Ioana plugged in the blanket. In a minute, she put Christina's hands between the folds.

A smile spread across Christina's face. "This is lovely. I might not want to get up in the mornings."

After accepting Christina's and Ioana's gratitude, Gideon had his own reason to be excited. "Let's eat the ham."

Over Christmas brunch, Gideon asked, "How do you usually celebrate Christmas?"

Ioana's face showed regret. "We just tried to stay warm the last few years. Before that, the communist government didn't encourage any religious celebrations."

Christina nodded and added, "Before communism, we children would go out dancing and carol singing from house to house on December sixth. That was our Christmas Eve. People would give us candy or fruit. My mother kept an oil lamp lit all night. In the morning, we would find Moş Nicolae had come and put gifts into our laced-up boots." Christina sighed. "That was a long time ago."

Three days after Christmas, Gideon stood with Ioana at his side watching hundreds of bears dance down a street to the beat of drums. Gideon had surprised his wife with a two-night getaway by train to Comăneşti. People paraded under bearskins to participate in an ancient festival called Ursul.

"Why bears?" Gideon asked.

Ioana smiled. "An ancient tribe who lived here, called Dacians, believed bears to be sacred. The Dacians became a big part of the genetic mix that makes modern Romanians.

Bears having power and magic to protect and heal became part of Romanian mythology. Some still believe bearskins can protect people from evil spirits. But most just enjoy dressing up in their best bearskin as a cultural tradition."

"Spirits are woven into Romanian culture, aren't they?"

"Yes. But real spirits can use Romanian customs as camouflage and do great harm without people recognizing the source. Like if your Santa Claus really existed but secretly incited children to be bad, not good."

Gideon thought for a few minutes. "Maybe that could also work in reverse."

"What do you mean?"

"We have many more in the Bible study now than the original spiritual warriors. They are all on our side, but most aren't supernaturally gifted at opposing spirits. When trouble returns, calling ourselves 'bears' could be a way to include everybody."

"You mean like a mascot? A way for a group to identify itself?"

Gideon nodded. "I guess so."

"The title 'spiritual warriors' isn't one we could publicize without inviting skepticism. Whereas the bear opposing evil spirits is part of our culture."

"Right."

* * *

Springtime brought joy to rural Romania. The sun warmed people tired of an especially cold winter. Trees budded. Flowers bloomed. New lambs with their mothers dotted green fields. Farmers and gardeners prepared ground in hope of a bountiful harvest.

Ioana woke unusually early even for herself. She felt Gideon's warmth as he slept undisturbed beside her. Yet she had a distinct feeling of unease. She deliberately reviewed her circumstances compared to a year earlier. *I have a loving husband. A good man. A man God brought to help us. He has provided medicines to help my patients. Gideon and I are traveling to places together just to have fun. Mama is happy. She and her widow friends have plenty of wool yarn for knitting. I expect to soon have children to love and nurture.*

She dwelt on those pleasant thoughts for a while then asked herself, *So why do you sense the approach of greater difficulties? Are you naturally pessimistic? Maybe. Concentrate on your good fortune.* Ioana remembered the warriors and growing number of villagers, including many young people, attending the Bible study. *They are all good friends and partners in God's service.* Still the ominous feeling remained. As she lay awake in the dark, the feeling grew and brought with it clarity.

She shook Gideon to wake him.

"Is there danger?" he asked in a groggy voice.

"No, I have something important to tell you."

His wife's urgent tone cleared Gideon's head. "What?"

"He is coming. He is coming."

"Who is coming?"

"A more powerful evil spirit. Baal. And soon."

Chapter Twenty-one

From his church's nave, Flavius observed through an aperture the assembly of collaborators the spirits had summoned. The men and a few women gathering in the narthex of the Orthodox church at midnight looked uncomfortable in each other's company. Gradually they coalesced into small groupings of self-identified characters: werewolf pack leaders, a couple of would-be prophets, a few females and one male calling themselves witches. Primar Serban and Prefect Lazar, apparently considering themselves better than the rabble, stood together apart from the others. Flavius knew them to be men of ambition like himself.

Flavius opened the royal doors between the nave and the narthex and waved those waiting into the area considered part of the church. He turned his back and walked down the dimly lit nave. He could hear rustling as those assembled followed. Standing before the Beautiful Gates between the inner sanctuary and the nave, he turned to face the group. Without the preamble of a welcome, he began, "Together we face a challenge. Foreign cultists are threatening the true church. Romania's church. They are duping the weak of heart into doing their will. The cultists are undermining the foundations of our culture and way of life."

Nods of approval acknowledged the priest's words, but no one dared speak. "But tonight, we will begin a new era," Flavius continued. "The true god has sent a powerful angel to join our struggle." He turned and opened wide the Beautiful Gates, exposing the sanctuary.

A few gasps came from those watching. None had ever seen those gates cast open before. From the darkened sanctuary came flickering lights. But not the greenish glimmers of light some present had seen associated with ordinary spirits. Multi-hued lights of stronger intensity reflected off the walls and ceiling. Gradually the colored lights outlined a dark man-like shape larger than the lesser apparitions seen previously. The shape glided without steps outward from the sanctuary and grew larger into a presence twice Flavius's height. The priest relinquished his place to the specter and joined Primar Serban and Prefect Lazar in the audience.

Those present stood motionless in awe and terror. They gasped when two yellow eyes opened where the shape's face would be. Some reflexively knelt.

The spirit spoke, his voice sounding like a chorus of many loud voices in unison. "You are the faithful ones. Remain faithful and you will prosper. The future belongs to those who obey their masters. I am Baal, your master and protector." The spirit's words reverberated around the nave.

The spirit remained motionless and silent for a minute, two minutes, three. Then the lights grew more intense and illuminated a werewolf leader. "I see you, He Who Kills," Baal addressed that individual. "Your leadership skills have gone unappreciated by most Romanians. Yet you have led men in attacks on the witch called Ioana and others. Remain true and many more men will heed your call."

The lights refocused onto the priest, before the apparition addressed him. "Father Flavius, you aspire to be Patriarch of Romania, yet the Holy Synod has not recognized your faithfulness and superior abilities. Through me you can attain your desire."

The lights highlighted one of the would-be witches. "You, daughter, aspire to be more than a peasant wife to an unimaginative laborer. Many have devalued you because of your poverty. I can give you wealth and the admiration of those who have despised you."

As the lights continued highlighting individuals, Baal looked at each person present and demonstrated that it intimately knew them. The spirit told secrets only the person could know, frequently referenced private grievances, and made promises in exchange for loyalty. *Only an angel could know that,* thought each one addressed. *The angel appreciates me. I can achieve my dreams.*

After acknowledging each one present, Baal paused again before speaking. "The so-called spiritual warriors in Horvata are our enemies. Together we must defeat them. If not, the American cultist called Gideon will destroy your culture and your heritage. He will make Romanians into impoverished slaves for foreigners. The witch-woman Ioana is the American's harlot. She will control your thoughts and put spells on your children unless you stop her."

Baal made further accusations against each warrior before concluding, "I hereby charge each of you to a glorious mission with eternal consequences. Together we will drive the intruders from our midst. Let us prepare, cooperate, and act decisively. You will thereby receive the rewards you desire."

The spirit's apparition and lights grew smaller until they disappeared. Flavius moved forward and closed the Beautiful Gates. He turned to face the group. "Now talk among yourselves. Coordinate your activities. Decide actions you will take."

A dozen reports of persecution and malicious lies against the spiritual warriors came to Gideon the following week. The town-cottage sustained broken windows. Somebody had painted CULTISTS, DEATH TO WITCHES, and TRAITORS on the whitewashed outside walls. The cottage's owner came to demand that Gideon pay for all the damage.

More ominously, threats against non-warrior attendees of the weekly Bible study began. Several formerly supportive parents forbade their teenagers from attending Bible study.

Gideon questioned himself. *The warriors know what risks they take for God. Am I endangering non-warriors by allowing them to attend the Bible lessons?*

On Saturday, the group gathered at Pastor Raphael's church for Bible study as usual. Gideon noticed with joy several newcomers among them. Andrei had identified several fallen warriors who had been previously granted supernatural gifts, but then spirits had intimidated them. Gideon had found them and encouraged them to return. Everyone welcomed Pastor Raphael, who took a seat near the back. Forgoing the usual entertaining Bible story, Gideon taught the group on spiritual gifts from 1 Corinthians, Romans, and Ephesians. He told stories of the Apostles using spiritual gifts from the book of Acts. He emphasized, "The Bible teaches that all believers have at least one special gift from God."

A teenage girl raised her hand. "What's your spiritual gift, Mr. Dixon?"

"I think my gift is bringing the Bible to life. Making Scripture meaningful to our lives."

Florin spoke out loud for all to hear. "We think so too, Pastor." A murmur of agreement and nodded heads affirmed his words.

"Thank you all," responded Gideon. "Jesus Himself warned that his followers would face opposition and persecution. The book of Acts records persecution the Apostles endured for Christ. Some in this meeting have been using their gifts to oppose evil and are suffering persecution. If you are attending this meeting, you deserve to know that you may also be subject to persecution along with them."

After a silence, Ioana spoke to support her husband's warning. "Men supposing themselves to be werewolves ransacked our farm. Some have tried to attack me when I've gone on medical calls." Several non-warriors in the group shuddered in fear.

After Ioana finished, other spiritual warriors recounted incidents of vandalism, harassment, and malicious lies. A non-warrior teenage boy volunteered, "Some classmates at school are calling me a 'cultist' for attending these meetings. They say I should instead be patriotic for Romania." A murmur of voices affirmed his concern. Other non-warriors added experiences of ostracization and criticism.

Pastor Raphael surprised the group by reporting, "I am receiving threats for allowing you to meet in our building. Someone reported falsely to Bucharest authorities that I am embezzling money from the post office." When he paused, they could tell that the pastor had more to say and waited in silence. "I had always thought evil spirits were only active during New Testament times. They had become superstition. The things I've seen and heard about have made me relook at Scripture. The maliciousness of many in the community has convinced me that we are under attack."

Gideon noted the words, "We are under attack." *Does that mean Pastor Raphael is joining us?* He and Pastor Raphael looked each other in the eyes for a long moment. Both nodded in solemn commitment. Gideon spoke to the group again. "Each of you have the right to know what is going on. Unfortunately, this may only be the beginning of trouble. Many of you have heard, may even believe, that my wife, Ioana, is a witch. Maybe you think she even put a spell on me." Guilty laughter confirmed that idea. Gideon himself smiled. "Ioana is not a witch. She casts no spells, nor does she work magic. I believe she is a prophetess as recorded in the Bible. She has a warning for us." He gestured for Ioana to stand before the group.

Ioana looked nervous as she stood and faced the group. "Baal has come. He seeks to destroy us all."

"Who is Baal?" a woman asked.

Pastor Raphael answered, "A powerful evil spirit posing as a god. Perhaps a surrogate for Satan himself."

Gideon scanned those present, making eye contact with many. "You had the right to know. By openly siding with us, you may be making yourself a target for Baal. We will not think less of you for withdrawing from among us."

"I will not run from evil," Eugen, the blacksmith and winemaker, asserted from the back. "I don't understand all the religious teachings," the man continued with his deep, gruff voice. "But I've heard enough to know that things aren't right in Horvata. Not right in the whole județe, probably. The revolution against Ceaușescu and the communists began putting things right. Now we need to finish the job."

The group clapped and roared in affirmation.

Gideon waited until the tumult diminished before speaking forcibly. "Doesn't Eugen remind you of a bear?"

Shouts affirmed Eugen's bear-like qualities. "Aren't bears part of Romania's tradition of opposing evil spirits?" More affirmation resounded with applause and waves. "Then we shall call ourselves 'the bears.'"

Cheers, clapping, and vocalized bear-roars came from the group.

*　*　*

Sofia wiped her mouth after throwing up early in the morning. A fifteen-year-old girl at the orphanage where Sofia had grown up had suffered a similar affliction. She had been quietly taken away for a medical treatment and refused to talk after being returned. A few months later the girl reached sixteen years old. The orphanage administrators had released her to find her own way in the world.

Other girls talked, though. They claimed that their classmate had gotten pregnant. Somehow one of the male custodians had been involved. Sofia hadn't understood all the details. But she knew that a man factored in, and that morning sickness was a symptom. *I hope I am pregnant. Father Flavius would marry me for certain then.*

That night she went to see him while he read in his study. After hearing about her sickness, he asked, "What about the days each month when you bleed a little? Has that continued?"

"No. Not for three months."

Father Flavius shook his head. "Too bad you're not a witch. I am seeking a witch for my wife. I would love a witch."

Sofia remembered Ioana being called a witch. The thought of being like Ioana thrilled her heart. "How could I become a witch?"

"Maybe we could help you."

"Would you, please?"

Flavius turned down the lights and pulled the window curtains together. "I will call an angel to make you a witch." Then he chanted three times, "Come, Enlightened One."

Sofia noticed green glimmers of light flashing around the room. The glimmers of light outlined a dark man-like shadow from behind. Cold seemed to emanate from it. She felt terror but stood motionless lest Father Flavius think poorly of her.

Father Flavius spoke to the shape. "The housekeeper you provided has missed her period. She wishes to become a witch. Will you help her?"

The figure spoke in a hollow voice. "Faith and obedience are required to be a witch, Sofia. I will give you the power to be a witch if you prove your trust. Do you understand?"

Sofia hid her surprise that the angel would know her name. "Yes, sir."

"Then take a broom to the highest place you can find and fly. The instant you leap off riding the broom, you will become a witch. The broom will become magical and bear you safely to the ground. Your mind will be filled with witches' lore. Then use the broom to fly back here to Father Flavius. He will be proud of you. He will marry you."

"I will," Sofia promised.

Chapter Twenty-two

Ioana received a summons for a baby delivery after supper the following week. Gideon had gone into the village to meet with Pastor Raphael. A well-dressed man she didn't know showed up at the farm and reported his wife to be in labor.

"I will guide you to her. The place is higher in the mountains," the man told her. When she put her medical bag into her bicycle's basket, the man added, "The way has no road, only a rocky path. The bike is not good."

She followed the man as he trudged along without speaking further. True to his claim, a steep and difficult path separated from the road outside Horvata and ascended into the mountains. As light dimmed after sunset, the man motioned her ahead of him and turned on a flashlight to illuminate the rough path at her feet. After a thirty-minute walk, they came to a remote shepherd's cottage surrounded by evergreen woods on a hillside. A rivulet of spring-melted snow babbled nearby.

He's nicely dressed for a shepherd, thought Ioana.

Another man, also dressed unusually well for a shepherd, warmed himself in the chilly spring air at an open fire before the cottage. "Is this her?" he asked.

"She is," the first man answered.

Ioana noticed a pot on the coals brewing coffee. *Why not use the stove inside?* Ioana wondered. She looked at the cottage. The light of an oil lamp came from within and revealed no curtains. Even in the low flickering firelight, the cottage's exterior made it appear uninhabited. Broken windows had not been repaired. Weeds had grown up before the front door.

The man who had summoned her pointed to the door. "My wife is in the bedroom. She's waiting for you."

Ioana approached the door. She smelled tobacco smoke coming from within. *Women in delivery don't smoke.* She listened and heard no groans from a woman in pain. *This is a trap,* she realized. *Keep your head.*

"My instruments need to be sterilized first. I'll only take a couple of minutes," she told the men, who appeared to leer at her. "Can I use the coffee pot?" Without waiting for an answer, she picked up the pot and added. "Where are your cups? You can drink the remainder while I boil water."

The men gestured to their mugs, and Ioana poured two cups of coffee. "I'll need to clean out the grounds and get fresh water," she told them and headed toward the rivulet, carrying her medical bag. The men turned back to the warm fire while sipping the coffee.

At the water's edge, she made noise banging the pot around. Then she laid down the pot, waded across the rivulet, and hurried into the woods, ducking behind some head-high fir trees to stay out of sight as she carefully snuck away.

A half-minute passed before she heard a shout from one of the men.

"Hey! What happened to her?"

The other man cursed before answering, "The witch is running. Come on out, Ivan," he called to a man inside the cottage. "We'll have to catch her."

The third man came outside and demanded, "Which way did she go?"

Ioana considered dropping her medical bag to run faster. *That would show them your direction.* She held onto the bag as she pushed through the woods in sparse light provided by a half-moon above the alpine treetops. As her eyes adjusted to near darkness, she told herself, *Flee in a straight line so they cannot cut corners on you. Slow down, lest you bump into something.*

She heard the voice of the third man berating the others. "You morons should have grabbed her by the fire."

Looking back, she saw three flashlights swinging back and forth searching for her. A faint patch of greenish light glimmers joined her pursuers. "The witch cultist went that way," a hollow voice told the three men. Ioana immediately saw the three flashlights turn in her direction.

Ioana burst out of the woods into a mountain meadow. The half-moon seemed bright compared to the shaded

215

darkness of the woods. She ran downhill. Looking backwards, she saw three flashlights emerge from the woods led by a dark man-like shape. Greenish glimmers outlined the spirit against the trees. At first, the men with their vision accustomed to the flashlights could not see her running in the dim moonlight.

"There! The witch cultist runs down the hill. Catch her," the spirit's hollow voice ordered.

The three men started after Ioana. "We're gaining on her," yelled one. Another man cursed after falling on a loose stone. Ioana could hear her pursuers' heavy footsteps getting closer. "Give up, witch," a man called. "We won't hurt you."

Ioana smelled wood smoke. *People!* After passing around a patch of trees, she saw a campfire with black silhouettes outlined against the flames. Short figures appeared to be children. She headed toward them. With her heart pounding and her lungs heaving, she reached the circle of firelight. A squatting figure before the fire stood and turned toward her. She saw a swarthy, slight-of-stature man.

"Help me, please. Bad men are chasing me."

Two women rushed into the firelight. The children hurried to them. Ioana saw a circle of wagons illuminated by the fire. She smelled manure from nearby horses. *Romani!* Two of her pursuers came out of darkness into the ring of light. They approached Ioana, who retreated to the far side of the fire.

"Please save me. They are trying to kidnap me," Ioana begged.

Three other Romani men, each carrying a stout stick, hurried over from the wagons to protect their families. Ioana remained behind the fire, huddled near the women and children. The man who had been squatting picked up a wrought-iron poker used to tend the fire and held it ready to strike.

"Give us that woman," one of the men chasing Ioana demanded as he struggled to catch his breath after the exertion. "We work for Prefect Lazar. He will send policemen to deal with you all if you don't cooperate with us. This woman is a witch." The third man who had fallen caught up, his face bleeding from the tumble. The three chasers moved around two sides of the fire toward Ioana.

"Stop!" The thin voice of an older woman pierced the tension. A tiny woman bent with age hobbled into the firelight. "If Prefect Lazar wants this woman, then let him come get her himself."

"The prefect is not—" started the man who had pretended to have a wife in labor.

"Come back tomorrow with the prefect and his police," the old woman interrupted. "You will not take this woman tonight."

Two teenage Romani armed with long machete-like knives joined the others protecting the women, children, and Ioana.

"We will come back in force tomorrow," threatened the one called Ivan. "The police will be hard on you." The three would-be kidnappers disappeared into the darkness.

With few words, the Romani started moving. The men collected their hobbled horses. Women picked up items around the fire and led the children to the wagons. The old woman approached Ioana. "So, you're a witch?"

"No, I am not a witch. I don't know. Maybe I am, depending on how you define a witch," Ioana answered.

The old woman investigated Ioana's bag. "These look like midwifery tools."

"Yes, they are. One of the men chasing me pretended to have a wife in labor."

"Uh-huh. But there was no woman having a baby?"

"Right."

"You felt trouble and ran before they caught you?"

"Yes, ma'am."

The Romani woman reached out to hold Ioana's chin and looked into her eyes. "You probably do have the second sight. Those men would likely have used you and then killed you."

"Yes, ma'am," Ioana answered. "Thank you for protecting me. What will you do when the police come tomorrow?"

"Oh, we won't be here tomorrow, daughter." Ioana heard men hitching the horses and loading the wagons. "And neither should you be," the old woman added. She pointed to marks the wagon wheels had left in the grass. "Follow our tracks in the moonlight to a dirt road. Take the road downhill to the paved highway. It will lead you to safety. Travel quietly and without light, and you will get home safe."

* * *

Ioana chafed at Gideon's shouts of anger.

"You followed a strange man alone to a place you didn't know? How could you be so reckless?"

Ioana, unaccustomed to being bossed or protected, reacted with a calmer, albeit defiant, voice. "I've always responded to every need. He said his wife was in labor. I had to go! I'm not a coward . . ." She left unsaid the words, *like you.*

Gideon recognized the accusation, though. The unsaid words made him furious. "You think you can do anything you want? There are others to consider."

"I *was* considering others. A woman alone, in pain, and fearful. How could I know the summons was a lie? I had to go."

"I thought you knew things supernaturally. Didn't you sense the danger?"

"I cannot call up supernatural foresight at will. I have already told you that!"

"Well, things are going to be different from now on. You told everyone that a powerful new spirit would seek to harm us. Baal in the Bible represents the vilest evil. He is a manipulative false god. You're going to take extra precautions, starting with telling me whenever someone wants your help."

219

Gideon's mention of Baal slowed Ioana. "You were not here when the man came for me," she protested.

"No, I wasn't. But I stand by my command. You said that wives in Romania oversee food and babies. Well, husbands take care of their families even if wives disagree. Starting now, you will first find me before you go to help people you don't know. Do you understand?"

"I understand," Ioana answered between clenched teeth.

Chapter Twenty-three

Although her relationship with Gideon had been cordial after their fight, Ioana still seethed with resentment. *How does that American think he knows better than me? I have lived here all my life. I have been on hundreds of medical calls. Risks are necessary to do good in Romania. My fellow Romanians will side with me, especially the women.*

After the Saturday Bible study, the original spiritual warriors and the newcomers who had supernatural gifts lingered. Unlike previous occasions, about half of the other bears also remained. Ioana noticed the non-warriors and thought with gratitude, *They are with us more than ever now.*

Gideon treated the entire group as combatants in a common cause. He started by asking for reports of trouble. Several recited intensified persecutions: public ridicule, loss of customers, and physical threats. One teenage boy talked about being pelted with garbage. A woman grieved because her cat had been poisoned. Gideon encouraged everyone for their faithfulness and for acts of turning the other cheek and loving their enemies.

Ioana waited until the reports trailed off. "I had a dangerous experience this week." She then recounted her near abduction. "One of the men was named Ivan." She described her flight through the night and rescue by the Romani. The group shuddered at her description of a dark, hollow-voiced shape with greenish glimmers of light helping her pursuers.

"You saw an evil spirit," said Florin. "I have seen them myself." The group shivered in horror.

"I've seen spirits too," added Gideon. "Although at the time I didn't recognize them as what they are." The group remained in shocked silence at the gravity of the threat.

Ioana indirectly appealed to the group for her freedom to respond to medical emergencies. "Danger is frequently involved in helping others. I hope you will all pray for me as I follow God's leading."

After a moment of silence, Florin addressed Gideon. "Pastor, we thank God for bringing you to us. We love and respect you. But you cannot allow your wife to go out alone anymore. We all love and need her."

Daniela reacted with more emotion. "Gideon, you should know better. I do not know how things are done in America. But here in Romania, husbands are responsible to watch out for their wives. You need to take care of Ioana, who is like the daughter I never had." Several others chimed in exhorting or mildly rebuking Gideon for his negligence.

Gideon glanced at Ioana, who met his eyes then looked away in shame. "I hear you all. You're right. From now on I'll go with Ioana on her calls. But what if there's an emergency and I'm not available?"

"Then I will go and protect your wife," volunteered Eugen.

"Or me," declared Andrei.

All the men then agreed to help watch over Ioana. "Or any of you other women. Call any of us if the situation is risky," Florin declared. The other men chorused agreement.

Eugen spoke again with grim determination. "Sounds like those men who chased Ioana are former secret police. They probably work for the prefect behind the scenes. Criminals like them tortured me under Ceauşescu when I complained about the difficulty of getting bottles for my wine. I would like to bust their heads." All the men voiced agreement. Several showed scars from wounds inflicted by Ceauşescu's enforcers.

Gideon summarized, "So we've agreed that we'll all protect Ioana and each other, especially each of the women. Let us hope and pray we can do that in Christian love and not by busting heads." Eugen grunted but didn't contradict him.

Walking with Gideon to the farm after the group dispersed, Ioana confessed, "You were right."

"You've been right many times too. Like when you wanted to get married before my father came. We can be better together as a team if we listen to each other."

"And I need to get used to having a wise husband look out for me."

* * *

God, please help me! Please help me, Ioana prayed over and over to herself on the train to Bucharest before meeting Gideon's parents at the airport. She could not control her fears. *Gideon's mother and father will see you as a peasant woman who has stolen their son. They will think you're not good enough for him. What if they discover you are considered a witch by many?*

Beside her, Gideon rode looking out the window like a condemned man on his way to be hanged. To allay her own trepidation, Ioana asked, "Are you looking forward to seeing your parents?"

"Sure. Of course. I'm also nervous."

"Why would you be nervous meeting your own parents?"

"Dad always had lofty expectations for me. Our Bible study group isn't very large. Dad measures success by numbers. And we're not even an official church." Gideon sighed deeply. "I need to warn you that my father is set in his beliefs and can be rather forceful."

"But you are leading a group of supernaturally gifted people opposing evil spirits. You are bringing young people to Christianity. Lives are different because of you. The

224

medicines you purchased are helping heal my patients. Your father should be proud."

Gideon nodded. "Most of that is good to share." Then he shook his head. "But we should keep the parts about evil spirits and supernatural gifts to ourselves. Mom and Dad wouldn't understand or believe that possible. I'm just glad they won't be able to understand people speaking in Romanian."

Ioana squeezed her husband's arm. "All the warriors will be trying to protect your parents from the spirits, though."

"Thank you. With the threats we're experiencing, I just wish Mom and Dad could have come at a different time."

"Maybe God sent them to help. To do something special."

"I don't see how they could help, but I hope you're right."

Ioana waited with Gideon at 8:00 a.m. outside the luggage claim at Bucharest's Henri Coandă International Airport. Around them a half-dozen drivers held signs with the names of their clients. Having flown first class from the US, Aaron and Madeline Dixon came through smiling among the first arrivals. They waved at Gideon and embraced him once clear of the exit. Ioana observed Aaron to be taller than his son, thin, and handsome with distinguished streaks of gray hair at his temples. Madeline stood slightly shorter than Ioana, was exceptionally pretty with a round face, and had a stylish American hairstyle. Aaron wore a well-cut pinstripe suit and Madeline a fashionable dress.

Ioana heard Gideon use her name and saw him direct his parents' attention to her. Then he spoke in Romanian, "These are my parents, Aaron and Madeline Dixon."

Ioana expected a kiss on both cheeks. Instead, Madeline wrapped two arms around her for an enthusiastic hug. After the squeeze, Madeline leaned back while holding Ioana by the elbows and gave her a broad smile showing flawless teeth. Madeline said something friendly in rapid English Ioana couldn't understand.

"I am happy to meet you," Ioana responded slowly with English words she had memorized. "I hope your visit to Romania is enjoyable. You have raised a fine son."

Madeline hugged her again. Then she stepped away for Aaron to greet his daughter-in-law. Ioana took his proffered hand for a gentle shake and reflexively curtsied. Aaron laughed and said something unintelligible but loud in the fashion of most American males. He put one arm around her shoulders and squeezed while continuing to speak loudly.

Gideon and his father went into an animated discussion, seeming to Ioana as if they mildly disagreed about something. Finally, Aaron nodded. Gideon picked up both of his parents' large suitcases and led them toward the bus they would take to the train station.

"Dad wanted to rent a car," Gideon whispered to Ioana. "I told them we had already purchased the train tickets and warned against driving on unfamiliar Romanian roads."

At the train station, Aaron and Madeline recoiled from the mob trying to board the second-class cars. Gideon directed his parents around the crowd to board a first-class car. With Aaron and Madeline's two bags on the luggage rack, the four settled into the private compartment.

Unlike Gideon's arrival in Romania, the senior Dixons barely looked at the Romanian countryside. Rather, they peppered Ioana with friendly questions using Gideon as a passible translator. They asked about her parents, living on the farm, midwifing, her education, her medical practice, and the wedding.

When Aaron commented about the wedding, Madeline responded with something that made her husband laugh. Then Aaron made more comments that started Madeline giggling. Gideon told Ioana, "First Dad said that the wedding looked like it had been quite a bash. Mom told him she wished their own had been as much fun. Then Dad asked her if she was referring to the 'later.' Mom and Dad must have paid to have our wedding video translated into English."

Ioana could feel herself liking her boisterous American in-laws. "Tell them the 'later' was the best part,"
she told Gideon.

Gideon blushed red but delivered her message. Aaron and Madeline laughed merrily.

In Braşov, while waiting for the bus to Horvata, Ioana saw Madeline hand Gideon a hundred American dollars. "Hire a professional translator, a woman, for a day. I want to talk to my new daughter without her husband translating."

"The translator will arrive in Horvata the day after tomorrow," Gideon told his mother upon returning from a pay phone. He returned the money to his mother. "You can pay her when she comes. She is very happy to work for thirty American dollars a day, plus her expenses."

Madeline tucked the money away. "Well, I'll probably tip her anyway."

As the four rode the bus to Horvata, Ioana considered her new in-laws. She expected them to be accustomed to American luxuries and wondered how they would adjust to humble Horvata. *At least we have a nice place for them to stay,* she thought. *I am glad the warriors and I fixed up the town-cottage while Gideon gave spiritual support to the bears.*

"This is where you'll stay," Gideon announced, once they arrived at the town-cottage. When his parents gave no reaction, he added, "This is where I lived until marrying Ioana. We use it for English language classes now."

"Charmingly rustic," said Madeline.

"There's no hotel?" asked Aaron.

"Only a tiny room in the local tavern."

Aaron nodded. "Okay, then. This will do."

Inside, Ioana saw Gideon admiring the improvements she and the others made. They had spruced up the town-cottage with a soft new couch, tablecloth, nicer bed furnishings, wall decorations, coffee tables with electric lamps, towels, and an odd American bathroom accessory Claudia called a washcloth. Andrei had replaced the two cot-like beds in Gideon's former bedroom with a comfortable bed for two. He had moved one of the cots to Gideon's office. Florin had installed a clothes rod and three shelves. Delicious Romanian dishes waited in a borrowed refrigerator. The microwave Gideon had given Ioana for Christmas rested on the counter by the sink. Daniela had put a small window air conditioner into the bedroom.

"This will be fine," said Madeline looking around.

Good, thought Ioana. *This is certainly the best furnished home in the village now.*

"We'll let you rest from your trip now," Gideon told his parents. "In the morning we'll tour the village and Ioana's farm. Tomorrow night you'll have the English language class here as guests. They're already excited to meet you."

Gideon is anxious that his parents do not learn everything about our battle against spirits, thought Ioana. *I hope the teenagers are careful in what they say.*

Chapter Twenty-four

Teenagers crammed into the cottage, eager to practice their English on fresh Americans. Aaron could not count the times he heard, "My English is not so good," followed by a series of jumbled sentences. To each student, he paid rapt attention and, speaking slowly, made suggestions. Madeline, he saw, managed her own group of hopeful English practitioners with graciousness.

After an hour, Gideon called for volunteers to retell the stories they had rehearsed. A dozen hands went up. For a half-hour, individuals took turns telling popular Bible stories in English. Good-natured laughter at mistakes filled the cottage. Teenagers coached each other while Gideon looked on. One boy gave a dramatic account of the death and resurrection of Christ, bringing tears to Aaron's eyes. At the conclusion, Aaron asked him, "Do you believe this story, Son?"

"Yes, sir." The teenager gestured toward Gideon. "Mr. Dixon, he told us it was true."

"Then what will happen when you die?"

"I'll go to heaven because Jesus paid for my sin."

Aaron and Madeline, sitting separately to allow more teenagers near each of them, exchanged glances and imperceptivity nodded appreciation of their son's ministry.

Meanwhile, Gideon announced the next phase of the class. "Those were rehearsed stories. Our best English speakers can tell a story without rehearsal." He waved a girl to the front and said to his parents, "Ask Nadia any question that doesn't require a simple answer."

Aaron and Madeline looked at each other again. Madeline gestured for her husband to proceed. "What's the most exciting thing you've seen happen in Horvata?" he asked.

Nadia didn't hesitate. She spoke in slow, careful English words. "Our village put Ioana Nagy—that was her name before she and Mr. Dixon married—on trial in the city square for being a witch." The girl stumbled through the story, occasionally asking the other teenagers in Romanian for help with an English word. She dramatized the part where Gideon told the mob they would have to kill him first.

Aaron and Madeline listened in speechless silence. They glanced at each other in wonder. Aaron looked at his son and saw him cringing uncomfortably while listening to Nadia. *I'll bet Gideon didn't want us to know about that,* he thought. *There's more going on here than we see on the surface.*

Nadia tried to recite Gideon's forceful words but couldn't remember them exactly. She finished with, "They set Ioana free. I was there and saw it all. I am glad they didn't burn Ioana." Aaron and Madeline, followed by the teenagers, rose to their feet to applaud Nadia's linguistic feat.

* * *

Knocking on the cottage door the next morning woke Madeline—still suffering from jetlag—at 9:00 a.m. Aaron opened the door to find Gideon and Ioana along with a short, stout, fortyish-year-old woman with a no-nonsense demeanor.

"This is the professional translator Mom wanted in order to talk privately with Ioana," Gideon explained. "Lana used to translate at international conferences for the communist government. Now she freelances mostly for foreign businessmen. She can do simultaneous translation. That means she listens with her ears and speaks at the same time. No long pauses like you get from me."

Madeline spoke around her husband at the door. "Come on in, Lana and Ioana. I'll make us some tea."

"Coffee in Romania, Mom."

"Right. I remember now. I'll make coffee." Madeline turned to her husband. "You get dressed and go off somewhere. Leave us women to talk."

"Come with me, Dad. I'll take you to meet some of my friends. Then we can go for a walk in the countryside," Gideon offered. After Aaron dressed, father and son departed together.

"What's delivering a baby like, Ioana?" Madeline asked through Lana.

"It is messy." After Madeline laughed, Ioana continued, "Birthing a baby is tiring for the mother and the midwife. After the baby is born, the mother gets to rest. I must go home and catch up on farm work."

"Don't the parents pay you enough to live on?"

"Usually I am given some vegetables or other farm produce. Money is scarce, especially for rural people. After one twenty-nine-hour delivery, I got a suckling pig. I raised the pig on garden debris and traded it to a crop farmer for enough hay to feed our goats through the winter. From the nannies I made butter and cheese to barter for things Mama and I needed."

"What was your most difficult delivery?"

"A breech baby. The umbilical cord became pinched. I had to do an emergency caesarian. The parents forgot to pay me anything that time. But the mother and baby are fine now. You'll likely meet Eugen, the baby's grandfather."

"And nobody paid you?"

"No, but I know my worth in helping people."

Madeline realized, *Ioana is a woman skillful enough to perform a caesarian. Yet she had to make butter and cheese to care for her elderly mother.* She thought of her two daughters, a little older than Ioana, living comparatively comfortable suburban lives. *Ioana is tougher, more compassionate, and more responsible than my own daughters.*

"Could I ask you a question?" asked Ioana.

"Of course, honey."

"Are all American men as stubborn as Gideon?"

"How has Gideon been stubborn?"

"At first, he refused to marry legally until his father could perform a ceremony. Only after an intruder tried to break into our house and I needed protection did he agree."

Madeline hadn't realized that Ioana needed protection and regretted urging Gideon to delay. "No, Gideon isn't naturally stubborn. He must have wanted his father to preside very much. But just because Gideon is a man of God doesn't mean he can't be difficult as a husband. Trust me. Aaron was, still is, hardheaded sometimes. The worst are the newly married men. I call it 'young husband syndrome.' They feel they must be right about everything, or their manhood is somehow threatened."

"Do young husbands get angry? I never remember my Poppa getting angry."

"If I understand correctly from what Gideon has told me, your father was in his fifties when you were born. He and Christina had already been married a long time. So, your Poppa wasn't a young husband."

"That is true."

"What does Gideon get angry about?"

Ioana told about her and Gideon's bitter argument after the narrow escape she had during the false summons. "He was right about me not going alone on calls anymore. But I had never seen him so angry. Gideon shouted at me and called me reckless."

"You may or may not have been reckless, honey. But you frightened your husband by making him think he couldn't protect you. You hurt him by asserting you didn't need his protection. Men of any age don't like to admit fear or hurt. They frequently channel those emotions into anger."

"I've got a lot to learn about marriage."

"Yes, you do. Especially being married to someone from such a different culture. Do you know the two most important things about marriage, Ioana?"

"No."

"Commitment to a good marriage and a common plan."

After talking to Ioana about marriage for over an hour, Madeline changed the subject. "Last night one of the English students talked about you being accused of witchcraft. Gideon came to your rescue. Was that story true?"

Ioana nodded.

"Are you a witch, honey?"

"I don't cast spells or practice magic. But I do sometimes know things that others don't."

"That could be a keen sense of intuition."

"No. I told Gideon of Aaron's surgery and the results before Gideon received any news."

"I did think it strange that Gideon phoned in the middle of that crisis."

"Gideon thinks I have the biblical gift of prophecy."

Madeline sat back. "Aah . . ."

* * *

Gideon led his father to Horvata's post office, where he found Pastor Raphael on duty. After introducing the two pastors he explained, "Pastor Raphael married us. Our Bible study meets on Saturdays at his congregation's building."

"Are most of your Bible study participants also members of Pastor Raphael's church?" Aaron asked.

Pastor Raphael surprised both Americans by answering in rough English. "No. Only nine. Sometimes I also attend on Saturday. A few of Gideon's bears go to Orthodox church. Most don't go to church anywhere." To answer Gideon's surprised look at his English, Pastor Raphael added, "During communist time I studied university in Budapest. Went to international English language church. Your Romanian much better my English."

"Why did you call Gideon's Bible study 'bears'?" asked Aaron.

Gideon broke in and answered for Pastor Raphael. "It's like a mascot name, Dad."

Aaron contemplated that for a moment, then shrugged and gestured to their surroundings. "So, you work here at the post office? You're a bi-vocational pastor?"

Pastor Raphael couldn't follow Aaron's rapid words. After Gideon translated, Raphael answered, "Yes. Small church. Little money."

"Our bi-vocational pastors in America are among the most dedicated Christians. You have my highest respect." Aaron reached out and shook the Romanian pastor's hand heartily.

"You preach my church? Sunday?" asked Pastor Raphael.

"I would be honored, Pastor."

As the two pastors exchanged parting words, Gideon thought, *Dad can be so magnificent dealing with people. I could never fill his shoes.* "You should preach at our Saturday Bible study too, Dad."

"I'd like to hear you preach, Son."

"I really don't preach, just teach. I could bring a Bible lesson, then you could deliver a short sermon."

"Alright."

"I'll ask Mom's translator, Lana, to simultaneously translate for you."

"Good idea." Aaron stared at the large, well-tended Orthodox church near the town center. "Have you been able to cooperate with the Orthodox?"

"They hate us. At least, the senior priest Father Flavius does. He calls us an American cult and a danger to Romanian culture. He is actively trying to turn the community against us." Gideon kept other thoughts to himself. *Andrei says Flavius is a vampire influenced by evil spirits. Dad wouldn't understand that.* Gideon continued, "A young priest, Father Marcă, seems more favorable to us. He gave our marriage an Orthodox blessing then came to our reception and

238

Thanksgiving dinner. I did attend one Orthodox service with Ioana's mother, Christina."

"What was that like?" After Gideon described the church interior and service, Aaron stopped walking and turned to face his son. "You're telling me the priests conduct the service behind closed doors? Don't they realize that the veil of the temple ripped from the top to the bottom when Jesus died?"

Gideon shrugged. "I don't know what the Orthodox realize, Dad. But I did observe how much the liturgy they delivered meant to Ioana's mother, Christina. Church services can be meaningful to people because of their comforting repetition. Even your services. Your program hardly changes week to week."

Aaron glared teasingly at his son. Then he smiled and pinched Gideon at his collar bone as if he were still a teenager. "Still open-minded, I see. But you're right about the meaningfulness of comforting repetition, especially to older people. And I haven't ever seen the youth in our church excited about sharing Bible stories like the kids in your language classes."

The two men resumed walking together. "Father Flavius has started condemning us in his services. Although most of the participants in our Bible study group don't go to church, the teenagers have heard the accusations. Our classes and Bible study appeal to the renegade quality common to young people. In that way, Father Flavius is helping us."

"My son, the leader of renegades," Aaron razzed Gideon.

If you only knew how true that is, thought Gideon before answering, "Jesus' disciples were renegades, of a sort."

"That they were, Son."

Chapter Twenty-five

On Saturday, Aaron watched Florin lead forty-two Bible study bears, half of them young adults, in melodic Christian songs. Then Gideon rose to retell one of Abraham's experiences with God using expressive voice embellishments. Lana whispered translation into Aaron's and Madeline's ears. The Romanians listening interrupted periodically with laughter and comments. Aaron saw Pastor Raphael seated in the rear and laughing with the rest. *They are hanging on Gideon's every word,* Aaron realized.

"Gideon is introducing you to preach now," Lana whispered. "He is describing you as a wise and influential pastor in America. He says that your congregation has enabled him to live in beautiful Transylvania among fun and lively Romanians. He finished by saying that God sent him here to find a wonderful Romanian wife."

Aaron heard the group murmur approval, then Ioana said something aloud that made everyone laugh. "Ioana responded with, 'Don't you forget that,'" Lana explained.

Aaron then stood to speak. The bears greeted him with an enthusiastic ovation. Lana picked up a live microphone to use during translation. Aaron began an elegant sermon about God's sovereignty. Lana skillfully mimicked his tone and voice. The bears listened and reacted politely. Aaron increased his inflection and pounded out the most important scriptures. He noticed listeners looking at their watches or out the windows. The sermon dribbled to an end. Aaron returned to his seat in dismay.

Most remained after a concluding song. Individual bears openly shared once again about injustices, threats, and persecution they had endured during the previous week. "Fight back with love, with mercy, with justice, and with prayer," Gideon counseled those wronged. "Let us prove to the world that we are Jesus' followers by our love and commitment to each other." Aaron and Madeline listened intently to Lana's translation.

Pastor Raphael moved his seat to sit beside Arron. He waved Lana away. "Your preaching very wise. Important Bible understanding," he whispered. "Use the same sermon for my congregation tomorrow. Better for my people."

Aaron stood before Pastor Raphael's congregation of over a hundred the following morning. The service had followed traditional Protestant patterns; announcements, hymns, prayers, and an offering. The congregants appeared older and more solemn than the Bible study group. Gideon and Ioana, along with their older friends from the Bible study, sat in the front row.

With Lana translating as before, Aaron delivered the same sermon about God's sovereignty. Those attending appeared mesmerized. Although not overtly reacting, not one person looked away. Some unconsciously leaned forward. Aaron felt his confidence increasing. He added extra biblical references and examples. He concluded with Jesus' powerful declaration before His arrest and crucifixion, "Not my will, but thine, be done."

The congregation seemed to let out its breath. Although Pastor Raphael had asked Aaron and Madeline to stand with him at the exit after the benediction, congregants mobbed Aaron at the front before he could join Pastor Raphael. Lana stood nearby translating comments.

"Best sermon I ever heard."

"God bless you."

"Thank you for coming to Romania."

"Will you pray for me?"

"Could we meet for you to tell me more about God?"

Eventually the group departed, leaving Pastor Raphael. "Your son was right. You are wise and learned in God's ways. Would you preach again next week?"

Outside the church, Gideon and Ioana waited with Madeline. "Great sermon, Dad. You should move to Romania."

"I never learned so much about God," Ioana added through Lana.

Madeline kissed her husband on the cheek. "I'm proud of you."

Aaron could not speak in the emotional moment.

"Ioana has Romanian cabbage rolls and meatball soup ready for our lunch at your cottage," said Gideon.

"Mama loves the microwave Gideon gave me for Christmas. She went ahead to warm the food up for us," added Ioana.

* * *

"Hand these out. Post them in strategic places," Gideon instructed the bears who dropped into the town-cottage to pick up flyers printed in Braşov. The flyers denounced the Caritas Ponzi scheme being run by Primar Serban and protected from scrutiny by the prefect's police. Another flyer disputed the malicious lies being circulated about the bears.

Sunday night Lana had returned to Braşov delighted with ninety American dollars pay for three days of translation services, plus her expenses and a thirty-dollar tip. Madeline then hired Nadia, the teenage English speaker, to take herself and Aaron shopping. Ten dollars for a day had stupefied the girl with joy.

Gideon conferred with Claudia, deciding which warriors and a few non-warrior bears to use in thwarting the most threatening spirit attacks. *Everybody still needs to make a living,* he reminded himself. *We're stretched thin. I'm glad some of the former warriors have returned with renewed faith.* Two restored warriors who, like Florin, could banish evil spirits had begun opposing serious nighttime attacks. Claudia coordinated around-the-clock prayers among the bears and members of pastor Raphael's congregation.

Eugen proved tireless protecting Ioana and others at risk. Each night he guarded places where physical attacks had been predicted. "I'll catch one of the former secret police," he had vowed. To that point, he had prevented harm but caught nobody.

I'll be glad to take Mom and Dad on a tourist trip tomorrow, Gideon told himself. *But I'm happy they're not here right now. They don't need to know about the supernatural activity going on. They wouldn't understand.*

* * *

A bus well past its prime bounced along on twisting roads to Bran, the location of "Dracula's Castle." Gideon could tell that his parents felt uncomfortable taking the decrepit public transport. He leaned over to add a positive perspective. "You know that oftentimes people first see the place where they're living when visitors arrive. This is the most famous historical site in Romania. I've never seen it."

"I've never seen the castle either," contributed Ioana after Gideon told her what he had said.

"How much farther?" asked Madeline.

"Maybe an hour," answered Gideon.

Aaron spoke over the road noise and grinding bus gears. "And we'll be staying at a guest house?"

"Right. It's like a hotel and a bed-and-breakfast. They'll probably have indoor plumbing and hot water."

Two hours later, the foursome found the guest house *did* have indoor plumbing and hot water, albeit in a bathroom serving a hallway full of other guests. They found the small monk-like rooms thoroughly cleaned. Windows looked out at pristine mountains like those shown in travel brochures of Switzerland.

Ioana bubbled with enthusiasm. "I never traveled much before marrying Gideon. Being a tourist is fun."

The next morning, breakfast included bread and butter, unsweetened yogurt over granola, a slice of salami, a boiled egg, and strong coffee in shot-glass-sized cups. Madeline and Aaron surprised Ioana by pouring their coffee into bigger cups, then adding milk and sugar.

"Romanian coffee is a bit too strong for us," Madeline explained.

The castle, perched on a cliff overlooking a road through a valley, could have been a Hollywood set. The inner castle contained a maze of compartments, winding stairs, low arches, and foot-tripping thresholds. From the castle's defensive ramparts, they looked down on the valley from a dizzying height.

"So, this is the castle that inspired the mythical Dracula," commented Aaron.

Ioana shook her head after hearing Gideon's translation. "No, there was a real Dracula, a ruler named Vlad. In the fifteenth century, our Transylvania had Germanic settlers. Like Saxons in what became England and Lombards in northern Italy and Slovenia. Aided by the Ottoman Turks, Vlad raided Transylvania, sacked villages, and carried away women and children as slaves. Vlad the Impaler became a legend for cruelty and ruthlessness. The Irish author Bram Stoker took vampires from Romania's culture and combined them with Vlad's reputation and childhood name, Dracula. Western Europe and America distorted Romania's real vampire lore to depict bloodsuckers. More suspenseful that way for books and cinema."

Gideon prayed silently, *Lord, please don't let Mom and Dad ask about "Romania's real vampire lore."* They aren't *ready to believe vampires exist.*

As an answer to his prayer, Ioana continued, "But Vlad, or Dracula, never inhabited this castle. The Germanic settlers built Bran Castle as a defense. They wanted to keep Vlad out of Transylvania. Mama and I named our ruthless cat Vlad. When Mama and I had no food, we made soup out of rats he caught."

"You ate rats?" Madeline asked in surprise.

"Yes, after Poppa died four years ago. I used them in meatballs instead of pork or beef."

The sun had just set when the bus arrived in Horvata bringing the Dixons back from touring the castle in Bran and the fortress town of Braşov. Madeline saw a male farmworker waiting at the town-cottage.

"A girl has been hurt and has great pain," he said to Ioana.

"What happened?" asked Ioana.

"I don't know. We heard her screaming and found her on the ground at the foot of a cliff."

"I'll go with you," Gideon insisted.

"Please do," Ioana agreed.

"What is it?" Madeline asked.

"An emergency," Gideon explained. "I don't know what kind. Ioana will try to help an injured girl."

"Could I go along?"

Gideon conveyed the request to Ioana, who answered in English, "Yes."

"I need some rest and would be in the way anyway. I'll stay here," Aaron asserted.

The farmworker led the Dixons on a path for about a mile. They heard groans of pain a hundred feet before reaching the girl, who lay at the foot of a cliff. Somebody had covered her with a tarp. A group of male farmworkers, not knowing anything else to do, stood anxiously watching. A broom of twigs lay on the ground nearby. Ioana pulled a flashlight out of her medical bag and shined it on the afflicted young woman.

Gideon recognized her as Sofia, the girl he had given food to at the wedding. He whispered to Ioana, "I know this girl. Her name is Sofia. She has no parents."

Ioana started talking to the stricken girl in a gentle voice. "Sofia, my name is Ioana. I can help you." She pulled away the tarp and started to examine Sofia. A discharge of water and blood from her vagina soiled the ground. A contraction during which Sofia screamed proved her to be pregnant and in premature labor.

"Build a fire and boil water to sterilize my instruments," Ioana demanded of the farmworkers and handed one a pot. The men scurried to comply.

Ioana gave Sofia a mild sedative shot and asked her questions while checking her for broken bones.

"What's going on?" Madeline asked Gideon.

He reported piecemeal, as the girl answered Ioana's questions. "The girl—her name is Sofia—is pregnant. Sofia doesn't know when the baby is due. The fall brought on labor." Gideon hesitated before reporting the cause. "She fell while trying to fly on a broom."

"What?" exclaimed Madeline.

"You're in rural Transylvania, Mom. Sofia thought a spirit promised her the power to fly if she proved her faith by trying. She wanted to be like Ioana."

Madeline interrupted Gideon's piecemeal report. "Ioana flies on a broom?"

"No. But Sofia probably thought she could." Gideon listened to Sofia, then continued translating as Ioana gently examined and questioned Sofia. "The father is the senior Orthodox priest who took her in as a housekeeper. Father Flavius promised to marry her if she became a witch." Gideon paused as he strained to hear Ioana's gentle words over the girl's continued sobs. "Ioana is certain the baby is dead. Sofia is losing a lot of blood."

Ioana pulled a half-liter bottle of sterilized water out of her bag. She unwrapped a sterile needle and tube then stuck Sofia. She said something and handed the bottle to Madeline.

"You're to hold the water, Mom."

Gideon took the flashlight when Ioana wordlessly handed it to him and moved to provide light for his wife. "Ioana is removing the fetus and placenta, trying to save Sofia's life," he explained to his mother. "Afterwards, Ioana will treat Sofia for cuts and a broken arm."

Fifteen minutes later, Ioana said something urgent to Gideon. He handed the flashlight to his mother. "I'm to go fetch Luca."

"Who is Luca?" Madeline asked. But Gideon had gone. Madeline held the saline solution and positioned the flashlight according to Ioana's hand instructions as she worked on Sofia. The sight of the bloody mess made Madeline woozy, but she kept holding the water and positioning the flashlight.

Twenty-five minutes later and gasping from running, Gideon reappeared with Luca.

"Who is this?" Madeline asked as Ioana instructed Luca.

Between gasps, Gideon took the flashlight back and answered, "Luca is here to pray. Ioana hasn't been able to stop the bleeding."

Luca knelt and put one hand on Sofia's foot. His face contorted with effort for four agonizing minutes. Suddenly, Ioana cried out in joy.

"The bleeding has stopped," Gideon told his mother.

Chapter Twenty-six

Aaron suffered a troubling dream. His dream-self recalled a true-life experience as a young, unmarried associate pastor. He became infatuated with a young, attractive wife named Suzy who attended the church. Suzy had asked him for marriage counseling. After hearing her story of neglect and emotional abuse, he developed a compulsion to protect her. She began phoning him at his apartment to talk. The senior pastor recognized danger in the situation and had forbidden Aaron to communicate with Suzy. "Let Suzy talk to my wife," the senior pastor instructed.

Aaron felt heartbroken at the time. Eventually Suzy divorced her husband and moved away. He heard she married a doctor twenty years her senior. Aaron had never revealed his young foolishness to anyone.

In the dream, Suzy appeared at his current day church and accused Aaron of adultery that broke up her first marriage. She brought proof in the form of recordings, pictures, and love letters with his signature. News media reported the scandal. His megachurch dismissed him. Madeline left him. His children avoided him. Aaron's dream-self felt shame and disgrace.

Aaron woke with a start. *It was only a dream,* he assured himself. But a feeling of deep despair remained. He looked at Madeline in a dead-like sleep next to him. He got up without disturbing his wife and left the bedroom. He saw 6:34 on the microwave oven clock. Aaron found Ioana sleeping on the couch, her face and clothes stained by blood. In the other bedroom, he found a teenage girl with a cast on her right arm and various bandages. She rested on the cot-like bed in what Aaron assumed was a drug-induced deep sleep.

An older woman sat in a chair beside the girl. The woman put her finger to her lips in the universal sign for quiet. She pointed to herself and whispered, "Claudia."

Quietly, lest he wake the sleepers, Aaron dressed and left the town-cottage. He walked to the farm, where he found Gideon looking exhausted yet resolutely milking goats. A gray cat, presumably Vlad who had caught rats for Ioana to eat, lapped milk from a saucer. Christina kept Gideon company while knitting and reciting village gossip. Aaron saw his son politely humoring his mother-in-law with nods and inconsequential verbal responses.

"What happened last night, Son?"

Gideon turned eyes of exhaustion toward his father. "I'm so tired . . . can I let Mom tell you later?"

"Okay. May I help you here, then?"

"Sure. Thanks. Start by collecting the eggs. Watch out for the big red hen, though."

Two dirty barn-work hours later, Aaron found himself churning goat milk for butter. A large man with a big dog approached him and said a string of Romanian words. Aaron remembered him from the Bible study. Aaron's ears picked up "Gideon" with the upward inflection of a question. Aaron pointed to the large garden where his son was harvesting vegetables and giving refuse to young pigs.

When called, Gideon wearily appeared. A fast-paced conversation followed. Then Gideon went to find Christina. He talked earnestly to her for a minute and sent her to Claudia's house. Gideon, the big man, and his dog approached Aaron.

"Dad, this is Andrei. He brings news that a raid on the farm is coming."

"How does he know this?"

"Claudia told him. Daniela says the men hope to catch us off guard during the day. Do as much damage as they can. Maybe even abduct someone."

"Where—" Aaron started.

Gideon interrupted his father. "Would you try herding the goats into the barn, Dad? Scatter the chickens into the woods? Lock up Ioana's piglings."

"What about the cat?"

"Vlad? He'll take care of himself." Gideon turned to make plans with Andrei. Aaron saw them gesturing in different directions.

Aaron found herding the goats, who had been leisurely grazing, difficult. After consulting with Andrei, Gideon came to assist his father. "Sorry to order you around, Dad. We're in a bit of a crisis. Normally we just frighten intruders away in the night. Since this is daytime, Andrei suggests we try to get a look at them, maybe capture one. I sent a message with Christina for reinforcements."

Aaron needed clarification. "You normally—" But the arrival of Eugen, Florin, and two other men all carrying stout sticks distracted Gideon. A flurry of urgent Romanian words followed. The men separated in pairs to set an ambush.

Gideon returned to Aaron, leading Andrei's dog on a short rope. "This is Dragon, Dad. He's friendly but can be noisy. Will you take him inside the farm-house and keep him quiet? We can't risk him barking and giving us away." Gideon handed his father the rope then followed Andrei, who had taken the pitchfork from the barn, into the edge of the woods.

"Come on, Dragon." Aaron led the dog inside.

Two hours passed. Aaron prayed for the safety of all involved as he waited. Then he heard low, unfamiliar Romanian voices. Looking out a window, he saw seven men enter the farmyard as a group from the nearby woods. They split up to approach the barn, house, and other farm structures.

Aaron recognized his son's voice shouting in Romanian. Gideon and his five allies charged out of hiding and converged on the barnyard, cutting off the intruders' escape into the woods. Eugen, wielding a massive club, and Andrei, carrying the pitchfork, forged ahead in their eagerness to take a prisoner. The werewolves simply fled in panic toward the road. Aaron, followed by barking Dragon, emerged from the house into their path. One fleeing intruder swerved toward Aaron to get around Dragon. Aaron hadn't played football in decades. But he remembered how to make a tackle and took the man to the ground.

The pursuing Romanians and Gideon surrounded Aaron and his capture on the ground in an instant. Andrei extended a hand to pull Aaron to his feet. The Romanians pounded Aaron on his shoulders and shouted praise into his face.

Eugen jerked the tackled man off the ground. "What is your name?"

"Darius."

Ioana checked over Sofia and found her stable although with serious injuries. "You must recuperate here until you are better. Try to eat some food." She stepped back to let the other women shower the girl with attention.

Madeline warmed up meatball soup previously prepared by Ioana for Aaron and herself. She served Ioana, Daniela, and Claudia, then sat on the bed and spoon-fed weak Sofia while the others ate and talked. Sofia didn't understand English but recognized Madeline's flow of words as loving.

After feeding Sofia and helping her to the toilet, Madeline approached Ioana. "Nadia. Bring Nadia."

Ioana realized, *Nadia is the best English speaker in Gideon's class. Madeline wants to understand what is happening. Nadia can explain to her.* She answered in English, "Nadia come?" Then she made a gesture of speaking by putting her fingers together to her mouth and extending them.

Madeline nodded enthusiastically.

Ioana spoke to Daniela and Claudia, "Gideon's mother can't understand what we're saying. Lana has returned to Brașov. She's asked for the teenager Nadia to translate."

"I'll go get Nadia," Claudia volunteered.

"Thank you."

After Claudia left, Daniela told Ioana, "They tried to murder Sofia because her pregnancy would prevent Father Flavius from becoming the Patriarch of Romania."

Ioana nodded to recognize Daniela's gift of discerning motives. "I think besides Father Flavius, Sofia also saw a spirit. She described one last night."

"What should we do?" asked Daniela.

"We should send a report to the current Patriarch immediately. We need to quote Sofia's exact words. But we will leave out mentions of the spirit. The Patriarch might think that impossible and discount Sofia's testimony."

Claudia returned with Nadia, who surveyed the scene with wide eyes. Seeing Sofia—a girl two years younger than herself—in dire condition frightened Nadia. Madeline shoved twenty American dollars into the teenager's hand. "Tell me what people are saying."

Nadia looked at the money with astonishment. "I'll try, Mrs. Dixon."

All the women watched and listened as Ioana sat by Sofia, coaxed out an account of her sordid experiences with Father Flavius, and made notes. Nadia whispered Sofia's story to Madeline, who grew angry at the injustices committed. When Sofia retold her encounter with the spirit, Madeline listened with open-mouthed astonishment.

After Ioana finished and gave Sofia a sedative to sleep, Madeline approached her daughter-in-law to ask through Nadia, "Do you think Sofia really saw a demon? Or did she have a hallucination?"

"She saw an evil spirit. Gideon has seen them too. I saw one once from a distance."

"Am I right that a boy named Luca prayed and healed her last night?"

"Of the bleeding, yes. I know you do not understand—"

Madeline stopped her. "I understand that you are dealing with serious issues beyond my experience."

Gideon allowed the Romanians to interrogate their prisoner. Darius, surrounded by five angry and armed Romanian men, talked. He started with a disclaimer regarding the gang-rape of the teenage girl Maria.

"I did not touch her. I tried to stop them. After that, I wanted to leave the werewolves but knew they would kill me." Under prodding, Darius went on to describe his initiation and various escapades. "I'd rather not repeat what the werewolves said about girls and women."

Gideon and Aaron stood apart from the Romanians as Gideon translated the gist of Darius's confession and story. Aaron rotated his shoulder to relieve an ache from making the unaccustomed tackle.

"Werewolves?" questioned Aaron. "Are you serious? How are werewolves possible?"

"Real werewolves don't change shape and grow wolf teeth under a full moon. Evil spirits or demons influence humans to think and act like werewolves. Incited by spirits, men become violent and vicious. They're causing trouble all over the region. This is the first one we've caught."

"They sound like thugs. The police should be notified."

"Thugs they are," admitted Gideon. "And they become maliciously aggressive when in a pack and incited by spirits. But police usually look the other way."

After Darius thought he had finished his confession, he begged the men not to turn him over to the police. "They would give me to the werewolves. I need protection." Eugen and Andrei continued questioning Darius, extracting details of werewolf escapades.

Aaron whispered to Gideon, "And you think the spirits are demons? Why aren't they active in America?"

"I'm not certain, Dad," Gideon whispered back. "All this is new to me too. But I've seen, heard, and experienced things that convince me that the supernatural aspect of spiritual warfare is more than I had realized. I'm working on a theory to explain the difference between Romania and America. The New Testament records plenty of demonic activity and doesn't exclude any region. In Transylvania, where many people already believe in evil spirits, the demons are more open. However, few Americans recognize the activity of spirits. Maybe evil spirits can do more harm by keeping a low profile. Maybe evil spirits just hide themselves to keep American Christians complacent."

Aaron spoke louder, "Are you insinuating that American Christians are complacent?"

"Most American Christians are sincere, but complacency is certainly one thing American Christians could struggle with. Demons revealing themselves would be powerful proof of the validity of the Bible to Christians and non-Christians alike. I've learned a lot here in Romania. And you remember that I always questioned overly simplistic biblical interpretations."

"Yes, you did," Aaron agreed. "Maybe that has made you adaptable to this situation." Aaron paused before continuing, "Well, I'm going to notify the police about these so-called werewolves."

"That might bring more trouble, Dad. The police could even accuse you of crimes."

"An honest man has nothing to fear from the authorities. They would know that any jury would see through their perfidy."

Gideon shrugged. "Romania doesn't have any jury trials, only judges. The judges are appointed by the same officials as the police."

"They have no juries? Then how—"

"What can I do?" Darius's anguished words drew both Aaron's and Gideon's attention back to the interrogation. Recounting the litany of evil committed by the werewolves had reduced him to guilty misery. He began to softly weep.

Chapter Twenty-seven

Gideon stepped toward Darius. The Romanians backed away to give him room. "We have all sinned, Darius. Jesus died to pay for our sins. His resurrection from death proved that He could forgive any and every sin. Jesus will wipe your slate clean if you will confess to Him that you are a sinner, believe in Him, and accept His death as payment for your sin. God will forgive you, and we will forgive you." Gideon looked from man to man among the Romanians. Starting with Florin, each nodded until only Eugen remained. "Eugen?" Gideon prompted.

After a long moment, Eugen nodded as well. "Yes, once God forgives Darius, I will too."

"If you want forgiveness, pray after me, Darius," said Gideon. All the Romanians and Americans put a hand on Darius.

After repeating a short prayer, Darius looked up, relieved. "Am I really forgiven?"

"Yes, you are. Come home with me now, young man," said Eugen. "I'll protect you and help you get started in a new life."

* * *

Gideon accompanied his father on the early bus to Brașov. He knew that his parents had stayed up late exchanging stories and reviewing the implausible things they had seen and heard about supernatural activity. Spirits, witches, vampires, werewolves, and spiritual gifts had fueled a vigorous discussion between them while Claudia sat watching over Sofia.

Gideon had gotten some sleep after hearing Ioana's account of the letter Pastor Raphael had posted to the Patriarch. Eugen had taken charge of Darius, who demonstrated no desire to go back to werewolf ways.

In Brașov, Gideon and Aaron located the regional police station to make a complaint about the werewolves. After they had waited for four hours, three plain-clothes officers met them in an interrogation room. Aaron spoke in short sentences, giving Gideon the opportunity to think and translate each statement carefully. Seated at a table opposite the police officers, Aaron described the thwarted raid on the farm. He added the confession by Darius and gave second-hand examples of other werewolf terrorism.

The police officers exchanged glances. One spoke for them. "Why are two Americans complaining about spirited young Romanians? Don't you have enough problems in America?"

"I thought you'd want to know," stammered Aaron.

"All we know is that foreigners detained a native Romanian and made him confess to something to save his life. We have that by your statement. That is illegal. We should arrest you."

"Arrest us?"

"Or you could pay a fine now. Say, a hundred American dollars."

Aaron failed to find words. Then Gideon, without speaking, pulled a hundred dollars out of his pocket and pushed it across the table.

The men grinned. "That's better," said one.

"I think the Americans should buy some protection," suggested another. "For five hundred dollars a month, we could make sure some of the locals left them alone."

Aaron sat flummoxed while Gideon spoke directly for the first time. "We don't have that much money with us. We'll leave now and see what we can arrange." The policemen laughed.

Gideon rose to go and pulled his father with him.

"Gideon, this is a protection racket. You are letting them extort us!" Aaron accused him once they had left the interrogation room.

"Would you rather spend several days in a Romanian jail cell? Or disappear into the system without access to an attorney or arraignment?" Gideon returned. "Corrupt police from the communist era remain in the government. These men report to the regional prefect. We know he's corrupt and may have tried to kidnap Ioana."

"I had no idea any police could be so corrupted."

Gideon nodded in agreement. "Before today I didn't realize how bad the system was myself."

* * *

The next morning Gideon and Ioana went to the town-cottage and knocked on the door. When Aaron opened the door, Gideon asked, "Dad, do you suppose you and Mom could watch over Sofia? We need Claudia for a meeting."

"Of course. What sort of meeting are you conducting, Son?" When Gideon hesitated, Aaron added, "Your mother and I have become aware that you're facing serious issues here. Challenges we have never experienced. Things we could not have imagined."

"It's a strategy meeting to decide how to deal with some of those challenges, Dad."

Madeline came to the door. "Did you talk to them, Aaron?"

Aaron opened the door wider and spoke to Gideon and Ioana. "Could you two come inside for a few moments?"

Inside, Madeline began, "Gideon, your father and I believe you and Ioana are in danger here. We think you should come home to the US. Ioana can emigrate and so can Christina. You can be a youth pastor at your father's church.

You and Ioana will be safe and can buy a nice home to raise your children."

"Thank you for your generous offer. But I will not leave Horvata," answered Ioana after Gideon had translated.

Madeline shook her head. "But you have your future children to consider, honey."

"Romanian mothers have faced dire situations for a thousand years."

"Gideon, tell your wife it would be best to leave," insisted Aaron.

"Ioana can go to the US with you if she decides best," answered Gideon. "But I'm staying here. My flock may be small, but a pastor doesn't leave his people in a crisis."

"This is more than a crisis. You are endangering both your lives by staying," Madeline pleaded.

Aaron's face showed remorse. "I agree with your mother, Son. You should come home with us. But I will respect your decision. After all I've seen, I respect *you*, Son."

The father and son looked at each other intensely until Gideon nodded. "I respect you too, Dad. I must stay."

Aaron called, "Claudia!" The older woman came out of the room where Sofia lay. "Madeline, you take care of Sofia. Lead the way to the meeting, Son."

"You're going with them?" Madeline asked.

"A father doesn't leave his son . . ." Aaron looked pointedly at Ioana, ". . . or his daughter."

* * *

Aaron saw a circle of chairs Pastor Raphael had set up at his church. The primary warriors and bears took seats. Gideon sent someone to bring Nadia to translate for his father. While they waited for Nadia, Luca inquired about Sofia.

"Her body is healing. But Sofia remains deeply despondent. I sense she has lost the will to live," Claudia answered. "We watch over her all the time. Madeline is with her now."

Upon Nadia's arrival, Gideon opened with a succinct, albeit fervent, prayer. "Lord, we ask you to give Sofia hope. And please show the rest of us what to do in our situation. Amen."

After looking up, Gideon started. "Those of you who supernaturally know something from God, tell the rest of us."

The answers came quickly.

"Prefect Lazar is using the police, mostly remnants of the Ceaușescu communist dictatorship, to conduct protection and favor-selling schemes. He also takes bribes to ignore Primar Serban and others conducting the Caritas Ponzi scheme."

"Father Flavius is a sexual predator. He is using his position in the church to spread false accusations and rumors about all who threaten to expose him."

"Gangs calling themselves werewolves are being incited by spirits to violence and destruction against the warriors and the bears."

"Mediums and a false prophet conduct meetings where secrets known by spirits are mixed with monstrous lies."

"Witches curse those who oppose evil spirits and attempt casting spells on anyone siding with us."

Eugen spoke up. "I cannot say I've heard from God. But I know in my bones that some of Ceauşescu's former secret police are mixed up in all this."

"Thank you all," said Gideon. "These things we know. Knowing and proving are different issues. Stopping these evils will be even harder. To go to the authorities in Bucharest, we need proof. Ioana has already sent evidence against Father Flavius to the Patriarch of Romania. Hopefully, he'll investigate. Prefect Lazar is covering for all the other abuses. How can we implicate him?"

"I have an idea," volunteered Aaron.

* * *

Gideon and Aaron sat before the same three police in Braşov as before. Aaron glared at the officers in defiance. Through Gideon he spoke loudly. "You offered us protection for five hundred dollars a month. Officers of the law have a duty to protect citizens."

"Well, you are not exactly citizens, are you?" returned one of the men in an equally loud voice.

"The protection isn't for us," Aaron insisted. "Romanians are the ones being harassed and threatened."

"Oh, then you will want the expanded protection package. That will be five hundred a month for you and another five hundred for your filthy peasant friends."

Gideon had stared at the table while translating. His hands held a backpack in his lap. He looked up at the three police officers with an anguished expression. "That's too much. We'll give you three hundred."

"An American with some sense," said one man. "But no. Like Ivan said, protection is one thousand dollars now. You are rich Americans."

Gideon recognized the name Ivan as possibly one of those who had tried to abduct Ioana. A harsh rebuke from Aaron interrupted him from processing that.

"Don't give in to extortion, Gideon. Show a backbone!" Aaron demanded. Even without translation, the trio opposite them understood the tone.

"He is afraid his pretty Romanian wife will not get away next time. If she had not run into the Romani scum, we would have caught the witch," said the third policeman.

Aaron looked defiantly at the men. "I'm going to report you to the regional prefect."

The men laughed. "He gets half. You go to Prefect Lazar, and he will up the payment to two thousand a month for bothering him. You better take our offer while you can."

"I don't believe you."

"We have been working for Prefect Lazar for a lot of years. Before the new government, he would have had us lock you up. We would do a little convincing in your cell. We still can."

Gideon reached into his backpack and pulled out a wad of American bills. He pushed the money across the table. "Here's four hundred and fifty dollars. That's all we have right now."

"That will do for two weeks. Now get out of here before we go back to our old ways of dealing with complainers. Bring the rest of the money, or we will come get you."

Without ever making eye contact, Gideon stood and opened the door to leave. Aaron gave the men one last glare and followed Gideon out while berating him. Outside the police station Aaron whispered, "Did you get it?"

"I think so. Holding the recorder under the table in my lap could have muffled the sound a little. But they spoke loudly. Good job inciting them, Dad."

"Take me to a phone. Congressman White is a member of our church. I'll call and ask him to arrange an appointment for me with the US ambassador. Our ambassador will know who in the elected Romanian government should get this evidence of Prefect Lazar's corruption."

Chapter Twenty-eight

At sunset three days later, Aaron and Gideon returned to Horvata from Bucharest. They had met with the American ambassador, who directed them to an official in the Romanian Department of Justice. The ambassador had described the official as honest. Aaron and Gideon had then delivered the evidence of Prefect Lazar's corruption.

They found the people of Horvata in hiding. Ioana with Madeline and Daniela heard their voices approaching. She opened the town-cottage door and met the men outside.

"Police from Braşov have been here," Ioana explained. "They are looking for Aaron. They harassed and threatened everybody who has been part of the bears. They went into Florin's shop and Pastor Raphael's church to break things. They busted in here," she gestured toward the town-cottage, "and smashed the microwave."

Gideon's face displayed alarm. "How did you escape?"

"God warned me. I relayed the warning to the warriors then took Mama, Madeline, and Sofia into the forest to hide. Daniela came to recall us after the police left the village."

Madeline appeared stricken. "At first, I didn't understand why Ioana dragged me toward the woods. But I could tell she was frightened about something. The big man, Eugen, came and carried Sofia behind us. Then he went back into the village." Madeline shook her head. "I never expected to be hiding in the woods from police."

Ioana spoke again as Gideon translated. "Later, Eugen verbally confronted the three policemen and took some nasty knocks. I stitched him up in places but found no broken bones. He is resting at the farm under Mama's care. Darius went to guard them," said Ioana.

"Where is Sofia now?" asked Gideon.

"Madeline and Daniela helped her walk gingerly back from the woods." Ioana pointed at the town-cottage door. "Sofia is safely back in her bed."

"Why were the police looking for me?" asked Aaron.

Madeline addressed her husband. "They claim you are an immoral phony, Aaron. News reports from America say that a woman named Suzy has come forward. She claims that as a young assistant pastor you had an affair with her, a married woman at the time and a member of your congregation. She claims to have recorded some romantic late-night phone conversations between you and her. Suzy is suing you and the church you served then, saying you seduced her, broke up her marriage, and ruined her life. Your senior pastor at the time, now retired, has confirmed that he intervened in a situation and assumed that nothing more had developed. The American news media is all over the story. Your church has suspended you pending a review of your pastoral qualifications upon your return to America."

Aaron stood stunned. "Madeline, I . . . I did develop a crush on a young wife for a couple of weeks. That was years before I met you. I foolishly tried to give her counseling without a female witness. But I swear there was no affair. I never touched her."

Madeline nodded. "I know that for certain, Aaron." She turned to Gideon and Ioana, who stood motionless, hardly daring to breathe. "Aaron never had any affair. He didn't know what to do on our wedding night. Neither did I."

After Gideon translated, Ioana's laughter broke the tension. "We didn't know what to do either." She gestured between herself and Gideon.

"Good for you, honey," said Madeline. "But, Aaron, this is a serious matter developing back home. And the police told people all over this village. Their report casts a shadow on you and on Gideon's work."

"Why would Suzy say these things? How would the Romanian police know, much less care, about something happening in America three decades ago?" wondered Aaron.

Ioana spoke gently to him through Gideon. "Spirits incite people to lie. They take a little truth, like the truth that you knew Suzy, and mix it with monstrous lies, like the affair.

275

Spirits may have even convinced Suzy that the affair happened."

Gideon could not help adding, "Still need evidence that demons are active in America, Dad?"

"But why did the Romanian police come now?" Aaron demanded.

"Evil spirits know things. They tell their followers secrets. Just like God's angels tell me things," answered Ioana. "Didn't you go to make a report against the police to the government in Bucharest? The spirits know and can inform those police that you are their adversary. The police came here today to punish and silence you."

Daniela interjected, "I can sense their motives. The policemen are angry and hateful. They want revenge. They want to intimidate anyone who opposes them. And the woman Suzy . . . her life has turned out poorly. She seeks someone other than herself to blame. She needs money and hopes she might get a quick settlement from you to end the bad publicity."

Aaron hung his head. "I've made trouble for everyone. The situation here is worse because of me."

Gideon put his hand on his father's shoulder. "No, Dad. You're standing up against the unseen forces of darkness. That brings trouble. And remember that we had all agreed to your plan to collect evidence against the prefect. They are reacting to what *we* did, not just to you."

* * *

Madeline watched Sofia, who showed signs of physical improvement, while Claudia rested at her home. Aaron had gone with Gideon and Eugen to record accounts of damage done in the village during the police incursion. Ioana was away tending to the labor and delivery of a mother she knew and trusted in the village.

Through Nadia, Madeline asked Sofia, "Would you like to sit up for a while, honey? I'll bet your back is sore from lying down nearly all the time."

Sofia remained listless and silent. Madeline stood over her. "Come on, honey. Let's get you up." When Sofia swung her feet around, Madeline and Nadia each took an arm and helped Sofia into Gideon's comfortable chair.

While Nadia talked and brushed Sofia's hair, Madeline used teabags, found while shopping earlier in the week, to make hot tea.

She placed a hot cup of tea with lemon and sugar by Sofia. Nadia sipped her own tea and smiled. "This is good, Sofia. Please try it."

Sofia sipped her cup and smiled for the first time since her injury. Nadia continued teenage-girl chatter. Sofia visibly relaxed as she listened. Nadia started to fuss around Sofia, braiding her hair and applying a little lipstick. She held a mirror for Sofia to see herself. "I told her she is pretty," Nadia told Madeline as Sofia admired her reflection.

A knock drew Madeline's attention to the door. Outside, she found a roughly dressed young man who asked something in Romanian. "He's looking for Eugen. Says his name is Darius," Nadia told her.

Through Nadia, Madeline told the young man that Eugen had gone with Gideon. Then she insisted that he wait inside. Upon entering, Darius immediately noticed Sofia. Nadia recognized his attraction to the injured girl and instinctively drifted toward Madeline to provide whispered translation.

"I heard about you and your accident," Darius said to Sofia. "Spirits victimized you, same as they have done to me. I am sorry. I've seen a spirit."

"I have too," answered Sofia. "A dark shape and lights."

"Yes! Were you afraid like me?"

"I was. Then I did what it told me."

Darius nodded. "I did what the spirit said too."

Sofia, although shy at first, conversed with their visitor. Madeline interrupted only to serve tea to the afflicted young adults, then followed Nadia outside to give them privacy. "Sounds like Darius and Sofia have a lot in common," she said to Nadia.

"They do. Both grew up orphans, earned food through farm work, had nothing but hay to sleep on, and were deceived by those serving spirits. Lucky that I had prettied Sofia up a little."

"Maybe not luck in this case. God might have prompted you to."

278

* * *

Ioana, exhausted from days of traumatic events, prepared to sleep in her own bed at the farm-house. Eugen had gone back to his home accompanied by Darius. Aaron and Madeline remained with Sofia in the town-cottage. Gideon had already fallen into an exhausted sleep, and she looked forward to joining him. A gentle nighttime knock at the door surprised her. After opening the door, young Father Marcă's presence surprised her even more.

"Could I come in?" he asked.

She opened the door wider and stepped back. "Of course, Father."

Inside, Father Marcă hardly looked around but stood rigidly. "I need to talk to you and Gideon, please."

"Certainly. Please sit down. Can I make you coffee?"

Father Marcă sat down, albeit uneasily. He looked grim. "No coffee, thank you."

"I will bring Gideon, then." In their bedroom, Ioana shook her husband. When he stirred and groaned lightly, she whispered, "Wake up. I know you are tired. But Father Marcă is here. This could be important."

"I'll need just a minute to be coherent," Gideon mumbled.

Ioana returned to Father Marcă. "Have you heard we sent a report to the Patriarch?"

"Yes. And I've seen the report."

279

"How can such things happen?" Ioana asked.

Father Marcă shrugged. "I can only say that a person, especially a priest, can twist the Holy Bible to say anything they want to believe."

Gideon emerged disheveled but determined. "Father Marcă, you are welcome here."

The young priest proceeded without preamble. "I have received a directive from our Patriarch to secretly investigate a complaint filed against Father Flavius. I'll need to personally interview you and Father Flavius's former housekeeper, Sofia. I understand you are caring for her after an injury."

Gideon and Ioana looked at each other. "She is at the cottage we rent in the village," answered Ioana. "Would tomorrow morning be adequate?"

Father Marcă sighed. "This is a matter of urgency. Tonight would be better."

"Alright, tonight it is," agreed Gideon. "Let us get dressed. Then we'll take you to Sofia. You can ask us anything you wish on the way."

The young priest smiled for the first time. "Thank you." He hesitated before continuing. "I need to tell you something else. Prefect Lazar has called a midnight meeting of all those who oppose what Father Flavius calls 'the American cult.'"

"Where will the meeting be held?" asked Gideon.

"In the dining hall of the old collective farm previously run by Primar Serban."

"When will the meeting occur?" asked Ioana

"At midnight tomorrow night."

Chapter Twenty-nine

The abandoned collective farm's low-ceilinged dining room smelled musty when Gideon slipped in just before midnight. Rudimentary fixtures cast dim light. He knew that all the warriors and bears had gathered at Pastor Raphael's church to pray for his invisibility. Even so, his stomach felt queasy from apprehension. *Low lighting will make recognizing me under this disguise more difficult,* he reassured himself and took a seat on a folding chair near the front. He checked the recorder in the bag he carried and found it ready.

Over a hundred—vampires, werewolves, witches, mediums, a false prophet, policemen from Braşov, Caritas-scheme promoters, and Primar Serban leading a gang of thugs—assembled in the semidarkness. Gideon activated the recorder as Prefect Lazar called their attention using a microphone.

"Welcome, Romanian patriots and those faithful to the church. We gather tonight to defend our homeland. Our way of life. Our church."

Prefect Lazar paused for a smattering of applause to die out before continuing, "An American cult is leading Romania's sons and daughters away from our traditions and our church, the very things that make us a nation. A people. God will hold us accountable if we allow a cult to thrive and deceive our fellow citizens. The center of the cult is in Horvata. Tomorrow night we will purge the cult and its supporters from among us."

Those assembled erupted in spontaneous acclamation. Shouts of "Kill them all!" rang out.

Prefect Lazar waited as the crowd expressed their support and used expletives to describe those they thought responsible for destroying Romania's values. Vows of retribution reverberated throughout the dining hall. After several minutes, Prefect Lazar quietened them and announced, "Our priest and a true son of Romania brings the blessings of the church on our commitment to cleanse our homeland."

Father Flavius walked from behind a partition in full ceremonial robes and carrying a clerical staff. He stepped before the microphone and gazed at the audience with an attitude of full authority from the Orthodox church. "In Deuteronomy 13:5, the Holy Scripture says, 'You must purge the evil from among you.'" He continued with a homily describing Gideon as an opportunistic cult leader misleading the weak-minded. Flavius called Ioana a sorcerous witch casting spells and bringing suffering to the community. He repeated the accusations against Aaron as an adulterer preying on weak wives and added sordid made-up details of abuse. He condemned Pastor Raphael, Florin, Andrei, Daniela, Claudia, and even Luca. He named others who had participated in Gideon's "so-called Bible studies" and called for their "reeducation."

The crowd seethed with barely contained anger. "Your outrage is justified," Father Flavius announced in a commanding voice. "But you are not alone in opposing this threat. A mighty angel will attend you now." He stood aside as multicolored glimmers of light flickered across the dining hall. A dark ten-foot-tall man-like shape with yellow eyes materialized. Two smaller man-like shapes outlined by green light appeared on either side of the monster. Everyone in the room felt a chill and remained as motionless as statues.

The largest shape outlined by multi-colors spoke with a chorus of deep voices. "Priest, throw down the staff you carry." Father Flavius did as he had been instructed, whereupon the staff became a black snake as large as a man's upper arm. The crowd gasped and recoiled as the reptile wriggled into the darkness. "Priest, pour out the sacred water." Father Flavius picked up a pitcher and poured. The clear water turned into scarlet-red blood.

The spirit then raised its arms to point over the heads of the crowd. The two smaller man-like shapes became balls of white light that didn't cast shadows. The balls moved to hover over the crowd, which cowered beneath them. "These are my servants and your guides," the chorus of voices announced. "I am your protector. I am Baal. Declare your allegiance to me."

Those assembled remained motionless and terrified. Father Flavius announced, "I declare allegiance to Baal." Another voice hollered the same from the crowd. Then another. Finally, every voice asserted their allegiance and loyalty.

"I hear your pledge," acknowledged Baal. "However, if you fail to expel the cultists, I will hold each of you accountable. Avoid my wrath." The large spirit outlined by multicolored lights and the two balls of white light grew smaller and disappeared.

The crowd buzzed with words of relief until Prefect Lazar retook the microphone. "We will drive the cultists from our land. Gather all those who will stand with us to save Romania. Meet me at the bridge south of Horvata tomorrow after dark. Together we will protect our heritage as Romanians or suffer Baal's wrath."

Gideon turned off the recorder and blended into the crowd as the people dispersed. His legs trembled with fear as he remained in the shadows and made his way home.

Early the following morning, forty-nine warriors and bears assembled inside Pastor Raphael's church. Aaron and Madeline watched their son play the recording to the group and listened while Nadia tried to simultaneously translate for them. The group sat numb at the conclusion.

"Should we run to the woods and hide?" Daniela asked.

"We," Gideon indicated himself, Ioana, Christina, and his parents, "could catch the bus and leave town. Everybody else could stay inside their homes. The attackers might declare victory and do no damage."

Pastor Raphael shook his head. "No, we Romanians remember how Ceaușescu's secret police busted down doors and arrested people in the dark night. Many so taken never returned. We know how thugs took retribution on the families of those who opposed them. Ceaușescu may be gone, but those who supported him are still around. They will make an example of Horvata. Nobody will be safe, including your children."

"Let us send copies of the recording to Bucharest," Ioana suggested. "There's still time to catch the bus to Brașov, then the train. Go to the honest official Aaron identified through the American Embassy."

"My husband's brother has a car," Daniela said. "My husband can borrow the car and drive me. I'll carry the tape to Bucharest and explain our danger."

Pastor Raphael quickly produced a church-owned recorder and made copies of the original recording. Gideon gave Daniela a hundred dollars to pay for gasoline and other expenses. Daniela hurried away.

"What should the rest of us do?" asked Florin.

"We should warn the rest of the villagers," said Gideon. "I'll stay at the town-cottage and play the recording for anyone who comes. Let the most vulnerable hide in the forest—"

Eugen interrupted him. "And let those willing defend our home, Horvata, until help comes."

"And everybody should pray for God to save us," suggested Claudia.

"Amen," answered Eugen.

Aaron and Madeline watched the situation unfolding with astonishment.

* * *

Ioana accompanied Gideon along with his parents to the town-cottage. The young Orthodox priest Father Marcă soon arrived to listen to the recording.

"Sofia's and Ioana's testimonies about Father Flavius are credible," he said. "I didn't know his intentions when I summoned Sofia on his behalf. But I had personal suspicions about Father Flavius's behavior afterwards. I included everything in a report and sent it by courier to the Patriarch this morning," he told Ioana and Gideon. After listening to the recording Gideon had made, Father Marcă went out warning the villagers about the impending attack.

Darius came to the town-cottage and offered to carry Sofia into the forest. "I want to go wherever you go, Darius," the girl responded.

Gideon looked at Ioana, who shrugged. "You can do whatever you feel strong enough to do," Ioana told Sofia.

286

"The cast should protect your broken arm as long as you're careful with it."

"We could both convince people in the village how dangerous the situation is," suggested Darius.

Sofia struggled to her feet and limped away with Darius.

Maria and Luca appeared. "School has been dismissed," Luca explained. They listened to the recording and asked, "What can we do?"

"Help families get their children into hiding," answered Ioana. "Make sure my mother, Christina, is safe in the woods."

By late afternoon, women with children and those infirm had been assisted into hiding and made as comfortable as possible. Warriors and bears, as well as many helped by Ioana and Gideon, and other victims of Ceaușescu's secret police, old and young, congregated in the village square.

"Speak to them, Gideon," Pastor Raphael urged.

Ioana received a prophetic impression. "No, let Aaron speak."

Aaron protested, "I don't know Romanian."

Ioana thrust a megaphone into his hands. "Speak anyway."

Aaron spoke into the megaphone in English, but the people heard his words in forceful, un-accented Romanian. He used his masterful voice and leadership to exhort those listening. "We face a determined enemy emboldened by evil spirits." Everyone could understand him plainly. The crowd marveled at the miracle before them. Aaron continued by citing Old Testament examples of standing up for God to defend home and family against a ruthless enemy. He concluded, "We must cling to the truth in a raging sea of lies. Satan is the father of liars. We are facing a tsunami of lies by his servants. People who believe these lies are a threat to you and your children. You can stand together tonight or let them hunt you down one by one. We are not alone. Jesus Christ is with us."

Amens and shouts of affirmation came from those assembled.

As Aaron finished, Ioana stepped close and took the megaphone from his hands. "They are coming. They are coming!" she screamed.

"Who is coming?" called a voice.

"A large mob of evil ones. Baal and a legion of spirits. They will come up the valley on the road tonight."

"Build a barricade to block the road!" Eugen's bellow could be heard without the megaphone. "Arm yourselves!"

The villagers worked frantically piling tables from the market to make an eighty-foot-long barricade across the road leading into Horvata. Town buildings anchored the barricade on both ends. They overturned wagons then added furniture, appliances, bags of feed, a derelict truck, and fences ripped away from cottage perimeters until an eight-to-ten-foot-high barricade blocked the road.

A surprising number of villagers produced firearms— World War II weapons hidden for generations and antique guns used to hunt or protect their poultry and livestock from predators. Andrei and one other man produced Kalashnikov AK-47 assault rifles. "Taken in the revolution four years ago," the two men explained.

"Don't use the guns," Gideon told those holding them. "But keep your firearms handy. Fire over the mob's heads if we need a demonstration."

Other villagers fashioned crude weapons from farm implements. They collected long poles to jab through the barricade. Darius used an axe to sharpen the poles before Sofia whittled a fine point using a knife. Luca and Maria, along with Nadia and other teenagers, fashioned crude slings and collected palm-sized rocks as ammunition. They practiced twirling the slings around their heads and flinging stones until they'd developed reasonable accuracy. Women and older men collected large rocks and bricks to throw over the barricade. Determined men made firebombs with glass bottles and gasoline.

Aaron and Madeline stood apart, watching the frenzied activity of the Romanians. "I can't believe this is happening," said Aaron.

"Sounded to me like you're the one who stirred them up."

Aaron tried to look penitent. "So it would seem."

"I just wish I could remember all you said."

Aaron shrugged. "I doubt I can recall my own words."

They looked over to see Gideon piling old tires into the barricade. "I don't think our son is leaving. If not Gideon, then we can't leave either," said Madeline.

"What do you suggest we do?" asked Aaron.

"Looks like the rock-gatherers need help."

"Let's get to it." *What would my congregation think if they could see me now?* thought Aaron.

As the sun set, Eugen told the defenders, "Lay a bonfire of wood and kerosene in front of the barricade. We will light it so our attackers can be seen." Defenders hurried to collect firewood left over from the winter.

Gideon used the megaphone to call, "Supernatural warriors, come to me." Once his flock gathered around him, he said, "Our fellow Romanians are not the greatest threat." All noticed that Gideon had counted himself among the Romanians. "Remember the Holy Scripture, 'For we are not contending against flesh and blood, but against the principalities, against the powers, against the world rulers of this present darkness, against the spiritual hosts of wickedness in the heavenly places.' Stay out of any physical fighting if you can. Your battle will be against the evil spirits who inspire those beyond the barricade and cause fear among the righteous. Tonight, you will all repel evil spirits. Tell them how, Florin."

Florin said, "Use the existence of the spirits themselves to strengthen your faith. They prove what the Bible says is true. Command them in the name of Christ Jesus to depart. Know by your faith that they must do so."

Chapter Thirty

Before midnight, Horvata's defenders saw a mass of flashlights and fiery torches approaching the village by the road. The headlights of vehicles mingled with the walkers. Ioana took the megaphone to shout. "They will take an hour or more to assemble. After that they will attack us."

Three village women approached Ioana. One pleaded, "Can't you put a witch's curse on them, Ioana?"

"I am not a witch. I may have a prophetic gift."

"We all know you are something good and magical. Please save our men and children, Ioana."

Ioana felt the weight of impossible responsibility and realized, *I cannot save them. God, please speak to me.* "I will do all I can. Only God can save any of us," she told the women.

Villagers clustered around Pastor Raphael and Father Marcă, asking for God's absolution and prayers for protection.

Andrei tied Dragon to a post behind the barricade. The dog sensed the excitement and started making noise with deep, threatening barks. Eugen heard and approached Andrei. "When will you turn your dog loose?"

Tension made Andrei laugh. "Dragon would not be able to tell friend from foe. He would be just as likely to bite our people."

"He sounds frightening, though. Dogs could make attackers reluctant to cross the barricade." Eugen used the megaphone to call, "If you have a big, loud dog, bring it." In fifteen minutes, nine vicious-sounding dogs produced a din of barking behind the barricade.

The attackers assembled slowly as those walking and lagging caught up to the vehicles. "They just keep coming," a farmer behind the barricade worried aloud. After an hour, a malice-filled mob of three hundred men and a hundred women had amassed in front of the barricade. Most had armed themselves with clubs and long knives. Those holding guns stood in the front.

Opposing the mob, seventy-nine village men and nineteen robust women waited silently behind the barricade. More women, older men, and teenagers continued to gather rocks. With a mighty heave, Eugen threw a lighted torch into the pile of kerosene-doused combustibles piled before the barricade. The bonfire roared up, illuminating the mob.

The werewolf leader He Who Kills called out to Darius. "You are one of us, Bloodthirsty. Rejoin your pack. You will be on the winning side." Other werewolf voices urged Darius to rejoin the werewolves. When Darius didn't respond, the werewolves taunted, "We will drink your blood tonight." Darius stood firm next to Eugen. He glanced back to see Sofia filling containers with water to carry to the defenders.

The mob parted, allowing Primar Serban, Father Flavius, and Prefect Lazar to step to the front. They stood visible in reddish-orange light from the bonfire burning between them and the barricade. Prefect Lazar demanded, "Take down this barricade and go to your homes. We will then remove the foreign cult from your midst." Some villagers glanced around anxiously.

"You'll set your thugs and criminals calling themselves werewolves free in our village, homes, and families," Eugen bellowed back.

"The police among us have guns."

Pastor Raphael answered, "We also have guns. But we will not use them unless you do. Hear our guns." At a signal, all the villagers with firearms fired into the air above the mob's heads. "Do not use guns, and you will go home alive. Use guns, and you will go home dead."

The villagers defending the barricade stood resolute. Behind them they heard dogs barking, the rock gatherers ripping up cobblestones for ammunition, and others praying fervently. Shouts from the warriors rebuked and expelled evil spirits who occasionally appeared behind the barricade to frighten the defenders.

"As the authority of this judeţe, I order you to remove this barricade and go to your homes," called Prefect Lazar.

Pastor Raphael answered, "We are in *our* home, Horvata. You are not welcome inside. We will clear the barricade when legitimate authorities from Bucharest arrive."

"I am the representative of Bucharest," asserted the former communist.

"I meant elected and non-corrupted authorities."

Prefect Lazar turned to the mob and demanded, "Clear the barricade and rout the rabble. Teach these peasants a lesson. Then take anything and do whatever you wish in the village."

The malice-filled mob gave a ragged cheer and started to advance.

"Hear our dogs?" Eugen shouted back. "They will kill any who pass this barricade." Behind him Dragon and the other dogs maintained the din of barking.

Ioana stood near the dogs watching and waiting, hoping for messages from God. She noticed some attackers slow their steps to allow others more determined to forge ahead. *They do not wish to be the first through and face death by the dogs.* She saw Gideon standing next to Father Marcă, who continually crossed himself. Other defenders followed the young priest's example. *God, please protect Gideon and the others. Please speak to me,* Ioana prayed.

Dozens of evil spirits indicated by balls of white light that didn't cast shadows appeared over the mob streaming around the bonfire to attack the barricade. Stones sling-thrown by Luca and other teenagers harassed the approaching attackers and brought down nine. Hand-thrown gasoline bombs broke on the ground in front of the mob and disrupted the advance. The bonfire's reddish-orange light created a hellish scene. Madeline handed a rock to Aaron, who arched it over the barricade into the oncoming mob. Soon a barrage of stones and bricks thrown by the rock gatherers rained down on the mob from out of darkness. Thirty or more attackers fell to the ground or dropped to their knees, having been struck by stones in the head or face.

Cries of pain mingled with the dog noise as the front rank of attackers reached and started to pull the barricade down. Defenders used short, quick thrusts with sharpened poles through openings to stab at those assaulting the barricade. Some attackers grabbed the poles. When tug-o-wars resulted, defenders stabbed additional poles at the grabbers, who released their grip.

Ioana saw Aaron and other rock throwers move closer to the barricade and start underhandedly lobbing heavy cobblestones, so they flew high and then fell onto the attackers' heads and collarbones. Shouts and curses of the combatants, moans of the wounded, thuds of thrown rocks blended together to make the battle a roar of indistinguishable noise.

"Follow the spirits over the barricade and kill the cultists," Prefect Lazar ordered using his own megaphone from behind the mob. Maria noted the location of his voice in the darkness, pointed, and shouted, "The prefect is over there." The teenagers slung stones at the place she indicated. Prefect Lazar retreated as rocks whizzed around him but continued to exhort the attackers out of range of the flying rocks. Father Flavius and Primar Serban stood at a safe distance with him.

The balls of white light descended onto the barricade and transformed into black man-like shapes outlined by greenish lights. Many of the defenders cried out in fear and edged backwards in terror, abandoning the barricade. Attackers started to climb the barricade behind the spirits. Ioana, who had been watching from the rear, approached the undefended barricade. Within a few feet of a spirit she demanded, "Begone in the name Jesus." The apparition shrunk in size until it disappeared.

Following Ioana's example, Florin moved closer and expelled a spirit. Gideon shouted above the tumult, "Stand firm, spiritual warriors of God!" The other warriors rallied, moved closer to the barricade, and began expelling the demonic forces one at a time. Wherever a spirit shrunk into nothingness, the attackers lost heart and hesitated. But a hundred of the mob had already mounted the barricade behind the presence of the spirits.

Gideon shouted again. "God is with us. Follow me!" He climbed the barricade from the inside and started clubbing assaulters who had reached the top. Eugen, Andre, and other stout men rallied and joined Gideon using cudgels and pitchforks to fight desperately on top of the barricade. Other defenders resumed thrusting the sharpened poles through the barricade to stab the midsections of assailants still trying to climb over. Aaron threw a fist-sized rock like a baseball to strike one attacker who had reached the top of the barricade. Other rock throwers aimed a fuselage of stones at other attackers who showed themselves above the barricade. The air buzzed with the sound of sling-thrown rocks whizzing by the heads of attackers. The assault began to waver. The mob's malice and fear of Baal had abated without the presence of the evil spirits. Those on their rearmost ranks started to flee into the darkness. Some attackers backed down from the barricade. The hail of rocks and stones from the defenders resumed. Finally, the leading attackers jumped down from the barricade and withdrew, chased by more sling-thrown stones.

A united cheer broke out among the defenders. Villagers, including those previously non-religious, shouted out thanks to God. Sofia and other women brought water to the defenders. None had sustained life-threatening injuries. Ioana, assisted by Luca, wrapped cuts tightly to be stitched later. She sent one man with a broken arm and two groggy from head blows into Daniela's shop to await treatment. Ioana then watched the villagers congratulating each other and celebrating. But as she glanced toward the barricade, she wondered if the battle was truly over.

Chapter Thirty-one

A third of the mob had lost heart and dispersed after the initial attack on the barricade. Prefect Lazar saw them disappear into the darkness, abandoning Baal's mission. The most seriously injured lay on the ground or limped away. Those remaining gathered around Primar Serban, Father Flavius, and Prefect Lazar. The three leaders argued about resuming the assault.

Prefect Lazar considered using gasoline firebombs on the barricade and those it protected. Flavius argued to fire the guns from a distance through the barricade and kill the villagers.

"There's a better, quicker way," suggested Primar Serban. "I know this area. I can show our toughest men a way around the village to attack from the rear while everybody else keeps the peasants busy at the barricade."

"I'm not going up to that barricade again," said one of the werewolves, who was bleeding from puncture wounds from the pointed sticks.

"You will not have to. You can stand off and occupy the peasants in a rock battle until we get behind them." Primar Serban gestured to the ground littered with stones thrown by the villagers. "Use their own ammunition against them."

* * *

Gideon stood exhausted by the exertion of the fight, yet he too realized it wasn't over. He gripped the pitchfork he carried firmly and resolved to repel another assault as the mob advanced. Rather than storm the barricade again, the mob started picking up and hurling rocks over the barricade. Defenders responded throwing rocks from behind the barricade. Gideon felt Ioana grab his arm to get his attention.

"I have felt a message from God," she warned. "This attack is a diversion. They are sending their toughest men around the village to attack from our rear while most of their mob distract us throwing rocks. The ones sneaking around behind us are mostly former secret police."

"How many?" asked Gideon. Those defending the barricade nearby stood listening.

"I am not sure. Twenty-five, maybe."

"Where will they attack?"

"Down this road where it leaves the village and passes by our farm. There is no barricade there."

Gideon shouted to all the defenders, "They are sending former secret police around Horvata to attack us from the rear. Who will fight them with me?"

300

Forty men gathered around him. "I need the younger and stronger men. The others are needed to stay here and hold the barricade." Gideon quickly picked out twenty-five young men, including Andrei, to match the number of rear attackers.

Eugen and four other tough-looking, mature men pushed forward. "You're not leaving me out," Eugen stated flatly. "I want a crack at the secret police pigs who terrorized us under Ceauşescu." Darius joined Eugen without speaking.

Another of those men insisted, "I was in the army for ten years."

"I served for eight," said another.

Gidon nodded assent. "Who is a father of young children to provide for?" he asked the twenty-five he had selected. Five of the young men he had picked raised their hands. "We want to expose you to the least danger. Will you men remain and defend the barricade instead, please?" They all agreed.

Gideon turned to Ioana. "We'll need you along to advise and warn us." He made eye contact with Pastor Raphael and Father Marcă. "Hold the barricade." They nodded assent. "Follow me, men."

Madeline pushed Aaron from behind. "You said, 'A father doesn't leave his son or daughter.' You go along and protect Gideon and Ioana."

Gideon with his men and Ioana approached her farm in darkness. They stopped after seeing a group of tough-looking thugs following a giant man-like shape advancing down the road. Glimmers of multicolored light reflected from behind the apparition.

"That must be Baal," someone exclaimed.

Even though he had seen Baal at the midnight meeting, Gideon felt his heart quaver at the sight. Fear passed through him. Body language indicated that the men around him felt even more terror. Most of his men unconsciously took a step or two backwards. "Ioana, you're a warrior. You'll have to take care of that thing," Gideon whispered.

"I am not gifted in banishing spirits. You need Florin to face Baal."

"Florin isn't here. You must try. We can't fight Baal. If we don't defeat those men here, the thugs will attack the barricade from behind. We'll all be doomed."

Ioana took several steps ahead of Gideon's men and shouted, "In the name of God, leave, evil one."

Baal wavered a second then continued its advance. Two yellow eyes opened and looked directly at Ioana. Malicious laughter mocked her failure. Baal's deep voice filled the air. "I am not a simple spirit. A mere witch such as yourself has not the power to repel me. I am Baal. My followers will burn you alive after the men have finished with you tonight."

Ioana visibly shook with fear. "God through me commands you to leave," she cried.

The menacing presence continued approaching as its laughter echoed and penetrated the hearts of the village men. Primar Serban's men cheered and followed Baal forward.

Gideon's men started to edge backwards, ready to flee the unstoppable monster. Suddenly Aaron pushed through the defenders, stopped midway between Ioana and the apparition, and spoke firmly. "By the blood of Jesus Christ, Baal, begone!"

The apparition quivered then shrank in size until in a couple of seconds it had completely disappeared.

The opposing groups of men stood silent for a moment. Then Eugen roared and charged forward, crashing into the attackers. Six former secret police converged on him. Eugen double-handedly flailed a five-foot pipe to which he had welded a maul head in wide arcs to keep them away. Darius ran forward and used a club to knock down one of those assaulting Eugen. The other four mature men followed Darius, shouting insults and curses at their former tormentors. No individual attacker could resist Eugen's fury. The rest of Gideon's men joined the fight. Thugs accustomed to terrorizing helpless victims proved no match for enraged farmers and craftsmen defending their homes and families. Several attackers managed to escape before the defenders beat the others to the ground.

Gideon participated in the short fight by keeping the attackers alive. "Stop! Don't kill them. Take them prisoner," he shouted and moved among his men as they ferociously beat their opponents. Gideon being their leader, the village men relented.

Eugen jerked an opponent to his feet using his collar. "Look who I've got." Eugen held Primar Serban, whose nose streamed blood.

"Hold onto him," Gideon said. "And don't kill him . . . yet."

He then went to where Ioana had collapsed to the ground sobbing with regret. She looked up at him with tears running down her cheeks. "I am sorry to fail you, Gideon. I was so afraid of Baal."

Gideon helped his wife up and wrapped his arms around her. "You had the courage to try, sweetheart. I couldn't even try to face Baal myself." He pulled back and dried her face with his sleeve. "We're near the farm. You can go home and rest."

"No," she answered. "Men are hurt. I can help them." Ioana pulled away and started to examine and treat the men's wounds.

In the moments of quiet that followed, the victorious men sagged in relief and caught their breath. All heard the door of Ioana's farmhouse opening.

"What's all the noise and ruckus about?" called Christina. "I'm trying to sleep."

Ioana shouted back, "What are you doing home, Mama?"

"I walked back. Did you expect an old woman like me to sleep in the woods?"

"Go back to bed, Mama," returned Ioana. "I'll tell you about it tomorrow." Their tension relieved, all the village men laughed and started to cheer.

Chapter Thirty-two

No attackers attempted to cross the barricade, making the fight a rock-throwing battle in the red glow of the diminished bonfire. The villagers with the barricade for protection and the advantage of slings held off their opponents. But the attackers greatly outnumbered them. Village casualties climbed.

Pastor Raphael saw a village woman holding her head with blood oozing between her fingers after being hit by a stone. *The mob is not trying to cross our barricade. They have lost heart for a person-to-person fight. A sortie could rout them,* he realized.

He gathered the stoutest defenders remaining behind the barricade. "Our people are being hurt. Let us end this." Pastor Raphael led twenty-one men and six women to the darkest section of the barricade. There they climbed over unobserved by opponents engaged in the rock battle. Several silenced and carried their dogs over the barrier with them.

Once the counter-attackers had assembled, Pastor Raphael shouted, "For our homes and families," and charged the mob.

The villagers roared in unison and followed him, surprising the attackers. Released dogs barked and ran ahead. The rock-throwing enemy, which still numbered nearly two hundred, panicked at the sudden threat and ran without a fight.

Dozens of seriously injured men and women attackers with head wounds from rocks and clubs and stab wounds from the pikes had been left behind. Luca's arrival from behind the barricade surprised Pastor Raphael. Luca knelt by an unconscious man who'd been hit in the head by a brick and prayed fervently. The man woke up and tried to stand. "Lie still awhile," Luca told him. "Get over your dizziness before standing."

Pastor Raphael had watched the healing. "There are more injured over here, Luca."

"I cannot. I have never done more than one healing in a day. I am worn out already," Luca replied.

A slight teenage girl, having followed Luca over the barricade, joined them. "You can, Luca," Maria said. "God used you to heal me once."

"When was that?"

"Werewolves had molested me."

"That was you, Maria?"

"Yes. And I know God can use you to help these hurt people. I will stay with you."

Pastor Raphael watched as the young pair started going to each seriously injured person. Maria held Luca's free hand in both of hers as he prayed fervently over each one stricken. Once healed, most stood and staggered away under the cover of darkness in the direction from which they had come. Pastor Raphael thought, *Nothing strengthens a man more than the confidence of a woman.*

* * *

Gideon walked back to where Aaron had confronted Baal. He found his father sitting on the ground cross-legged and exhausted with his hands on his knees. "Dad, you saved us."

"No, God saved us."

"Well, God used you."

"God used all of us tonight." Then Aaron added, "You're doing a great job here, Son. And you've found an amazing wife. I didn't believe in spiritual warfare like this."

"The timing of your surgery couldn't have been coincidental. We needed you here now, not at our wedding. You've done a world of good despite your initial doubts, Dad."

"Not the best I could have, though. What you don't know won't hurt you as much as something you know for certain and are wrong about. I think the spirits in America have deceived many, including myself. With us deceived, the spirits keep a low profile to do the most harm. They incite humans to do terrible things like murdering school children."

"You're right, Dad."

*   *   *

Pastor Raphael saw cars and large military trucks entering Horvata the next afternoon. Led by Daniela, the elected federal authorities with the Orthodox bishop and four truckloads of armed Romanian soldiers stopped in the square. The barricade had already been cleared where the road passed through the village. The new arrivals saw evidence of the fight. A large circle of ashes smoldered where the bonfire had burned. Pastor Raphael and Father Marcă, along with village elders, met them. As a foreigner, Gideon stayed away.

"What happened here?" asked a government official from Bucharest.

"The village was attacked by marauders. We fought back," answered Father Marcă.

"What marauders?"

Pastor Raphael pointed to a group of fifty guarded men and women sitting or lying on the ground under the shadow of a tree. "We took some prisoners. Ask them. There were no fatalities."

"Where are their leaders?"

"The first ones to run away. But we captured one." Pastor Raphael pointed to his church. "One of their leaders is in there."

The federal authorities found Primar Serban surrounded by five grim Horvata men. Gideon's hint that he might be killed had made him willing to cooperate. Primar Serban spoke into Aaron's recorder, confessing misdeeds, naming accomplices, and revealing the crimes of Father Flavius and Prefect Lazar.

* * *

I've never seen Aaron so drained, thought Madeline as they rested in the town-cottage. "Can I get you anything to eat, honey?" she asked.

Aaron lay flat on his back on the bed. Without moving, he whispered, "I'm too weak to chew anything."

She sat on the bed beside him. "I imagine facing off Baal could take something out of a man."

Aaron turned his head to look at her. "I would never have believed Gideon could be so resolute. He was always uncertain of advanced spiritual matters. How could he have adapted and discovered a side of spiritual warfare we never recognized?"

Madeline suggested, "Maybe Gideon being somewhat uncertain allowed him to adapt."

Aaron grunted in agreement.

She waited a moment before continuing. "You, on the other hand, have always been rather certain of everything you did. Maybe that's what enabled you to banish Baal."

"I didn't think, just acted."

"My point exactly. God used both you and Gideon differently in spiritual situations beyond our previous experience."

Aaron managed to raise himself to lean on one elbow. "But in America, we have the best seminaries in the world and churches galore. Why aren't we leading the charge in spiritual warfare?"

Madeline remembered seeing Father Marcă, Pastor Raphael, and her son, Gideon, rejoicing together after the battle. "Maybe spirits hide themselves in America. Then the Christians have no one to fight against except each other and those with different values."

Aaron remembered Florin's words that the existence of spirits could prove the supernatural and thereby strengthen faith. "Spirits revealing themselves would give Christians a common enemy. Proof of the supernatural would boost everyone's confidence in Scriptures."

Madeline teased her husband. "Then you'll be happy that evil spirits are active in your absence back home."

"Not happy. But made resolute. Let's pack up and head home, sweetheart. We have business to address there. And our son is doing fine in Romania."

* * *

Two months later

"Hello, Mom and Dad!" Gideon said over the phone in Braşov. "How are things working out back home?"

Aaron didn't miss the implied question. "The woman, Suzy, has withdrawn her lawsuit. The recorded phone messages revealed that she had called me at home unsolicited on several occasions. They prove I gave her heartfelt sympathy and encouragement but made no romantic suggestions. I was young and naïve, but not immoral. The romantic notes Suzy offered as proof didn't match my handwriting. She had no pictures of us together."

"How did your church react?"

"They accepted the evidence, or lack of evidence. Then your mother talking about my lack of experience on our wedding night helped convince everybody."

Madeline broke in from the extension phone. "Aaron, you know that doubts would have persisted otherwise."

"You're right," Aaron agreed. "And getting married without sexual experience isn't anything to be ashamed of."

"No, it isn't." Madeline continued, "Gideon, you should have heard the sermon your father delivered when reinstated as senior pastor."

"About the allegations?" Gideon asked.

His mother answered, "No about stepping up everyone's spirituality. Let me see if I can remember his words. Your father preached . . ." Madeline mimicked her husband's

311

voice, "'I'm not going to dwell in the cozy confines of our comfortable church life. I'm going to foray into where Satan rules and face our enemy. Who among you will go with me to become a more-than-ordinary Christian?' The congregation sat thunderstruck. You could have heard a feather drop. Then your father shared some of our experiences in Romania. He saved the violence and scarier spirit stuff for later."

"How has the congregation reacted since?" asked Gideon.

"Too early to tell. But they realize God has somehow changed their senior pastor."

Aaron broke in, "Enough about me. What's happening in Horvata, Son?"

"Well, people in Horvata are calling our confrontation 'The Second Revolution.' The shaky federal government shushed the fight up to avoid violence elsewhere. And I think they feared ridicule by Western Europe and America if mention of spirit involvement leaked out."

"Before our trip, I wouldn't have believed any account blaming spirits," Aaron confirmed. "But the last time a person changed his or her mind about something, is when they stopped growing."

Gideon murmured agreement and continued, "But the government has started an investigation of corruption across the country. Primar Serban has been arrested for fraud regarding the Caritas Ponzi scheme and the assault on Horvata. His thugs disappeared into the populace."

"What about Prefect Lazar?" asked Aaron.

"He vanished somewhere. Maybe he escaped the country. But most people think somebody had him killed to prevent him from implicating them and hid his body. The federal government did listen to the tape you and I made and arrested the three policemen who extorted you. You won't need to testify. Other victims came forward to implicate them."

"And Father Flavius?"

"Defrocked. Father Marcă is Horvata's interim priest."

"How about the young man I tackled, Darius?"

"Darius's testimony implicated the werewolves, including He Who Kills, for assaulting Maria. The werewolves are going to prison, except Darius himself. Maria testified that Darius tried to save her. Her boyfriend Luca emotionally supported her during the trials. They've become inseparable. Anyway, at Maria's request, the judge released Darius on probation. He and Sofia are smitten with each other and perhaps the most fervent members of our Bible study. They also attend services at Pastor Raphael's church."

"Well, the Bible says that one forgiven much loves much," explained Aaron.

Gideon continued, "Ioana hired Darius and Sofia to work on her farm. Ioana and I will concentrate on medical and missionary work. After they're married by Pastor Raphael next month, Darius and Sofia will live in the town-cottage."

"Tell him about the church offering Ioana a job, Aaron," insisted Madeline.

"Right! Your mother talked to the women of our church. They are insisting that Ioana be offered the same salary as you to be our medical missionary. If she accepts, you'll find her salary deposited in your US bank account, and her medical expenses will be reimbursable through the church."

Gideon laughed. "I'm sure she'll accept. That would be beyond her wildest dreams. Ioana, Christina, and I have talked about having a new house built on the farm property. We'll be able to afford that now."

"Let's talk about some more cooperation, Son. I think our church here would benefit from becoming more involved in your and Ioana's work in Romania. Maybe funding for some projects. Maybe some short-term missionary trips: students, workers, medical staff to assist Ioana."

"Sure, Dad!"

Epilogue

Three years later

Madeline saw Gideon and Ioana waiting at the barrier when she emerged from baggage claim at Bucharest's airport. Slightly behind her son and daughter-in-law, she recognized twenty-one-year-old Nadia who, as a teenager, had translated for her and Aaron. Ioana saw Madeline first and waved. Gideon smiled broadly.

Ioana spoke before Madeline reached her. "See, I can speak more English now. I learned in the English classes."

Madeline noticed Ioana's slightly distended abdomen and hugged her first. "You are speaking well, third daughter. When are you due?"

Ioana beamed with joy. "Twenty-two more weeks. We saved the news until you came."

Gideon also received a hug from his mother. Then Madeline turned to Nadia. "I remember you. Are you here to translate for us again?"

Gideon shook his head. "Nadia works with us now. She teaches the English classes and ministers to village children. The best of her English students will translate for you. Nadia herself will take charge of the teen mission-trippers you've brought with you."

"I'm glad to see you again, Mrs. Dixon," said Nadia. "My pupils are eager to talk in English to Americans their age."

Madeline hugged Nadia. "Our kids are excited too, honey."

Aaron emerged leading six girls and five boys, ages fifteen to eighteen, dragging suitcases. The American teenagers looked wide-eyed all around them. After everybody exchanged names, Gideon told the Americans, "Nadia will be your hostess and director while you're in Romania."

"I'm glad to meet you all," Nadia said in perfect, albeit accented, English. "We will get some hard work done doing chores and helping those less fortunate in our village. We'll have Bible lessons and get to know each other. Each week we will have some fun making a field trip to someplace in Romania, starting with Dracula's Castle. Some Romanians your age are learning English. They are on a spiritual retreat for these three weeks and will be part of our activities."

"When do we get to meet the witch who turned out to be a prophetess?" one girl asked.

Nadia pointed at Ioana, who stood talking to Madeline in halting English. "That is her. Ask your Romanian counterparts tonight to tell you the story. Many of them fought in the Second Revolution. So did Mr. Dixon, your pastor, and

Mrs. Dixon." The American teenagers looked at their pastor and his wife in awe.

Uh-oh, thought Madeline. *Aaron warned Gideon to be circumspect about the more dramatic details of our visit three years ago with the earlier adult mission-trippers. But teenager-to-teenager, nothing will be held back. And our kids will tell everyone at home. Aaron will have a lot of questions to answer.* She mentally shrugged. *Well, the truth is the truth.*

Outside the airport, a bus Gideon had chartered waited. Most of the American teenagers fell asleep from jetlag on the four-hour ride to Horvata. In the late afternoon, the bus stopped in Horvata's square, where a welcoming crowd waited. Banners proclaimed in English WELCOME BACK, THANK YOU, and WE LOVE YOU.

Madeline and Aaron descended the bus steps to applause and cheering. Eugen, the newly elected primar, greeted them. Then bears and quite a few townsfolk thronged around them. The American teenagers watched from the bus windows in wonder while their pastor and his wife shook hands and hugged individuals.

After ten minutes, Gideon interrupted the reunion by shouting. "Our guests have been on a long journey. We need to let them rest. My parents will be here for three weeks."

As they returned to the bus, Aaron heard one of the American teenagers ask Nadia, "Why are Mr. and Mrs. Dixon so popular?"

317

"God used Aaron to save Horvata from spirits and a hateful mob. Madeline gave us a medical clinic. Ask the Romanian friends you will soon meet."

A few minutes later the bus pulled in front of a newly constructed Christian center on the outskirts of Horvata. Nadia took charge of the American teenagers, showing them two rooms acting as boys' and girls' dormitories. Sleeping pallets lined the walls. Eighteen Romanian teenagers met them there.

"They all speak some English," Nadia explained to the Americans. "Speak slowly and help them when they don't know a word. Try to learn a little Romanian from them."

Gideon eagerly showed his father and mother around the Christian center that Aaron's American church had funded. Aaron's eyes seemed to sparkle as he envisioned the work God could do there. "And you did all this with only a hundred and seventy thousand dollars?"

Gideon smiled. "Three hundred twenty thousand, including the clinic. Prices are rising here even with American currency. So, it was your money *and* the teams of mission-trip workers from your church in America who worked to help build the structures."

"Those mission-trippers said that coming here was one of the greatest experiences of their lives. They came home revering the Romanian Christians they met. They've injected tremendous energy into our congregation, especially in raising money for Romania."

"I want to see the clinic," Madeline demanded.

Ioana laughed. "You will certainly see it. It is just next door, and you will stay there. We moved two of the beds into the private examination room for you and Aaron."

Madeline recognized immense joy in Ioana as she proudly showed off the clinic. "When medical teams come from your church in America, we offer free examinations and treatment. People come from all over the region. Same when the dental teams come."

Two expectant mothers relaxed in a large waiting room complete with home-like furniture and a kitchenette. Anxious-looking family members kept them company. Ioana spoke to each pregnant woman then explained, "They are due and could start labor any moment. But they live a long way from any medical help. We brought them here to be ready."

One bed in an eight-bed ward held a young man in a leg traction. "He fell off a roof on a construction job," Ioana explained. "The others are a man passing a kidney stone and a woman recovering from food poisoning." Then she gestured at the clinic. "Please thank the people of your church in America for providing this. And the medicines."

"We are privileged to be your partners, Ioana," answered Madeline.

"How's your new house coming, Son?" asked Aaron.

"Slowly. We've saved money to build it but couldn't handle managing all the construction. We prioritized the Christian center and the clinic. Now that they're finished, the house should come more quickly. Hopefully we'll be in before Ioana's baby comes."

"Our baby," Ioana corrected him.

A pretty girl in a simple nurse's uniform had been bustling about, caring for the patients, and watching over the mothers-to-be. Ioana waved her over. "This is Maria. She was in the Second Revolution battle. She is engaged to Luca, whom God used to heal those injured after the battle. He is attending college and medical school in Bucharest now."

Maria curtseyed and spoke in accented English. "Happy to see you again, Mr. and Mrs. Dixon."

"I remember you, Maria. I saw you help Luca attend to wounded men and women after the fight," answered Madeline. "When are you getting married, honey?"

Maria smiled in response to Madeline's recognition. "When Luca is home on school break. Three months, two weeks, and six days from now."

Madeline looked at Ioana and raised her eyebrows. "Why is Luca in medical school . . ." she left *when he can miraculously heal?* unverbalized.

Ioana recognized the implied question. "Luca can only heal occasionally and only in an emergency. He says healing takes fervent prayer that exhausts him for days. He expects to do more as a trained doctor and has promised to join us at this clinic when he graduates."

Aaron nodded in approval. "God wants us to do what we can with the talents He gives us. We should not expect Him to do what we can do ourselves."

"I haven't received any foreknowledge from God in more than two years," Ioana confessed.

"But you had the gift when you needed it," said Gideon.

"Yes, I did," agreed Ioana. She smiled at Gideon, and then turned to address Madeline and Aaron. "While Nadia takes care of your young church members, all our Romanian friends want to see you. Tonight, you will have dinner at our farm-house and see Mama."

"How is Christina?" asked Madeline.

"Getting older, but still knitting. Darius and Sofia manage the farm now," said Ioana. "They have a six-month-old baby boy. They have asked to host you for dinner too. It would mean so much to them."

"We will go, of course."

"Eugen—you saw that he is now Horvata's primar—will be at the dinner with Darius and Sofia too. He's the godfather of their baby. He'll be offering you his best wines."

Aaron laughed. "We don't know much about wine. But we'll taste and praise his gift."

Ioana continued, "Each of the warriors hopes to entertain you somehow. Florin, Claudia, Daniela, and Andrei—who is married now."

"Yes, we will be grateful for everybody's hospitality."

"You'll have work to do too, if you're willing, Dad," said Gideon. "Paster Raphael's church has grown so much that he is now a full-time pastor. He asks that you preach every Sunday you're in Romania."

"I would be honored, Son. I have a new sermon based on Will Roger's quip, 'It isn't what we don't know that gives us trouble, it's what we know that ain't so.' That applied to me before I visited Romania."

"Me too, Dad." Gideon remained silent for a moment, remembering his initial naïveté in Romania. "Father Marcă also asks that you teach at the Orthodox church. He's the senior priest now. The Patriarch tried to replace Father Flavius with a man older than Father Marcă, but the Orthodox of Horvata demanded Father Marcă. He had fought with them three years ago. He's married now and they're expecting a child. He'll be a Father and a father." Gideon smiled at his own joke.

Aaron shook his head. "I wouldn't know how to teach in an Orthodox service."

"I didn't mean their worship service. Father Marcă has started a weekday Bible study for his congregants. He asks me to teach sometimes. I have him teach here at the Christian center as well. Those who attend Father Marcă's class are mostly older congregants. But Father Marcă also encourages younger people to attend Bible classes at our Christian center."

"Then I'd be happy to serve Father Marcă," Aaron agreed. "You still don't offer worship services here?"

"No, we don't. But we do gather people together who attend worship elsewhere. God is helping and reaching people through our work."

"Yes, He is."

Authors' Note

All the characters depicted in *Missionary and the Witch* are purely fictional and from the imagination of the authors. Romania and its people, including many dedicated Christians, are truly remarkable. Locations, cultural descriptions, and historical backgrounds are as accurate as space and most readers' attentions will allow.

Although biblical interpretations can vary widely, we have tried to apply Scripture accurately and never contradict Scripture regarding fictional elaborations of demonic activities.

About the Authors

Kit and Drew Coons met while living in Africa as humanitarian missionaries in 1980. "Kit was living in a mud house with a metal roof and no running water or electricity," Drew recalls. "She is as tough as a hickory nut." There Kit taught in a teachers college while Drew worked to provide clean water to nineteen cities and towns.

As humorous speakers specializing in strengthening relationships, they have taught in every part of the US and in thirty-nine other countries. For two years, the Coonses lived and taught in New Zealand and Australia. They are keen cultural observers and incorporate their many adventures into their writing and speaking. The Coonses are unique in that they speak and write as a team.

Drew received honors degrees in engineering from both Auburn and Georgia Tech. He worked on the Delta Rocket program and designed critical components for the Space Shuttle. Later he served as a researcher for BASF Corporation and received twenty-three US and several international patents.

Kit has an honors degree in education from the University of Minnesota. She is a gifted teacher and blogger with a undaunted spirit regardless of the circumstances.

The Coonses are unique in that they speak and write as a team. Kit and Drew live in Washington State and are available as speakers for a wide variety of entertaining and meaningful topics.

Other Books by Kit and Drew Coons

Challenge Series of Mystery–Destination Novels with Dave and Katie

Dave and Katie Parker are an early-60s-aged couple forced into premature retirement and recovering from difficult circumstances. "I feel like our old life was a boat that went over a waterfall with us inside. Now we're bobbing up in the pool below, glad to be alive, but without a boat," says Katie.

The *Challenge Series* of novels follow the Parkers as they solve mysteries and find new adventures. Dave and Katie's relationship and ability to work as a team is deepened by each fish-out-of-water experience. They meet and help many colorful characters in charming settings. The situations frequently require the Parkers to face difficult choices and undergo personal growth. Readers will experience new places and cultures with Dave and Katie.

Admirable characters in each story and some redemptive themes make the stories meaningful. All the *Challenge* novels have been professionally illustrated.

Please see the Coonses' website for descriptions of each *Challenge Series* novel.

https://morethanordinarylives.com

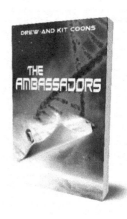

"The Ambassadors combines elements of science fiction and real-life genetics into a story that is smart, witty, and completely unique. Drew and Kit Coons navigate complex issues of humanity in a way that will leave you pondering the implications long after the book is over. If you're ready for a compelling adventure with humor, suspense, and protagonists you can really root for, don't miss out on this one!" Jayna Richardson

Two genetically engineered beings unexpectedly arrive on Earth. Unlike most extraterrestrials depicted in science fiction, the pair is attractive, personable, and telegenic–the perfect talk show guests. They have come to Earth as ambassadors bringing an offer of partnership in a confederation of civilizations. Technological advances are offered as part of the partnership. But humans must learn to cooperate among themselves to join.

Molly, a young reporter, and Paul, a NASA scientist, have each suffered personal tragedy and carry emotional baggage. They are asked to tutor the ambassadors in human ways and to guide them on a worldwide goodwill tour. Molly and Paul observe as the extraterrestrials commit faux pas while experiencing human culture. They struggle trying to define a romance and partnership while dealing with burdens of the past.

However, mankind finds implementing actual change difficult. Clashing value systems and conflicts among subgroups of humanity erupt. Inevitably, rather than face difficult choices, fearmongers in the media start to blame the messengers. Then an uncontrolled biological weapon previously created by a rogue country tips the world into chaos. Molly, Paul, and the others must face complex moral decisions about what being human means and the future of mankind.

What is a more than ordinary life?

Each person's life is unique and special. In that sense, there is no such thing as an ordinary life. However, many people yearn for lives more special: excitement, adventure, romance, purpose, character. Our site is dedicated to the premise that any life can be more than ordinary.

At **MoreThanOrdinaryLives.com** you will find:

- inspiring stories
- ideas and resources
- entertaining novels
- free downloads

https://morethanordinarylives.com/

Life-skills Books

Life-skills books give practical and biblical advice dealing with issues related to living a More-Than-Ordinary Life.

More Than Ordinary *Challenges*—Dealing with the Unexpected (Group Discussion Questions Included)

Many heartwarming stories share about difficult situations that worked out miraculously or through iron-willed determination. The stories are useful in that they inspire hope. But sometimes life just doesn't work out the way we expected. Many people's lives will never be what they had hoped. What does a person do then? This life-skills book uses our personal struggle with infertility as an example.

More Than Ordinary *Choices*—Making Good Decisions (Group Discussion Questions Included)

Every moment separates our lives into before and after. Some moments divide our lives into never before and always after. Many of those life-changing moments are based on the choices we make. God allows us to make choices through free will. Making good choices at those moments is for our good and ultimately reflects on God as we represent Him.

More Than Ordinary *Marriage*—A Higher Level

Some might suggest that any marriage surviving in these times is more than ordinary. Unfortunately, many marriages don't last a lifetime. But by more than ordinary, we mean a marriage that goes beyond basic survival and is more than successful. This type of relationship can cause others to ask, "What makes their marriage so special?" Such marriages glorify God and represent Christ and the church well.

More Than Ordinary *Faith*—Why Does God Allow Suffering? (Group Discussion Questions Included)

Why does God allow suffering? This is a universal question in every heart. The question is both reasonable and valid. Lack of a meaningful answer is a faith barrier for many people. Shallow answers can undermine faith. Fortunately, the Bible gives clear reasons that God allows suffering. But the best time to learn about God's purposes and strengthen our faith is *before* a crisis.

More Than Ordinary *Wisdom*—Stories of Faith and Folly

Jesus told story after story to communicate God's truth. Personal stories create hope and change lives by speaking to the heart. The following collection of Drew's stories is offered for your amusement and so that you can learn from his experiences. These stories can motivate you to consider your own life experiences. What was God teaching you? "Let the redeemed of the Lord tell their story." (Psalm 107:2)

More Than Ordinary *Abundance*—From Kit's Heart

Abundance means, "richly or plentifully supplied; ample." Kit's personal devotions in this mini book record her experiences of God's abundant goodness and offer insights into godly living. Her hope is that you will rejoice with her and marvel at God's provision in your own life. "They celebrate

your abundant goodness and joyfully sing of your
righteousness." (Psalm 145:7)